Marcel Möring

is one of Holland's most exciting, young literary authors. Publication in Holland of his first novel, *Mendel*, was an instant success, winning the country's Geertjan Lubber-huizen Prize for the Best Debut of 1990. His second novel, *The Great Longing*, received extraordinary critical praise and was *the* Dutch bestseller of 1992. Already established as one of Holland's great works of literature, it will be published in translation throughout Europe in 1995.

The Great Longing, a novel about memory, stays in the reader's memory with all the magical tracings of a butterfly wing pinned to the page before flying away, or dissolving. An impossible book to forget.'

MARIANNE WIGGINS, author of *John Dollar*

ORIGINAL

MARCEL MÖRING

The Great Longing

Translated by
Stacey Knecht

Flamingo
An Imprint of HarperCollins*Publishers*

f l a m i n g o	The term 'Original' signifies publication direct into paperback with no preceding British hardback edition.
ORIGINAL	The Flamingo Original series publishes fine writing at an affordable price at the point of first publication.

Flamingo
An Imprint of HarperCollins*Publishers*
77–85 Fulham Palace Road,
Hammersmith, London W6 8JB

First published in Great Britain by Flamingo 1995
9 8 7 6 5 4 3 2 1

Copyright © Marcel Möring 1992

English translation copyright © HarperCollins*Publishers* 1995

Author photograph © Harry Cock

The Author asserts the moral right to
be identified as the author of this work

The Publishers gratefully acknowledge the financial support of the
Foundation for the Production and Translation of Dutch Literature

A catalogue record for this book
is available from the British Library

ISBN 0 00 654749 4

Set in Galliard

Printed in Great Britain by
HarperCollinsManufacturing Glasgow

CONTENTS

Lord, it is time. The summer was so great.
Lay down long shadows on the sundials.
Let loose the winds to run across the plain.

Command the lingering fruits to ripen:
Grant them two southerly days yet
Then drive them to fulfilment and compel
The final sweetness in the heavy wine.

Who has no house, will build himself none now;
Who is alone now, will stay so —
Wake, read, write long letters, go
Back and forth along bare avenues,
Restlessly wandering, where the fallen leaves blow.

STEPHEN SPENDER, *Autumn Day, after Rilke*

I Remember Everything

'It was a warm summer, the warmest warm summer of the century. Nineteen fifty-seven. Mama sat in the cellar, among the shelves of pickled cucumbers and jars of string beans and barrels of sauerkraut and bottles of ginger beer and empty potato sacks and lumps of butter wrapped in wax paper and half cheeses and crates of tulip bulbs, and she had a belly like the world itself. Never before had anyone been so fat. Every time we kicked, it was like somebody doing a puppet show under her dress. Papa wrote his thesis, the Sputnik was launched, Grandpa had cancer, but didn't know it yet, Grandma was to die five years later, when John Glenn was circling the earth. Nineteen fifty-seven. August. The warmest August in the history of mankind.'

'This is my memory of us,' said Lisa. 'This is us: you, Raph and I, on our way home. It's a warm afternoon, they're burning off ditches in the distance. We're walking home and I'm thinking: this will never come back. While we're walking, I think: this will never come back, and I see us as three brightly coloured specks in the green of the lane. This is my memory, but I'm also thinking of what happened later, at the top of this lane, when I lay on my back under an oak, bathed in flecks of shadow, my head in the tall grass and he on top of me. Stretched out in the grass, the big tree above me and the singing of the silence and my body filled and yet not filled. I wished he were three, that afternoon, three times he. I wanted him everywhere.

'They're burning off the ditches and the shadow of the treetops glides over my head and we walk down the lane and I'm thinking: this is my memory of us, of you and Raph and me, and I know it will all disappear, the smoke, the evening about to fall, the

1

grass where we lay, which will rise again. I look at your faces, I smell the scent of burning hay and I think: this is my memory of us.'

But there were no burning ditches, Raph wasn't here either, and though evening fell, we never saw the sun sink below the horizon. This was where I lived, a shoebox hewn from stone, one and a half storeys of warehouse with grey wooden floors and crumbling ceilings and sawn-off pieces of pipe sticking out of bare brick walls.

A few hours earlier I had climbed the worn stairs with my bag full of groceries, into the light of the algae-covered cupola in the roof, and when I opened the door I saw her, huddled on the edge of the bed, her legs crossed, a saucer of butts in one hand, a cigarette in the other. I stood in the doorway and looked at my sister, way down at the other end of the room, almost sixty feet away from me. I thought: God, she's small.

Sometimes we haven't seen each other for a while, my sister and I, and when we meet again there's always that moment when it seems as if we're going to hold out our hands, a bit awkwardly, shrugging our shoulders, saying each other's names and: how are you, you look good, you've put on a little weight. This evening was no different. I walked towards her and she jumped up, brushing off ashes, shaking the hair out of her face as if she were shooing away a mosquito. We stood opposite each other, looking and nodding. Then she came up close, kissed me on the cheek and asked where I'd been all that time, and just as I was answering her she tossed her jacket on the sofa and began straightening up the room. I shrugged my shoulders and went into the kitchen, where I pushed open the windows, unpacked the groceries and started supper.

Lisa is my twin sister. She's the family conscience. Every other week she and Raph, our brother, come to visit me. We drink, we eat, we talk about the past, when our parents were still alive, and Raph and I listen to the stories Lisa tells. When it comes to our past, she's the authority. I used to think she had made it all up, her memories are so detailed, but since Raph can often confirm her stories (he's two years older), I'm now convinced that she

2

hasn't invented a thing. 'Did I do that?' I ask, when she comes up with yet another unfamiliar memory, and then she nods, my sister, yes, you really did, and we laugh. We laugh about the time Raph and I climbed into the bookcase and imitated chimpanzees and came crashing down, bookcase and all, about the time she punched me in the nose because I'd locked her out of the bathroom. We listen to her tell The Man Who Forgot Everything, a story our mother told us so often that in the end, we knew every line. We knew it so well, we'd even correct her. We'd say: No, no, that's not how it goes, first he went to the market vendor and *then* he went to the rich man. We listen till midnight. Then we sit in silence. Then we've arrived at the twelfth and fourteenth year of our lives, when our parents drove into a tree on their way home. Every one of Lisa's visits ends with us sitting around the table, three dancing shadows on the candlelit wall. 'God, Lisa, I miss them,' I say, and Raph nods, dramatically. 'So do I, guys,' she says, 'so do I', and she reaches across the table to grasp our hands and hold them, for a long, long time, her head bowed, just as Raph and I have bowed ours. Three sorrowing spiritists after a failed seance. At one o'clock she goes home, to Simon, her husband, and Raph and I stand in the doorway, in the rampant greenery, in a night filled with mosquitoes and muffled city sounds, and we wave and wave. We wave as though it's our last farewell, as though she, too, is about to meet her tree. When Raph has gone home, an hour later, after the last glass, after the last cigarette, I sit down at the table in my room with a bottle of beer and go over the things Lisa has said, the things I mustn't allow myself to forget.

But it wasn't like that now. We sat across from each other, at the table in front of one of the big windows at the back of my house, we ate the omelette I'd made, and then we drank beer and Lisa smoked the row of hash cigarettes she'd rolled while I was fixing supper. She began one of her stories, as though she felt obliged to make at least some attempt at one of our seances, but it didn't last long and the story was incoherent and implausible.

How could she know it had been so warm that summer, and that our mother had sat in her mother's cellar with the biggest belly in history? The launching of the Sputnik, that part was right, that much I knew, but from then on I was lost. We sat there, without Raph, without memories that sounded like good old stories about the good old days. The dishes were still on the table, and now and then I heard the hissing of hot ash as she stubbed out a brown-stained cigarette on her plate. Soon there were so many squashed butts among the yellow-green scraps of omelette that her plate looked like the scale model of a ravaged planetary surface. And all that time I saw her drifting away and understood less and less of what she was saying.

She sipped her tea. A badly rolled cigarette dangled from her fingers. She brought it to her mouth, inhaled and, still holding the smoke in her lungs, gave me a piercing look. Her large brown eyes were bloodshot, her reddish-brown hair lay in unruly curls on her forehead.

'Lisa?'

A puff of smoke escaped. She put an index finger to her lips.

'The first time was summer,' she said. 'The height of summer. I wore a blue linen skirt and a white blouse with lace trim and a yellow cardigan. I was a waitress. I kissed him on the ear and he said the ear is a reflection of the human embryo and then I felt his tongue in my ear and my belly filled and all I could think of was: let everything go, everything, no more thoughts, nothing, everything. And there he was, his hand on my breast, his lips on my throat. I felt the hollow of his back, where the back flows into the buttocks, there, and I felt the warmth of his body and I said: yes, and he grew in my hand, he lay in my hand and grew, and I spread my legs and there he was and my mind reeled, my mind reeled from his tongue in my ear and his lips on my throat and on my breast, yes, I said, yes, I felt him and I didn't and then I did, he was an animal and his mouth slid between my breasts, over my belly, my thighs, it was like swimming in the sea. It was like spilling over. I saw all kinds of things: a house, rooms, a forest, meadows, a dead horse. There he was and I felt him inside me and I said: I want it now, I want you. And afterwards we bicycled into town, I sat on the back of his bike, and we rode down the forest path and I hummed and I thought: why do they

4

always say the first time isn't good, this was the best. The air smelled of honeysuckle.'

Her eyes were still on me. It was almost as if she saw something, I didn't know what, I also didn't know if I wanted to know what, but she saw something.

'I dreamed we were in a house,' she said. 'You and Raph and Papa and Mama and I. The doors were open. A storm was blowing and the windows moved. It was night, and I dreamed there were people walking through the rooms. One morning you and I were in the cellars and you were beside me, we walked through the smoke of smouldering wood, and I turned my head and I saw your face in and out of the smoke, we glided like sailboats through the smoke, through the corridor. You looked up and sideways and your face turned, it tilted backward, your eyes squeezed shut, and you looked as if you wanted to say something, as if you wanted to call me but you couldn't see me, couldn't hear me. Then, very slowly, your mouth opened, it was like a hole opening up in the middle of your face and the hole got bigger and bigger and your face disappeared into the hole of your mouth. There's a photograph of you, at Grandpa and Grandma's house, standing between Grandma's legs. You're taking a step forward, you can't really walk yet, you're holding onto the garden gate with one little hand and Grandma's got you between her legs, her hands are on your shoulders. You can see she loved you very much. You can't see Grandpa. I have another photograph, of him, with me riding on his back, and he's smiling. When I look at these photographs I think of two things. The first is: they're all gone. That's hard for me to understand. They can't be gone. How can everything just vanish? The lives, the images in the photographs, everything they've felt and thought. It's impossible. The second thing is what Mama told me about Grandpa's death. He lay dying and she stood at his bedside and he said: You know what the worst part is, all these insects, and she said: Insects? and he said: The whole floor, full of insects, and then he said: I know they're not really there, I know that, but I still think it. Does a person have to die like that, Sam? Delirious, in a bed on a floor full of insects? I look at those photographs and I think of dying.

5

Even though I know they're about a boy learning to walk between his grandmother's legs and a girl riding on her grandfather's back.'

Her eyes strayed over my face. I thought: if I don't move, she can see me better. I sat at the table like a mannequin.

'It's as though it's nighttime and I'm sitting and painting and listening to music, and the radio hovers between two stations. You come and go and I look for you. I don't know where you are. Now and then I pick you up, I hear you in the distance, whispering in static. Lisa, you call, Lisa. I say: I miss them so. I miss them too, you say, and in my mind we embrace each other, in the static between two distant stations we embrace each other. And then you're gone again. I stand in the room with empty arms. I embrace the dusk.

'But this is where I want to be, this is my place, in the dusky room, in the static between two stations, holding out my arms and whispering: I miss them too I miss them so I miss them.

'I wanted all of him in me. I wanted him in me and I was content with part of him, because I couldn't have all of him, because that's what I wanted, I wanted him in me, a person in a person. I wanted to be two people, his body in my body, he and I.

'This is my memory of us: on our way home, I look at your faces. They're burning off ditches in the distance. Smoke drifts across the path between the trees and we pass through the smoke and I turn my head and your face disappears and comes back again and you open your mouth.

'Three lives cross in my mind,' she said. 'Where we walked, I walked with him. But I went away. And when I came back, days later, and he asked: Where have you been, I told a long story, a journey to the end of the world, the expulsion from Paradise. He said: Okay, but where have you been, and then I said I had to be alone. How, he said, how could you just leave, couldn't you have thought about me, I don't want you to go. But I said: I had to, I had to, and then he bowed his head and he banged it against the table, boom boom boom boom, blood splattered all over the place and I flew to his side and I threw my arms around him and I said: Oh God I love you oh God don't, don't be so sad, and

6

boom boom boom, his head against the table, he howled like a sick cat, and I said . . .

'I remember everything,' she said. 'That night I sat on top of him, as if he weren't there, I straddled him, his hands on my breasts and my head thrown back and I rode him as if it made no difference who he was and somewhere in the darkness it started to whirl and my head turned this way and that and light burned between my eyes and I saw horses, a meadow, forest, a whirlpool in which everything disappeared. Bang. And afterwards I wondered whether or not it really did matter who was lying under me and I didn't know.

'When I got home I thought of Papa and Mama. I didn't know where they were, they got in the car and they drove down the street and they never came back, and there was nothing I could do, I couldn't bring them back. Later on you had dreams, you saw the car lying in a ditch along the road, their car, with its nose crushed against a tree. You said you didn't know where they'd gone. They're dead, I said. But you already knew that, we were old enough to understand that much. But where had they gone? You just couldn't believe that they were never coming back. Maybe it's easier if it happens gradually, if the body declines and the skin shrivels and the eyes grow yellow and the voice weak.

'And then I thought of those photographs and I saw them as a moment in which a life began, and that life unfolded, it reeled itself off like film that's tossed in the street. Up until this moment, here: we're walking among the trees, it smells of burning grass, we're going home.'

But we weren't going home. We sat at the table by the window and she smoked and drank and I listened and asked myself what this was all about, what she was trying to tell me.

'One day he just stopped feeling like my lover,' she said. 'Without the mystery, love is a series of motions. I felt his tongue, but the magic was gone, I didn't drift away, I didn't float around in some great mysterious night and something came down and touched me. I felt his hand on my stomach, and there was a band-aid on his finger. Where have you gone, I thought, where has it all gone? That night I tied a handkerchief around my eyes and I stretched out on the bed and he ran his tongue over my body, but it didn't come back. I saw myself lying there. I asked him to tie my hands and feet to the bedposts and as he fucked me I floated around in nothingness and I thought: here I am lying in a bed with the man I wanted above all else and there's nothing left. It was all gone. I couldn't find it anymore.

'You know, don't you?' she said. She was no longer looking at me. Her head was bowed, a broken cigarette lay among the butts on the plate and smouldered. The spicy scent of hashish curled up around us. 'You know what's gone.'

She raised her head and opened her eyes wide.

'Papa and Mama,' she said, 'and God, and the mystery of love.' Her eyes filled.

'All that's left is the memory,' she said, 'and the memory's not enough, the memory is one great longing.'

You Have to Forget

Papa, Mama, God, the mystery of love. That, said my sister, was all gone. Then she fell asleep with her head next to the plate of leftover omelette, and I picked her up and carried her to the other side of the room, where I undressed her and slid her under the quilt. She curled up like a kitten. I bent over her and looked at the comet's tail of curls flared out on the pillow, her pale face in the mass of red-brown hair like . . . like something out of place, a pale pink pearl in a box of coloured cotton. I tucked the quilt around her and brushed a few stray curls from her forehead. Lisa shivered and raised her eyes.

'I saw you walking away,' she said.

'What?'

'That time on the country road, when they were burning off the ditches.'

'Oh?'

'You walked away and you looked over your shoulder.'

'Do you want something to drink?' I asked. 'Do you want some tea?'

'And I thought: you're all alone.'

I leaned over and stroked her cheek.

'Lisa wants to sleep,' she said. She closed her eyes and slipped away.

I stood there for a while looking at her, at the rising and falling quilt, the face that was suddenly empty, lifeless. I wondered what it was she was trying to tell me.

I pulled my sleeping bag out from under the bed, went to the table and switched off the lamp. The mugginess of the late summer evening hung in the room, and behind the window, a faint starry sky shimmered above the houses. I suddenly felt like the loneliest man in the world.

Sometimes I have this strong awareness that my spirit, my soul, is something which just happens to be travelling along, at this particular moment, in the vehicle of my body, as if, with one small movement, the right movement, I could rise up out of it, as if all I have to do is hold my breath, two, three seconds, and then, pfff . . . I escape from myself. Like a bottle of soda when you open it. The carbon dioxide hovers briefly above the neck, then dissolves into the air. Free, free from the world, from people, from history. That's how I felt that night.

The murmur of voices and televisions rose from the floor below, feet shuffled through a room. In the stairwell I heard the despondent thumping of people coming home and going out, and behind me, Lisa's even breathing. I sat down and rubbed my eyes. I know you're in there, I said to the void inside my head, wake up, don't leave me alone. I looked at the dark square of the window.

Next to the window is a patch of wall where I've tacked up the kinds of things a person saves: torn sheets of paper with notes scribbled on them, photographs (a blurred Voyager shot of Neptune, two strips of pictures of Raph and Lisa, taken in a photo booth one night when we were walking through the station), a xeroxed page from a book about drilling accidents, a newspaper clipping about the mortality rate in big cities, a page from a yellowed book, postcards I received long ago and hung up for reasons I've long since forgotten. Stuck up among all these curling and fading scraps of paper is something I once copied down, a passage written by an Italian monk in the fifteenth century. I sat there with my sleeping bag on my lap and read the passage for the thirtieth, maybe fortieth time, mechanically, as if that might help me restrain my escaping spirit.

Oh the unlimited generosity of God the Father, Oh the boundless good fortune of man: to whom it has been granted that he may have what he chooses and be what he desires. The beasts of the field at the moment of their birth

10

bring with them from their mother's womb all that they can ever become. The company of heaven, from the first moment of time or soon afterwards, are already that which they will remain through all eternity. But man is born having within himself, by the gift of God, the seed from which any created being may arise. So that whatsoever seed he chooses to cultivate, that for him will grow and bear fruit. If he chooses to lead a purely vegetative existence, then his life will have no more significance than that of the grass of the field. If he chooses to delight in sensuality, then he can become as one of the animal creation. If he chooses the way of understanding, then he can escape from his brutish nature and be turned towards heavenly things. If he becomes a true lover of wisdom, then he is like one of the angels and a child of God. But if every form of separate and individual existence fails to contain his spirit, then in the very centre of his soul is he made one with the Holy Spirit, in the mystery of God's unity which is the centre of all things and before all things had its being.

I'm not religious, far from it, and most philosophy has always gone in one ear and out the other. Questions like: what is man, and why, make me more impatient than curious. People are born, people die, but it's the same with ants. There's no master plan behind it all. Why does there always have to be cause and effect? Why can't we get used to the idea that sometimes, or usually, there just isn't any purpose, that we just move along from beginning to end and it doesn't mean a thing?

I'd hung up that passage by Pico della Mirandola — that was the monk's name — because there was a memory attached to it. The first time I read it I thought of a story Lisa once told.

One evening, the four of us were sitting in the room I shared with Raph. On the big table was a model airplane with a broken wing, surrounded by pieces of plastic and bits of paper smeared with glue. The radio hummed faintly in the background. We drank tea and talked about a leaflet which had fallen through the letterbox and which Lisa had picked up off the floor. It said the

11

Messiah was coming, very very soon. The good would be separated from the bad and the Millennium would begin. Now that we were all sitting together, Lisa and our mother on my bed, Raph and I at the table, we were determined to find out what this meant.

'Where does he come from, the Messiah?' Lisa wanted to know.

'He doesn't come from anywhere,' said Mama.

'That's impossible. Everybody's somewhere,' said Raph.

'He's somewhere, too. He's never been away.'

'Then where is he?' I asked.

According to Lisa, my mother told this story. A young man asks his master these same questions, and he answers that the Messiah has never been away: in fact, he's been here all along. But where? asks the young man. You'll find him among the beggars at the gates of Rome. But how can you tell it's him? All the beggars, says his master, have clean clothes to wear at the end of the day, and this is how they do it: they get undressed, go down to the river, wash their clothes, dry them and put them back on again. But not the Messiah. He removes one article of clothing at a time, washes it, dries it, puts it back on and begins on the next one. Why? asks the young man. Because he wants to be ready to come at any time, says his master.

'And when's that?' asked Lisa.

'When enough people want him to,' our mother had answered.

I looked out at the dark gardens and thought: the Messiah in rags and Pico's Man of Multiple Possibilities, what could they possibly have to do with each other?

The strange thing about Pico's passage is that he follows a sequence that everybody knows – from grass, to beast, to man, from the absence of all feeling, via the absence of reason, to knowledge, but just when we think he's reached the top, knowledge, he goes a step further. Higher still is the restless, homeless soul, which becomes one with the Holy Spirit.

Downstairs, a fan of light swept across the grass in one of the gardens. A door opened, somebody stepped out, and a hazy silhouette moved in the lamplit doorway. It was nearly ten, a large pale moon floated above the city. I straightened my back and peered into the darkness. In the mist of light, I saw the girl with the polka-dots. She was no more than a black figure, a long way off, but I recognized her instantly.

I first saw her a year ago, almost a year ago, when I was sitting at my table one afternoon and looked out the window and noticed a young woman in a white chair. She had her legs stretched out in the grass, her arms on the armrests, her head back. Though I couldn't see her face very clearly, she was too far away, my whole body was drawn to her. For an hour, maybe two, I sat and stared, squinting my eyes, my pencil poised in mid-air. When she got up and dragged her chair behind her into the house, a bubble burst inside my head.

From then on I saw her come out every day at around two in the afternoon. She usually sat there till about five, on a chair in the grass, reading, sleeping, always alone. Since her garden was almost completely enclosed by trees and shrubs, I had to use my binoculars to see her.

Two black circles merge, a green haze melts into the glittering brilliance of highly magnified birch leaf. Branches, leaves, rhododendrons. Grass goes shooting by. A newspaper, carelessly tossed aside ('RIOTS AT ELEC'), a glass ashtray, three broken filter tips with red lipstick rings, a knee, the gentle slope of a thigh, a piece of white fabric with black polka-dots, big black buttons (one, two, three), a gleaming triangle of skin, two taut tendons, a chin. Face.

What happens when a man gets up from his table one summer afternoon, takes his binoculars out of the closet, holds them up to his eyes and focuses on a woman he doesn't know, ten yards down, fifty yards away, basking in the sun? That man thinks he's seeing the whole world in the magnification of his binoculars. Like an atomic physicist, who nods approvingly when an astronomer shows him a picture of a nebula. I've seen this before, he thinks, the same laws, the same structure.

Behind me, Lisa mumbled something unintelligible. I picked up the sleeping bag and climbed the stairs to the attic, which I had always left empty because I preferred to live and work in one space. I unrolled the sleeping bag onto Raph's old bed, got undressed and slid into the musty envelope. As I gazed up at the window in the roof, trying to remember which constellation that was in the zinc frame, the questions Lisa had landed me with came washing up like driftwood. What road was she talking about, and why was it all gone: God, Papa and Mama, the mystery of love?

I fell asleep before I could ask myself any more questions I didn't know the answer to.

When I came down the next morning, Lisa had already left. On my table was a mug with a red lipstick mark and a plate of crumbs. I went into the kitchen, made fresh coffee, buttered some toast and ate breakfast. Then I sat down at the table and read through the pile of index cards I'd filled in over the last months.

I worked until late in the afternoon, stopping only for lunch: two sandwiches made with tuna from a can with no label, washed down with a mug of strong tea. Just before five I ran outside, where the June heat clung to the dusty pavement, and did my shopping. A few hours later I ducked into the kitchen to make spaghetti and tomato sauce and fix my usual bowl of salad (A single guy has to make sure he gets his vitamins, says Lisa). I put the plate on the index cards and the bowl on my notepad and ate, gazing out at the dusk as it settled hesitantly among the apartment buildings.

There isn't a single comfortable chair in this house. I read on my bed, I work and eat at the table by the window. I never get down to just sitting around. My view is always the same: the walled-in gardens behind my house, the gardens I can see through the window above the table. There's always someone to watch, and when it's late and dark and everyone's gone inside, there are birds fighting in the bushes, cats chasing leaves, and windows behind which people walk back and forth and talk and eat. It's the whole world, in a space of fifty by a hundred yards: around it, the bare brick walls of dilapidated buildings and houses; above it, the veiled night sky of the city. It's the home of the beast.

I have a very clear image of memory, my memory. It's an animal

14

that lives in the gardens and, in the evening, when everything's dark and seems peaceful, when I sit at the open window listening to the city (the soft wailing of sirens, the grating of iron against iron of the trams, a freight train passing through Central Station and sounding its plaintive, nasal horn) ... an animal that, on evenings like this, arches its back and rears up out of the darkness and opens its jaws at the window and soundlessly roars. Other people see a golden light, as on an autumn afternoon, a low, ageing sun, a sky iridescent as weathered glass. Or a gentle shower that spatters down and leaves you agreeably wet. Something pleasant, in any case, a moment in which the things you lost long ago seem, if only briefly, to return. Maybe even happiness itself.

I have a memory like a sieve. For Raph and Lisa, my forgetfulness is a constant source of annoyance and amusement. I remember nothing about our youth, very little about the time I spent in foster homes and only a few highlights from the year Raph and I roamed around the provinces. Yet I can walk through the oil company archives with my eyes closed and go straight to the file containing the drilling schedule of the L–4 well. What I do know about our youth comes from Lisa. She's had such a strong influence on my memory that there are times when I think I remember something and then realize I'm just chewing over one of her stories.

I went into the kitchen to get a beer. When I came back, the first lights were burning in the towering brick cliffs that surrounded the gardens.

Which road was it, where we walked, where it smelled of burning grass and the trees cast flecks of shadow on our clothes? Come on, I said to the beast, show yourself.

An enormous moon rose over the warehouses on the other side of the gardens. Mare Serenitatis, Mare Imbrium, Oceanus Procellarum, Mare Nubium, Mare Nectaris, Mare Tranquillitatis, you could see them all.

Strictly speaking, my memory ends, or begins, at the age of twelve. Before that everything is empty and grey and I find myself staring into a house where the paintings have been taken off the walls, the furniture removed and the carpets rolled up and carried

15

out. A few wisps of dust drift across the bare floor, pale stains glimmer on the wallpaper. Sometimes I look inside and there's a vague sense of recognition. Over there, in the corner, where the wall's scratched, didn't there used to be a . . . But then everything goes blurry. I reach for something and when my fingers close I'm a traveller lost in the desert who runs to an oasis and discovers only after he's dived into the water that he's the victim of a mirage.

We were twelve, Lisa and I, when our parents died. Raph was two years older. After the accident we were placed in different foster homes, since we had no family and nobody wanted two moody boys and a stubborn little girl. We didn't see each other for nine years. In all that time, Raph and I spoke only once. That was when he phoned and told my foster mother he was a friend from school.

It happened one evening. I was called to the phone, and when I was standing in the hall and picked up the heavy bakelite receiver I heard a voice I recognized instantly. If God Himself had phoned, I couldn't have been more surprised.

'Sam? It's me, Raph. I said I was in your class. This is a secret. They're not supposed to know it's me. I told her my name was Johnny.'

' "Johnny"?'

'How are you?'

'Okay,' I said. 'Fine.'

I could hear myself breathing. I thought: why does he have to pretend to be someone else, and where in the world did he come up with 'Johnny'?

'Are they listening in?'

'Yes,' I said. I looked around at my foster mother, who was standing behind me with her arms folded, frowning.

'Pretend I'm asking you something about homework.'

'Yes.'

'It's three years ago today, did you know that?'

'Chemistry?'

'Papa and Mama,' he said. 'Have you been thinking about them?'

'Yes,' I said.

16

'Don't think about them. You have to forget.'

'What?'

He sighed. There was a long silence.

'You have to forget everything,' said Raph. 'Everything.'

'Yes,' I said. 'Chapter One.'

'It's better to forget. You have to go on.'

'Okay.'

'Do what I say,' he said. 'I've got to hang up.'

I had no time to reply. There was a dry click and I stood in the hall with the heavy receiver pressed against my ear, listening to the monotonous hum of the dial tone.

In the six years that followed, I didn't hear another word from Raph. I would've phoned him, but I didn't know where he was.

His question, whether I'd been thinking about our parents, was right on target. I'd thought of nothing else. Until that phone call. From then on I began to forget, just like Raph told me to.

I have vague memories of that time. I see myself coming home from school, in a house that isn't mine, with people I mistrust. I see three staircases, leading to three bedrooms (I've lived in three foster homes), I see my schoolbag being chucked under three different beds. After that everything fades into the daydream that takes hold of me. Whatever I may have been dreaming in all those rooms on the edge of all those beds, I can't remember. I assume I was thinking back to the time when Raph and Lisa and I were still together, when our parents were still alive and the world was orderly and neat.

Nine years and three foster homes later, a letter arrived informing me that as of my next birthday, I no longer needed a guardian. I was to report to a lawyer's office to discuss such matters as inheritance and orphan's allowance. That day – it was October, the air was mild and warm – I stuffed my two pairs of jeans and the few shirts I owned, faded and worn, into my knapsack, and set off for the address given in the letter. I walked through the centre of town, the canvas pouch on my back, and looked at my shoes, which sent up little clouds of dust each time they hit the pavement: with every step, a puff of fine yellow sand. I walked past a large pond, down sagging sidewalks, past buildings in scaffolding, and I felt like a radio that hadn't been properly tuned, kind of like the way Lisa described: somewhere in the space between two stations, nothing around you but the barely audible whisper of soundlessness. I was floating, that's what I thought that day. I was floating around between two worlds and I didn't know where I was going.

At the lawyer's office, on a broad canal lined with shedding plane trees, I sat and waited on a chair screwed to the wall until my name was called and a secretary took me up in the elevator to the top floor, where she opened a carved door and showed me into a large office. On the other side of the room, his back to a semi-circular window that reached from floor to ceiling, was a heavyset man, sitting behind a teakwood desk. He rose with difficulty. He held out his hand, and smiled when I walked across the river of carpet to shake it.

'Have a seat,' he said.

I took hold of the metal chair in front of the desk and sat down. The man lowered himself into his leather armchair and mopped his forehead with a white handkerchief. I watched him as he swept a few papers together and wondered what it would be like to have such an enormous body, fingers like sausages, a head like a Dutch cheese, eyes sunken in fat.

'Why don't we get the formalities over with first,' said the man. 'Have you got a passport, driver's licence, anything like that?'

I shook my head.

'Nothing at all to show who you are?'

I took my wallet out of my knapsack and pulled out my library card. He compared me with the picture on the card and smiled.

'Well well, Sam van Dijk,' he said, 'I see it's your birthday today. Hope it's a good one.'

I nodded.

'Your brother was in here two years ago. He asked me to give you this address.'

He picked up the torn-off corner of a sheet of typing paper and handed it to me. I looked at it and read an address scribbled in pencil, in handwriting I didn't recognize.

'I'll tell you the same thing I told him. Your parents had a will.

18

That will provided for sale of the house, if anything were to happen to them, and payment of your father's life insurance. All that money has run out. It was used to pay for your upbringing and education.' He raised his hand, as if he expected me to say something. 'Your brother was furious when he heard that. I should tell you, though, it wasn't very much money. The house brought in a little over two hundred thousand guilders, the life insurance, a hundred fifty thousand. Two hundred thousand wasn't much for a house like that, I told your brother that too, but the estate had to be liquidated, so you can't expect much more.' He reached for the white handkerchief and wiped his forehead again. 'That means there was three hundred and fifty thousand guilders, around fifty thousand of which went for expenses, including our services, and nearly half on taxes. Not only have we settled all the financial matters, we've also been keeping ourselves informed about your upbringing and schooling over the years, and we've saved a number of personal possessions for you. The household effects have already been sold, in accordance with the terms of the will.' He stopped talking and looked at me. Then he returned to the documents in front of him. 'In other words, there's no inheritance. All you can expect are the usual provisions that apply in cases like these, study grants, social security benefits, that kind of thing.' He straightened up and pressed his lips together. 'I'm sorry,' he said. 'I advised your father at the time to make other arrangements, but he refused. He said, and I told your brother this too, that people had to earn their own money. I think he just didn't want you to have money at your disposal without having done anything to get it.'

I nodded.

'Coffee?' he said.

I shook my head.

'I had your brother sign for the box of personal belongings we've been saving for you. Here's a list of the contents. Now, if you'll just sign this, we're all done.'

He placed a form and a black ballpoint in front of me. I picked up the pen and looked at the sheet of paper. At the bottom was a bold flourish in which I could clearly make out the name 'Raph'.

19

I wrote my name down next to it and laid the pen on top of the paper.

'That's it,' said the man. 'Please don't hesitate to get in touch if there's anything we can do for you. I'll send the box along with your sister after she's checked the contents.'

An hour later I arrived at the address Raph had left for me, a big dilapidated house in the centre of town. On the battered green door hung a note: 'sam the red bell is mine top floor.' I pressed the red button, the door flew open and I stumbled up the stairs, bumping back and forth between the dented walls of the narrow staircase. On the top floor, in the dim light, like an echo of the dreams I'd sometimes had of him in the years when I was living with all those foster families, I saw Raph towering above me. I looked up at him and squeezed my eyes shut to dispel the memory of those dreams, and when I opened them again we were standing face to face and he held out his hand and I held out mine. He cleared his throat and asked if I wanted something to drink and I said I'd have some tea and we went inside, into the room he had rented after he 'got out', as he put it.

A green window with smudged glass was propped open, the sound of cars and the smell of warm asphalt and rubber and diesel wafted in. While Raph was filling a kettle at a cracked sink and lighting the stove, I put down my knapsack and went over to the window. I leaned out and looked at the urban anthill, the people, the cars, the tangle of tramrails and overhead wires and street-lamps, the withered leaves and newspapers in the gutters and the sand lying in small pools around the manholes, in yellowy white tongues in the gutters, like a skin across the pavingstones. Sand and windswept old newspapers and trampled paper milkshake cups and styrofoam clamshells and crumpled beer cans and lying among them, I was sure: tram tickets and crushed cigarette filters and bottle caps and receipts. I turned and looked around at the room, a space which most closely resembled a cavern hewn out of rock. Paint was peeling off the walls, on the bare floor stood a metal bed with a striped mattress and, in the middle of the room, a kitchen table and an unpainted wooden chair. Next to the door was the sink, and next to that, a small formica table with a hotplate on top. Raph was standing by the table, staring at the kettle. I turned around again and leaned out the window and told him, half shouting, everything that had happened in the past nine years, and that I needed a place to live, a room, and then the kettle sang. I looked over my shoulder. Raph, who was still standing with his back to me, took the kettle off the fire and poured boiling water into a mug. He lowered a teabag into the water and moved it up and down, up and down, and when he'd finished doing that and had dropped the teabag into the sink, he picked up the mug and set it on the kitchen table. He looked at me.

'So what are your plans?' he asked.

I shrugged. 'Don't have any. What about you?'

'Me? I wanna be free, really free, no house, no obligations. I wanna travel around, for a year or so, nobody hassling me, no school or foster homes or any of that shit.'

I nodded. 'And Lisa,' I said. 'Where's Lisa?'

'Lisa's staying where she is, till she finishes school.'

'What school?'

'Art school, she wants to paint.'

I raised my eyebrows. I could hardly remember anything about her. They say there's always something special between twins, telepathy, empathy for all I know, but for the last nine years I had hardly even thought about her or Raph. I mean: I'd thought about them every now and again, but in an abstract kind of way, without ever seeing their faces, without ever longing for them. Somehow I was always too busy adapting, always ducking and evading, in the hopes that, for a while anyway, I would be left in peace, that I'd be allowed to stay in one place for at least a year or two so I could get used to the rules and the do's and don'ts that differed from one family to the next. So while there may very well have been some kind of telepathy between Lisa and me, my daily worries had weakened that invisible bond to the point where I could no longer feel it.

'How do you know she's at art school?' I asked.

'I heard it from that lawyer, the notary, whatever the hell he is . . .'

21

The sounds of the city poured in through the open window. The room smelled of dust and dry wood. I looked at my brother, who had gone to sit on the edge of the bed and was staring down at the floor. I went over to the kitchen chair and took a seat. I kicked the knapsack standing between us and asked: 'Where to? Where do you want to go?'

I never had the feeling that *we* set off. Raph left, I trailed along after him. For Raph, our journey was one huge sigh of relief. I was a follower. Sure, I had a goal (I wanted my family back, I wanted to know what it was like to have a brother and a sister), but I didn't need to travel around the provinces for that. I needed a relative, and since Raph was the only one available, my search for the past followed the footsteps he left behind as he wandered into the future.

During that year on the road I learned what it meant to have a brother. That knowledge confused me. I had never thought you could have so much in common (same parents, twelve years of the same upbringing) and at the same time be so different. Raph was talkative, self-assured, wild, hungry, I was the opposite. The foster families I was sent to live with after my parents died had made me feel insecure. In one home I had to spend all my free time in my room ('A person must learn to amuse himself'), in another I was taught domesticity, and had to spend every evening with the family. I was sent into town to buy my own clothes, I was forbidden to even think about what I wanted to wear. I had to shower in the evening, I had to shower in the morning. I was allowed to leave food on my plate, I had to eat every bite. Each new rule was a sledgehammer blow to the foundation of my existence, and the shakier that foundation grew, the further I withdrew into my shell, the more I began to look at things from a distance. My whole life, as I discovered on the road, consisted of waiting, waiting to see what they wanted and only then taking action. Or steering clear.

Lisa, who had her teacher's certificate, once told me about an assignment she'd done with another student teacher that had got slightly out of hand. They were supposed to read to two groups of ten-year-olds and then have them draw pictures based on the story. Lisa read a fairy tale by the Brothers Grimm. Her fellow student told the other group a horror story she had made up herself, with plenty of blood and gore. Halfway through, two children were cowering in their chairs and another was sobbing uncontrollably. Soon after that the whole class broke down. Lisa's supervisor said later that they hadn't been paying enough attention. You can tell if you're going too far, he explained, at a certain point there's a change in a child's eyes: his gaze grows empty, his face expressionless. The child is then a victim, powerless, that's how he feels, he's waiting to see what's going to happen to him.

And that's how I felt in my foster years: like a child forced to submit to something too great for his soul.

What kept me going in all those families was the thought of my knapsack. The dingy canvas pouch my parents had given me for my tenth birthday lay ready and waiting at the bottom of my closet. All I had to do was fill it with a pair of jeans, a shirt, an extra pair of shoes, a bar of chocolate nicked from the cupboard and a hunk of bread, and I could flee, out of the house, into the street, away from this life. I didn't go, and I probably never would have, but it was enough just knowing that the knapsack was there and that I could leave if I wanted to.

Perhaps Raph and Lisa were victims of the same disorientation and helplessness, but while they surfaced at the end of their foster phase with the vigour of swimmers who, having dived off the edge, come up for air and get down to business, I remained distant, almost invisible.

When Raph and I were trekking from one village to the next, the only thing we seemed to have in common was a sense of loss. We talked about our parents, about Lisa, about the stuff he still remembered and I didn't, and all that time I knew we were both using the same words but meaning different things. Gradually I realized that Raph's sense of loss stemmed from bereavement, and mine, from longing.

At night, as we lay on our lumpy beds in some boarding-house in the provinces, tired of traipsing, tired of odd jobs, as Raph's

23

breathing deepened and I slipped down into the borderland between waking and dreaming, an image would appear in the darkness of one of those flea-bitten holes in Blackbird Inn or Bel-Air Lodge, the image of a long, winding road, lined with old oak trees, and somewhere in a gentle curve I'd see a big black car that had bored its nose into one of the trees, the windshield crystallized, the faint green glow of the car radio in the dark interior. A soft woman's voice rose in the still of the night, singing:

> *You must remember this,*
> *a kiss is just a kiss,*
> *a sigh is just a sigh,*
> *the fundamental things apply*
> *as time goes by.*

Each time, I'd lean over to look in the car, but just when my face was close enough to the driver's seat to be able to see anything, the image would slip away into the darkness and I'd be left staring at the chalky blue stripes on the wallpaper, the squashed flies and brown mildew stains that we'd seen in the last boarding-house and the one before that and God knows how many others.

'Happens to everyone,' said Raph, when I told him what I saw. 'It's just your imagination. Don't think about it. You'll make yourself miserable with all that daydreaming, and you're supposed to be happy, and satisfied. You are happy, aren't you?'

'Yes,' I said, 'of course I'm happy.' But all year long I walked behind him and stared at his back, at the boundless satisfaction radiating from that back, the happiness our wandering so obviously gave him, and I thought: why do I feel nothing but loss?

When the year was over we came back and went searching for Lisa. It took us almost a month to find her. Raph had got her address from the lawyer, but the bit of paper he'd scribbled it down on had disappeared. He said he had stuck it in a printing-paper box which he'd stored, together with his cameras, prints and negatives, at his foster parents' house, but when we went over to have a look, it was gone. We stood there among the heavy oak furniture of the elderly couple who, rather nervously, offered us coffee and biscuits, and looked at each other with raised eyebrows. Later, when Raph's foster parents were rummaging around somewhere in the house, searching for a suitcase that we could carry the cameras and the rest of the stuff in, I asked, 'When did you store that junk here?' 'Oh, ages ago,' he said. 'A couple of weeks before you came to see me.' I wondered how he could've known that I would look him up straight away and then go along without a struggle.

It didn't surprise me that he couldn't find the address. During our year on the road together, I had discovered that Raph was not the most orderly person I'd ever met. Every night I'd hang my trousers over a chair and my shirt by the window, while Raph lost his clothes on the way to bed and put them back on again, in reverse order, the following morning. We had even argued about this, barely a week after we'd left. I'd said to him that the trail of fabric running through our rooms was driving me crazy, and he just shrugged his shoulders and went to bed. The next morning I brought it up again. 'Okay,' he said, 'so it drives you crazy. Does that mean I'm supposed to change the way I am?' I said: 'Jesus, Raph, it's only normal to straighten up.' He nodded, and then he said maybe that was true, but he didn't feel like being normal, and anyway, who said my neatly folded trousers didn't drive *him* crazy? Who said I shouldn't do things *his* way? 'Because picking up your clothes is the goddamn norm!' I shouted. He'd raised his eyebrows and looked at me, and then said: 'Would you mind repeating that last sentence? And this time, listen to yourself.' I stood there looking at him, half dressed, my shirt over one shoulder, and I ran the sentence I'd just spoken through my mind and thought: I'm sure I'm right, but it does sound pretty bad, it sounds like an unreasonable parent saying you have to because they tell you to.

Since Raph couldn't find the bit of paper (though he did later, much later, after we had already been to see Lisa and she turned out to live somewhere else), I went back to the lawyer's office

25

where my independence had been confirmed a year earlier.

The fat man was sitting, just like the time before, behind his desk, the enormous window at his back, and he smiled broadly when I came in. He held up his hand, said hello and motioned toward the chair in front of the desk, but I remained standing and said that Raph and I needed Lisa's address, that we'd lost it.

'You mean you haven't got in touch with her yet?' He frowned.

I told him we'd been away for a while.

'She's married,' he said. 'Did you know that?'

'No.'

He stared past me. There was a long silence. Then he looked at me again. 'Try that black cabinet over there, under "D".'

I turned around and went to the row of filing cabinets next to the door. I pulled open the drawer that said 'C/D' and read through the labels on the files until I found our surname. I pulled out the file and went back to the desk. The fat man took the file and opened it. He went through the papers, muttering softly under his breath.

'Here it is,' he said after a while. 'Write it down.'

He pushed a cup of pencils toward me and pointed to a plastic holder with little squares of paper. I took a pencil and a piece of paper and copied down the address as he read it aloud. When I was finished, he closed the file and gave me a long look.

'How are things with you and your brother?'

I shrugged my shoulders: 'Too soon to say.'

He laughed.

'Your sister was in here a month ago,' he said. 'She wanted to know where she could reach the two of you and she left behind this address. I don't know where it is. I've never even heard of the street.' He scanned my face. 'I really hope you look after each other. I know it's none of my business, and I can't help you in any way, but still . . .'

I nodded and held out my hand. He leaned heavily across the desk and laid four chubby fingers in my palm.

That night we bent over the map, Raph and I, looking for the street where Lisa lived. It was somewhere in the industrial estate.

'What the hell is she doing in the middle of all those factories?' said Raph.

'You said she wanted to paint, didn't you?' I said. 'That she was going to art school? Maybe she's got a studio there. She'd never be able to find a room with a high enough ceiling here in town.'

He raised his eyebrows and stared into space.

'So what's next?' I asked. 'Do we go visit her?'

Raph nodded. He stood up and got his jacket, which was lying on the bed, and I got mine from the hook on the door and we walked down the stairs, into the street, off to find our sister.

The industrial estate was a shock. We'd seen our share of deterioration, mostly in small towns in the provinces, where factories had moved out and all kinds of old halls and depots were left vacant. But this was total decrepitude. There was practically nothing left. The roads were neglected, lampposts sagged and either didn't work or had been sawn down. Young birch trees poked up through the asphalt, grass grew rank between the tiles, and smashed, blackened windows revealed empty halls where there had once been a fire and the air still smelled vaguely of charred wood. Only twice did we see signs of human life. First, an old man on a bicycle laden with scrap, and later, on a barren field, a group of teenagers racing around in a kind of car without a body, just a motor and chairs in a frame made of steel tubes. Here and there were patches of burning grass and they were driving that prehistoric thing through the flames and each time one of them burst out of the fire in a shower of sparks they all started yelling their heads off. Yahoo! Yeah!

We'd brought along the map so we could get a rough idea of where we were every now and then, but it wasn't easy finding our way in that post-industrial inferno. There were hardly any signs, some of the roads were blocked with barricades of rubble and empty oil drums and wrecked cars, and so many factories had been torn down that we mistook several of the vacant lots for streets. After an hour of wandering around, we found a fairly intact piece of road where a couple of Nissen huts stood next to a huge empty building. This had to be where Lisa lived. We walked along the high black front of the building, past boarded-up windows, charred window-ledges and jagged holes with chimney pots sticking out. In the middle of the wall we found a yellow door covered with names on bits of paper. There was a large brass plate with a button. Raph pressed it. Several minutes went by. Then we heard footsteps, bolts were pushed back, a chain fell, a lock groaned. The door opened slightly and a guy with a Mohican peered through the crack.

'We're here for Lisa,' I said.

'Don't know her.'

'We heard she lived here, with her husband. She paints.'

'Everybody paints,' he said.

'Very witty,' said Raph. 'Now if you'll just step aside, we'd like to see our sister.'

'How do I know you aren't cops?'

'Want me to show you my prick?' said Raph.

The guy with the Mohican looked at me.

I said: 'What does a person have to do to get into this place?'

'I don't know any Lisa,' he said again.

'We've already been through that,' said Raph.

I said: 'Are we supposed to identify ourselves or something? We're here to visit our sister, dammit! What is this, a prison?'

Just then Raph kicked the door as hard as he could, right by the handle. I shot forward and rammed my shoulder against the wood. I fell inside, against the Mohican, dragging him down with me. We went crashing to the floor. I scrambled to my feet and pulled him up by his T-shirt. Raph grabbed his arms and pinned them behind his back.

'Mission accomplished, Agent 41,' said Raph.

'Right-o,' I said.

The guy tried to wrest himself free, but Raph pushed his arms up to his shoulderblades and made him stand with his face to the wall, while I let go of his shirt.

'Caution is an admirable quality,' said Raph. 'You just have to know who you're being cautious *with*. Now, where is she?'

28

'Upstairs,' he said. 'Jesus, let go of me. I thought you were cops.'

'Where upstairs?'

'Three flights up and to the left, somewhere at the back.'

Raph gave his arms another tug and then released him. We turned around and walked through the dimly lit hallway to a wide staircase, a bit farther down.

This staircase had once been the company's pride and joy. Now the beige stone was cracked in places, and parts of the wooden banister were missing. The wall alongside it had been painted and written on by the new occupants. On the third floor we came across a spraypaint fresco, late twentieth century, of Paradise. Adam and Eve looked like the airbrush barbarians you see on pinball machines, forefathers of Conan. Adam had a cord around his brawny right arm and an erection you could slam nails into a wall with. Eve was an Amazonian body builder with granite breasts. There was a creamy white unicorn, a tree with a kind of boa constrictor wriggling among gleaming apples, and in one corner, partly hidden by an exotic fern, Tintin was buggering Bianca Castafiore. Raph clicked his tongue as we walked past.

'You think Lisa painted this?' I said.

'I don't know,' said Raph, 'but if she did, we'd better not count on white ankle socks.'

All the way at the back of the building, on the fourth floor, we knocked on a black door that said 'Lisa/Simon'. It was a while before we heard footsteps. Then the door opened and we found ourselves staring into our sister's face.

If you haven't seen someone for a long time, there are two possible ways of greeting each other: either you just stand there, avoiding each other's eyes, hands held out shyly, mumbling unintelligible things, or you rush into each other's arms, embrace fervently and let the tears flow. In our case, it was a combination of both. We like to be different. Lisa stood in the doorway, we stood opposite her, and for a full thirty seconds we stared at each other in total silence. Then she took a step forward, our sister, and flung herself at us, hugging Raph with her right arm and me with her left. She lowered her head and shoved it between us, and there we were with this sobbing girl wedged under our armpits. Raph looked at me. He made an unhappy face. I pressed my lips together and shook my head. Then we leaned over and patted her awkwardly on the back. We stood there like that for a while, waiting for the storm of emotion to subside.

When we had finally gone inside and sat down at an ink-stained wooden table, wormlike squiggles of dried paint running across the top, as if somebody had been using it as a palette, Lisa told us how long she'd been searching for us, that she'd even put ads in the paper and all she'd got were dirty letters. Raph and I sat and listened and drank the bottles of beer she opened. When she was through talking, Raph explained how we'd managed to find her. Now and then she moved her head: uh uh, uh-huh. I looked at her, at the unkempt, reddish brown curls, the pale face and the dark eyes with smudged mascara, the peculiar outfit she was wearing: a voluminous pair of pants the colour of three rainbows, a faded black tank top and a baggy red shirt that kept slipping down one shoulder. She looked up and smiled, I smiled back. As we sat there grinning at each other, she suddenly froze. She put an index finger to her lips and looked over our heads to the wall, where someone had tacked up a yellowed reproduction of Breughel's *Tower of Babel*. 'Hold on, you guys,' she said. 'I just thought of something.' She stood up and walked out of the room, through a sort of hole in the wall. The frame was still there, but the door was gone. Raph turned to me and raised his eyebrows. I drank the cold beer and looked around.

It was a square room we were sitting in, twenty by twenty, something like that. Large flakes of paint were peeling from the high moulded ceiling, a thick pipe with a hook on the end wrapped with electrical wire stuck out of a ring of grapevines. The walls had been whitewashed, but large dark patches showed through the paint. Next to the door hung a black telephone which was missing its bakelite casing, so you could see right inside. The wall around the phone was scribbled over with addresses, numbers and notes. Against the back wall of the room was a wobbly set of cupboards and shelves with a steel counter and sink across the top. On top of a small painted refrigerator, green with wriggly black lines, was the gas burner.

'Great space,' said Raph. 'Perfect height.'

In the distance, we heard Lisa's voice. We got up and walked through the hole in the wall.

We found ourselves in a large room with a mattress on the floor. Just below the ceiling, suspended between two entwined steel wires, was an aluminium pipe with clothes hanging from it.

'That's just the thing for you,' said Raph. 'Not only could you hang up your clothes, you could hoist them all the way up in the air!'

We walked across the floor, pushed aside a curtain and entered a long room that was almost completely shrouded in darkness. One wall was covered with sheets of black plastic. A trickle of light came in through the brownish glass sawtooth roof, just enough to see Lisa, at the other end of the room, standing next to a table. She reached up and pulled a cord. Two fluorescent tubes came on, crackling and sputtering.

On the table was a box made of heavy grey cardboard, all taped up and sealed in three places with strips of paper.

'The lawyer gave me this box, but he said I wasn't allowed to open it unless you were there,' said Lisa.

'Go ahead,' said Raph.

Lisa looked from him to me. The fluorescent lights hummed. In the distance I heard the muffled screech of an electric guitar. I nodded.

She picked up a pallet knife, stuck it in the tape, where the flaps met, and pressed down. She drew the knife back and forth and cut through the seal. She pushed back the flaps and looked inside.

This is the secret of our life, I thought, the moment we've all been waiting for, the ultimate magic trick.

Lisa stuck her hand in the box and pulled out a pile of paper. She put it on the table and peered at the typewritten letters dancing across the white surface.

'List of contents,' she said, pushing aside the top sheet of paper. 'We don't want to see that.' She picked up the pile again and

31

leafed through it. 'Deeds, a will, all kinds of official stuff.' She put the paper down next to the list of contents and looked back in the box. She groped around in the cardboard muzzle and drew out something greyish.

'Jesus!' said Raph. 'The Mercury!'

It was a space capsule, a half diabolo made of plastic, with faint lines running across it that suggested hatches and plates. I reached out and took the thing from Lisa.

'You're touching it!' said Raph. 'He's holding it in his hand! Sing! Dance!'

I looked at Raph.

'You're not going to tell me you don't recognise the Mercury?' he said.

'I do, but . . .'

Lisa said: 'Dad gave you guys a Dakota kit, remember? Because you weren't allowed to play with the Mercury.'

Raph shook his head. 'He doesn't remember a thing. He's got the memory of an ant.'

Lisa looked at me for a long time. Then she shifted her gaze to Raph. For a moment it seemed as if they were trying to tell each other something.

I stood there with the model of the Mercury in my hand and tried to remember what the damn thing meant.

I knew what the Mercury was, and that Glenn and Carpenter had made their first flights in it. I even remembered that they'd insisted on it having a window, after the designers had shown them a model that was completely sealed up, and that they had also wanted hand controls so they would feel like real pilots, not just hunks of flesh being shot off into space for the sake of an experiment. I knew all of this, but I couldn't connect the object I was holding in my hand with my father.

'Tapes,' said Lisa. 'A whole pile of tapes.' She scooped up two or three handfuls of plastic boxes.

Raph sighed. 'Jesus,' he said, 'some inheritance. Model space-ships and badly recorded music. Who the hell put those tapes in there? They were ours! You call that an inheritance?'

'Maybe there's a message on them,' I said.

Raph pressed his lips together and stared at the heap of plastic boxes. 'There's nothing on there but fragments of classical music. Mendelssohn's Violin Concerto, the first few minutes. One lousy excerpt from the *St Matthew Passion*, *O Haupt voll Blut und Wunden*. That kind of crap. Rita Reys singing "As Time Goes By". He was always recording junk like that for us.'

'Who?'

'Our father!' said Raph. 'Jesus, use your brains. Nobody's that much of a moron.'

Lisa's eyes wandered from me to Raph. 'Why don't we just tell him what happened?' she said.

'First look in the box,' said Raph.

Lisa took hold of the flaps and turned the box upside down. A dark green Leatherette photo album dropped out and fell open on the table before us, its pages beckoning. The first thing I saw was a photograph of a tall old man with a shock of white hair. He was carrying a child on his shoulders. Lisa picked up the album and stared at the photo.

'Who's that?' asked Raph.

'That's Sam, with our grandfather.'

'Jesus,' said Raph, 'I can't even remember the man.'

'Neither can I,' said Lisa. 'Mama used to tell me about him. His name was Sam too.'

I leaned over Raph's shoulder. The man in the picture was a giant. He radiated strength and a zest for living, even on paper. The little boy on his shoulders had his hands on the old man's head and was peering nearsightedly at the photographer.

There was a noise behind us. Somebody stumbled across the room and called out something unintelligible. Lisa threw everything back in the box and gestured to us to follow her.

In the other room, a man about our age was bent over the table, reading the front page of a newspaper.

'Simon? My brothers are here.'

The man jumped. His eyes went from Lisa to Raph and then to me. Raph stepped forward and held out his hand. As they said their names and smiled at each other, I felt Lisa's eyes on me. Her husband turned around and shook my hand.

33

'You two look alike,' he said, nodding toward my sister.

I glanced at Lisa, as if to verify this statement, then looked back at him.

'How did you find us?' he asked.

Raph began telling the story of our search. Lisa grabbed my arm and dragged me towards the hole in the wall.

'Let's go clean up that mess,' she said. She spoke loudly, as if she wanted to make sure everyone knew we were leaving.

In the long room with the covered windows, I picked up the bottle of beer I'd left behind and drank down the last two or three gulps. Then I looked at my sister. She was leaning against the table, her hands grasping the tabletop. Her eyebrows were raised and she was studying my face.

'What's the matter?' I asked.

'Do we really look alike?'

'I don't know. Is that a problem?'

She shook her head.

'What have you guys been up to since you've been living on your own?'

I turned my back to the table and pushed myself up, until I was sitting. I ran my eyes over the brick walls, over the ceiling, some four or five yards above me. I swung my legs onto the table and turned to face Lisa. 'I don't live alone,' I said. 'As soon as I was free I went to Raph's and I spent one night there and then we took off. And you?'

She shrugged. She stuck her hands in her pockets and looked down at her shoes.

'I just stayed with my parents, my foster parents, and finished school.'

She kept on staring down.

And then? What happened then? I thought.

'You want another drink?' she asked.

I nodded.

She reached for the cord hanging from the tray of fluorescent light, but before she could pull it I asked: 'When did you get married?'

'Just before exams. I was working as a waitress in a pub, to

34

earn a little extra money. Simon and his friends used to hang out there a lot. He was studying anthropology.'

'Was?'

'He quit.'

I waited for her to tell me what he was doing now, but she said nothing. She reached out and pulled the cord. The light went 'spet'. The walls withdrew into the shadows. I slid down from the table and shuffled along behind her to the door.

She said: 'I'm the breadwinner. I work for a publishing company that makes calendars. Porno calendars, male pin-ups.'

'Where do you get your models?'

'I've got a wild imagination.'

In the other room Raph and Simon were sitting at the table drinking beer. Raph turned around when we came in. He looked at Lisa and me and grinned.

'The twins have found each other,' he said. 'Everything's gonna be all right.'

The gardens behind my house were dark. The moon had reached the highest point of its arc and cast bluish parallelograms on the floor. Which road was it, where we walked? I shut my eyes and tried to remember.

The asphalt we walked along, Raph and I, as cars whooshed by in clouds of rain. Winding paths of tamped sand, bordered with meadows of buttercups and fresh green grass. Long, endless brick roads between two villages, nothing but timber forest to the right of us and parcel after parcel of farmland to the left. I saw a whole encyclopedia of roads. Lisa's wasn't among them.

I finished my beer, straightened up the room and went to bed. As I lay on my back and stared at the ceiling, I suddenly saw, for the first time since my travels with Raph, the gentle curve with the wreck bored into the tree.

If you try to remember something, you always end up with something you could do without.

How Did It All Begin?

The next morning I walked downtown to the oil company. I said hello to the porter, got myself a cup of coffee and opened the door to the well archives. I switched on the fluorescent lights, took out the box of index cards and pulled my chair over to the cabinet that contained the file I was working on.

Usually I'll work in the archives for a month or two, maybe three, until my notes have grown into a spaghetti of sentences and lines and arrows. Then I take my index cards home and write the umpteenth report on things I couldn't care less about: 'A Summary of Casing and Piping in the Great Field; K-14, a Case History'.

I could just as easily have worked at a municipal archives, or for an insurance company. The subject isn't important. What matters to me is the search, slowly penetrating into an unfamiliar world whose pathways, short cuts and secret chambers I gradually come to know.

I owe my occupation to the man in charge of the archives, Mr Huizinga. A month or so after our return, when Raph and I had rented a loft, a large rectangular space in an old warehouse on the edge of the city centre, the place I stayed behind in when Raph moved to a factory in the abandoned industrial estate, I ran into him at an employment agency. He was looking for an archivist. Was I interested? I'd ummed and ah'd, saying that I wasn't an archivist, that I hadn't studied anything in particular (nothing at all, to be exact). Huizinga told me he already knew that (he was an old friend of my father's), but surely a clever guy like me could sort out a thing or two? And the pay wasn't bad either. It was nothing permanent, he said, just an odd job which, if I were to do it well, might be followed by other odd jobs. I said, 'I'm not sure' and 'how long?' and 'in what way?', the things people say to put off making a decision, and then Huizinga said he wasn't doing it for me, goddammit, he just couldn't make heads or tails of those archives, they weren't even alphabetized yet! I told him I'd drop by and we could talk about it. That was the beginning. From then on I had a profession, got regular assignments from the oil company and even began doing the same kind of work for other companies, since Huizinga was quite pleased with my first efforts and recommended me to his business associates. It wasn't exactly what I'd expected to be doing with my life (Raph's a photographer, Lisa paints, my father was an astrophysicist and my mother filled in as an executive secretary for companies in chaos; everyone in my family has made something of themselves) but at least I was alive.

I was sitting on the floor between the tall carousel cabinets, surrounded by paper, when Huizinga came in. He leaned against a cabinet and looked around at the mess.

'Everything okay?'

I nodded.

'When can you be done?'

'In a week or two, if necessary.'

It was the first time he had ever asked me when I'd be through with a study.

'Take a month, a month and a half if you like.'

I put down my pile of index cards and looked at him.

'We're stopping the project,' he said. 'The money's run out. We're going to limit ourselves to preserving the files. I've told them that Kopakker is an exceptionally complex study that could go on for quite some time.'

He was feeling guilty, I could tell.

'What will you do when you're finished here?' he asked.

I shrugged my shoulders. I stacked up a bunch of files and got to my feet. 'No idea,' I said. 'Something new always comes along.'

Huizinga nodded. We stood there awkwardly and thought the things that people wish they could say at times like those: I'm sorry, it's not your fault, I just wanted . . .

'When are you going to write your report?'

'What?'

'Kopakker. When do you start writing?'

'I've already started. I'll get back to it next week. I have to Xerox some stuff first.'

We talked a bit more about the archives, I showed him a cabinet that kept turning to the wrong row of files, we looked over the projects I'd done in the last few months, and then, after a few more half apologies, he left. The air-conditioning hummed in the little archives. I heard footsteps up and down the corridor, the tea trolley coming out of the elevator and starting its rounds, clinking and clattering. I walked back to the files and paused for a moment at the window, the one overlooking the car park. I thought about Kopakker, the site where a drilling rig had sunk right into the ground, buildings, trucks, equipment and all.

I think it was then that I realized that I was living in a different world from the one I'd always thought.

I came from a youth full of uncertainties, had let myself be dragged along toward adulthood in my brother's slipstream and waited, once I got there, for life to begin, on the assumption that there was a moment in everyone's lives when the dust settled and the chaos and uncertainty disappeared.

I stood at the window and gazed out at the slide puzzle of cars. Life hasn't begun, I thought, it'll never be calm and clear. This is Plato's Cave. I'm watching the shadows moving across the cave wall.

For someone who has learned not to rely on his memory, who doesn't know his own past and is dependent on the stories his sister and brother tell him, that's a shocking discovery. A discovery I probably could've lived with, I think I could've got used to a world that wasn't what it seemed, if I hadn't remembered, at that very moment, what had happened to Echo, a week, maybe a week and a half earlier.

I can't say I really knew Echo, but somehow, because of everything that happened, he's become part of my permanent collection of ghosts: Echo, the girl with the polka dots, the faceless figures of my parents and grandparents and a couple of girlfriends who, except for some trivial detail, I've totally forgotten.

The first time I saw him, at least I thought it was the first time, was when Raph and I were standing and waiting for someone in the hospital quarantine, in a long corridor with grey walls and cream-coloured iron doors wide enough for a bed, and a bluish glass wall. We were talking about who that could possibly be for, all that glass, in a ward where everyone was lying behind blank doors with no numbers, no door handles, in high beds under tents of milky plastic, below which you could see the outlines of chrome tubes and motionless bodies, as if they had tucked in a bunch of dolls. Raph was fiddling around with his camera. He was turning the lens and focusing on everything in sight, and suddenly he nudged me. I followed his nod, out the window, and there, on the slope that rose up steeply just behind the glass, I saw two pairs of legs taking the kind of little steps you often see in hospitals, something halfway between walking slowly and shuffling. We couldn't see who they were, the people who belonged to those legs, because the quarantine was a semibasement, so we had to squat down and look up, and when we had done that and could finally see their faces, Raph said he knew them. 'That's Echo, the guitar player,' he said. 'Echo and his sister. She's a patient here. She committed suicide, for the tenth or twentieth time.' I looked up at the shuffling pair, and as it began to dawn on me what a strange situation this was, the two of them above ground and the two of us squatting below, craning our necks to be able to see them, Echo's sister suddenly buried her face in her hands and began sobbing, sobbing her heart out, with shaking shoulders and a head that said 'no', and Echo looked around as if he was afraid somebody might see him. He rubbed his forehead and pressed his lips together and then he put his hand on her shoulder and pushed her onto a bench and sat down beside her, and he stroked her hair and looked the other way, somewhat absently, as though he knew as well as anybody else that there was nothing to be done. Just then, the man we were waiting for showed up, and Raph grabbed his bag and his cameras and followed him down that peculiar corridor, to a short flight

39

of stairs that led to the ground floor. I bent down to pick up my stuff, rather slowly, because I couldn't tear myself away from the sight of the musician and his sister sitting there on that bench in the hospital garden, so alone, side by side yet so alone, and as I stood there, half-stooped, I heard Raph asking what was taking me so long. I grabbed the tripod and the dented lights, called out that I was coming and walked to the end of the corridor, but when I reached the stairs, I bent down to take one last look at the people on the bench, and suddenly I knew that I'd seen him before, and I knew where and when.

Years ago, when Raph used to photograph musicians and I, following in his wake, would find myself in all kinds of dreary halls, giant shoeboxes with fake wood wainscoting on the walls and cracked bowl-shaped lamps hanging from filthy ceilings and torn linoleum floors, that was really the first time I'd ever seen him, in a dressing room. He was sitting on a battered zinc dustbin, strumming a slow flamenco on his electric guitar. 'Echo used to be in Willie's band,' Raph had said, as he screwed a fifty-millimetre lens onto his camera, held it to his eye and focused. The man with the guitar looked up and stopped the chord he'd just struck, Raph pressed the shutter release. 'Willie's band . . .' said Echo bitterly, and he told us that Willie, whoever that was, used to be in his band, but that he'd left and gone on tour in America, which was why everybody had got the wrong idea about things. I listened to him telling the story of his rise and fall, because that's what it was, the classic rise and fall, and I remember thinking, even then: why isn't he making it? He can do anything! Later, on the way home, Raph told me that Echo wasn't his real name, but that the musicians in town called him that because he always blasted the reverb up to ten and then, his head thrown back and his eyes shut, played question and answer with his own notes. 'He talks to his guitar,' said Raph. 'You can see his lips moving as he plays, and his guitar talks back.' He also told me that Echo was descended from an old Armenian family that had come here by way of North Africa and Spain and I wondered what he meant by that, what that explained.

By this time I was upstairs, in a low dark corridor where Raph

40

and the man from the hospital were waiting. Raph held up his exposure meter and looked at the dial of numbers and every now and then he nodded at the man. I started setting up the lamps. I opened the tripod and followed the instructions that Raph muttered under his breath, moving one lamp, raising or lowering another.

I didn't run into Echo again for at least another year. I forgot what I'd seen, in the hospital and that time at the Bellevue, until one morning when I walked into the Molenaarsteeg and there he stood, at the end of the cleft of brick and concrete formed by the back of a large office building and the windowless walls of a cafe and a couple of shops. His hair was greasy and black and wispy and hung about his head in swaying tendrils. He was wearing an old blue jacket that had slid halfway down one shoulder, and a pair of shapeless jeans that sagged between his legs like a wet diaper. On the pavement was a half-empty bottle of wine which he was shuffling around with his shoes hanging open, the laces trailing behind him. He turned round and round like a ballerina in a music box, his left hand hovering in the air somewhere near his shoulder, his right hand plucking vaguely at his stomach, and I heard his broken voice making meowing sounds. I stood all the way at the other end of the alley and could see every detail, as though he were standing in a spot of great clarity, a place where the air was made of glass, or water. His face glowed in the light of the low morning sun, and I could see that his eyes were slightly crossed and his mouth contorted, not in a cruel or sad way, more as if he had tried to smile but wasn't very good at it anymore and was making a face that came as close as possible. Just then, I remembered what Raph had said, that day in the hospital, when we'd seen him walking with his sister: 'Losers, a whole family of losers. They've all got some vague talent or other, but none of 'em knows what to do with it,' and I thought of the fate of that other Echo, the first one, the real one, the nymph who withered away into a voice and saw her beloved Narcissus heading for disaster, while all she could do was repeat his desperate last words.

The last time I saw him was one evening, when I went along

41

with Raph to hand in photographs to a newspaper, a week or two before Huizinga came to tell me they were stopping the project. Raph stood talking to an editor, while I stared out the studio window. I was gazing down at the empty parking lot, the graffiti-covered walls, the big cardboard boxes of rubbish, when all of a sudden a hazy figure tottered into the light of the sodium lamps. His right hand was slightly raised, as if he were looking for something to hold on to, only there was nothing that offered support. He made his way to one of the walls and leaned his back against it, then slid down and bowed his head. As he sat there on the ground, a pile of forgotten laundry, his legs stretched out in front of him, a beam of light danced over the pavingstones, and first one, then another, and then a third motorcycle came gliding through the gap between the office buildings. The three bikes rode smoothly onto the parking lot and began a ballet of quivering beams that crossed each other, curved slowly down-ward, and then suddenly, in one flowing movement, shot across the walls of the parking lot. One of the motorcycles made a lazy semi-circle and stopped in front of the heap of clothes that lay slumped against the wall. The others circled around the car park. I couldn't hear anything, the windows were well insulated, but I wondered why the man down below didn't look up. The three bikes must have been making an incredible racket. The motorcycle standing in front of the tramp rode forward, until he was so close to the man against the wall, I was sure he was touching him. 'Jesus,' I said. Raph and the editor came over and stood next to me. In the sodium light, the black leather hand of the biker moved rhythmically back and forth. 'What do they want?' I asked. 'Noth-ing,' said the man from the newspaper. 'They're just playing around.' Something in his voice told me he wasn't sure. The right leg of the man on the motorcycle swung back, dangled briefly next to the chrome-plated exhaust pipe, then swept forward and planted a boot in the tramp's side, just below the ribs. The man on the ground, who had just glanced up, bashed his head against the wall. His body seemed to lift slightly, then slumped forward. The motorcycle jolted, the front wheel tipped and rode straight over the tramp's outstretched leg onto the car park. 'Oh God,' said Raph. 'I'm calling the police!' shouted the man from the paper. 'Don't go away!' He turned around and ran out of the studio. The motorcycle made a graceful curve, until it was standing between the other two. The gloved claws lay on the throttles and moved back and forth, back and forth, at exactly the same time. Gas on, gas off, gas on, gas off. The tramp pressed himself up along the wall until he was standing, one hand on his chest, the other behind him. He bent over and spit something on the ground. The first motorcycle started riding forward again. The tiny figure standing there in the pit of coloured light and stone raised his head and shook a slow, vague 'no'. He inched his way along the wall. The other two motorcycles started up. The tramp began to walk, half staggering, first along the wall ('Don't go left!' I shouted. 'Don't go left!'), and then in an unsteady zigzag over the car park, towards an open shed with a couple of big zinc skips. He'd gone no more than five yards when the first motorcycle overtook him and a boot hit him full in the back. He spun halfway around. He stumbled and fell to his knees. I saw him pause to catch his breath. A few seconds later he began crawling forward. No sooner had he started moving than the next motorcycle came towards him, and as the bike went past, just missing him, a black boot caught him behind the leg. The tramp made the limp, slow movement of a rag doll tossed in the air. He turned around and landed flat on his back. At the same time, the third motorcycle ran over his arm. The arm turned under the wheel and the tramp's mouth opened, wider and wider. His body curled like paper on fire. He lay there for a moment on the pavement, then slowly got to his feet. When he was standing again, half stooped, his hands on his knees, he raised his head, first in the direction of the three circling bikes, then higher. His eyes travelled over the wall of the building, toward our window. 'Echo,' said Raph. 'My God, Echo.' I beat my hand against the window and screamed. Echo lowered his head and shuffled slowly toward the skips. The motorcycles advanced. They rode in smooth arcs over the oil- and rubber-stained pavingstones. The first one missed him, the second kicked him in the side, and when the third motorcycle rode up and Echo was stretched out on the ground, his cheek against the pavement and his arms spread wide, the wheels ran him over from head to toe and he lay still.

'Sam?'

One of the department secretaries was standing in the doorway.

'You wouldn't happen to be going down to the basement?'

I nodded.

'Do me a favour, bring me up a box of printer paper?'

'Okay.'

She blew me a kiss and disappeared. I went to my chair, swept the index cards into a pile, locked the filing cabinets and walked out of the archives. I wandered down the gleaming linoleum in the corridor, to the elevator. Behind the open doors, secretaries sat typing and men in white shirts peered at their computer screens. When I passed Huizinga's office, he was sitting at his desk doing something with a paper clip and a rubber band. He held up his hand as I walked by.

I rang for the elevator and watched the numbers light up over the doors. Everything's happening at once, I thought. Lisa talks about something I don't understand and I suddenly start worrying about my blank memory, Huizinga tells me the project's ending and I think of Echo. What is this? The soul telling me enough is enough? Wake up, Sam? Look around you? I am looking, I said to my thoughts, and I believe the world is different than I thought it was. I believe! Hallelujah!

I got in the elevator and pressed 'B' for basement. The elevator went down (or the building went up – in a Platonic world, they're both equally true) and I felt around in my jacket pocket to see if I had any cigarettes. I found an old pack of Lisa's with a transparent plastic lighter wedged in. The doors slid open, the fluorescent lights went on in the dark cellar. The concrete gleamed softly, the smell of wood and paper crept into my nostrils. At the back of the cellar, where barrels of shredded paper stood against the wall and a hand truck waited obediently for something to do, I pulled a cardboard box of printer paper off a rack. I sat down on top of it and lit a cigarette.

We took the train to the east, Raph and I, to the most easterly place we could reach by rail, a spot where the tracks ended under a bumper. Then we got out and started to walk. We followed a road that ran square to the tracks, and as we walked along in silence, thinking about all the things we were going to do – at least, I was – and trying to figure out where we were walking and whether we'd ever get out of this godforsaken wilderness of stone and asphalt and one-storey houses, as we walked we automatically fell in line, in an order that hasn't really changed since: Raph in front, slightly stooped, sauntering; me at the back, thumbs hooked behind the straps of my knapsack, staring at a spot between his shoulderblades.

We trekked through sparsely populated regions, from odd job to odd job (and if there was no work, we tried to find a generous soul), for nearly a year. Until the end finally arrived, in the form of a red Chevrolet.

That was in October. We'd been working for a month or two in a potato starch plant. Raph stood at the sorting machine under a dusty window, and if he looked outside he was always the first to see it, the red dot on the grey strip of road through the potato fields, a matchhead gliding slowly over a vast expanse of flint. It was eleven-thirty by then. The weary Chevy would come to a halt on a bumpy piece of side road, between two interminable fields that breathed sad mists and were empty and grey.

At a quarter to twelve, the manager reported to the hazy red fleck. We'd see him, blowing on his hands, his jacket hanging loosely about his sinewy body, standing awkwardly at the right-hand door until it swung open and swallowed him up. Gulp. Sometimes the car would start rocking gently, as if somebody were in there dancing, which wasn't the case. Everyone, the entire plant, knew what was going on. Inside that Chevy was Rika. She did it wholesale.

The manager took a quarter of an hour, then tumbled out the door, every time, and hurried back to the plant, half walking half running, as if he'd suddenly remembered something very important. Once he was inside, the whistle blew.

Over the years a kind of pecking order had evolved in the line

45

that formed outside the car during the break. How long you'd worked at the plant, how strong you were, how smart, how good you were at boasting about it: all these were factors that determined your place in the line. When we worked there the line consisted of fifteen men, and whoever came last needed a pretty strong stomach. Rika may still have looked like a young boy's dream, but after thirteen men the car reeked of mushrooms and Rika's clothes stuck to every inch of her body. The last few had to literally work their way through the sperm of those who had gone before them. Raph and I stood at the end of the line.

Looking back, you wonder why the hell you'd want to share a ten-dollar whore, week in, week out, with a whole potato starch plant, but after a year of wandering around and sleeping in mouldy little rooms and sheds full of rats and wearing the same clothes day after day and sometimes nothing but ditchwater to wash your hands and face, it not only seemed perfectly normal for us to go to the Chevy along with thirteen other workers, it was something we deeply and passionately craved.

Rika was forty, a little over forty maybe, and she had thick black hair that we figured was probably pinned up when the manager got there and, in the course of the next thirteen clients, sagged lower and lower, until it was our turn and she lay sprawled across the wide leather front seat with an absent, weary expression on her face, damp wisps along her cheeks, groaning, saying: 'Hurry up, boys. Rika's tired.' The first time, Raph couldn't do it. She was so far away, he said later, so 'lifeless', that it never occurred to him that he was expected to do anything. Somehow he just couldn't imagine making love to 'that'.

Where the ritual came from, we didn't know. Nobody did. Everyone, from foreman to unloader, could remember how he'd started out at the end of the line and through the years worked his way up to more desirable places. Raph thought it must've started with the manager, since he was unmarried and a little weird, but I was sure Rika had been there long before the plant was even built and that she had more addresses like this. There must've been other places in the area where in the mornings, at an appointed time, the red Chevy came rolling up and the whole

46

plant, first the manager and then the workers, had their weekly fuck.

One day, Raph and I were walking home, discussing our usual 'Friday topic': how unfair it was that we'd have to stay at the back of the line until somebody died or went to work somewhere else. That is, if we hadn't already left by then.

'Those guys all have wives!' Raph cried, by which he meant that they could do it whenever they wanted.

We were twenty-one and twenty-three and could count our sexual experiences on the fingers of one hand. We roamed around, living off the odd jobs we picked up here and there, we were unshaven and, most of the time, unwashed, and we had no women at our disposal.

'We've got to get to the front of the line,' I said, thinking, as I did every Friday, about Rika, about the plant, about the millions of potatoes that rolled past you in a single day and where they were going and who would be eating them – in short: about life itself.

We walked along the asphalt road to a village, about three miles down. There was a bus stop and a pub, where we always began trying to wash off the dust from the Astartes, the Ostaras and all the other potatoes that were named after fertility goddesses who had long since died out. The dust got in your clothes, in your hair, in your eyes, in the tiny lines in your hands, and eventually, in your flesh. You could never get really clean. If you were unlucky enough to have to climb onto the conveyor belt because something was jammed, you had to crawl on all fours through the potatoes, some of which were already so bruised that you ended up covered with juice, and the juice turned black, so that by evening you had black hands, black streaks across your face, black feet, even black knees. The longer the season lasted, the dirtier you got. Some of the men washed themselves with Biotex, since that was the only thing that helped, but the problem was, the stuff dried you out so badly that after a few days the skin on your hands felt like paper and started cracking and the potato juice seeped right into your body. It was murder.

At the pub we ordered the usual: coffee and gin. We were so

cold and tired after that three mile walk that we could only warm up by drinking both these things at the same time. Raph sat across from me, slouched in his chair, which he had tipped back against the dark wood wainscoting. That day he was even more sullen than usual.

'And the worst part is,' he said, as though we were having a conversation and he was finishing a sentence he had started earlier, 'the worst part is that the season ends next week and that's all we're going to get.'

I didn't think that was so terrible. True, Rika did have a certain appeal (it was a sort of masturbation; she lay there so indifferently, you never had the feeling you were doing it with somebody else, which, at the time, I found greatly reassuring), but the idea of having to share her with thirteen others, of having to possess her after all that, made me sick. Even just having to wait on that line, stamping in the cold, a silent, steaming row of men blowing on their hands, jackets buttoned up to their chins, that alone was bad enough to make me almost glad we were leaving. I knew Raph felt the same way, but that his disgust was buried under a thick layer of desire and envy. I'd found this out about him in the course of that year, that he was the type of person who did things because he'd taken it into his head to do so, half the time he'd forgotten why, yet something drove him on, an engine that ran on stubbornness, desire and envy.

Every time we sat there like that, Fridays, and I looked at him, slumped against the wall, taking alternate sips of his coffee and gin, I could understand why people always knew immediately that we were brothers. We had all the ingredients: we resembled each other, but not too much, we differed, but also not that much. Raph was of average height, five foot ten, five eleven, and he had gentle features, though you'd never call him soft. His large hooked nose was a friendly beak in a somewhat owlish face. I was about two inches shorter, with more or less the same face, the difference being that I had a stubbly beard and wore smudged, battered glasses and lacked his olive complexion, and I mean *lacked*, because I was so pale, people were always asking me if I was sick. As we walked along the road, from one hole in the ground to the next, from potato starch plant to sugar refinery, we usually got lifts pretty fast, because with those good-natured faces of ours and those innocent, hooked noses and the fact that we looked like two lost boy scouts, we gave the impression of being a rather friendly, somewhat sheepish pair.

'We've got to come up with a scheme,' said Raph. He held up his hand for two more coffees and gin and slumped a bit lower in his chair, which was still tipped against the wall.

'A scheme,' I said.

'The ultimate ruse,' he said, 'the final fuckover.' He leaned forward and his chair landed with a thud. 'Listen,' he said. 'Listen.'

In that part of the country, the weather turns at the end of the season, before autumn has really begun and the storms and showers come. The first few weeks the North wind combs the barren fields like a sheet of steel, but after a month or so you wake up with a dry mouth and a pounding head and when you look outside you see great clouds of dust, like huge yellowy brown wheels, rolling across the horizon. Without warning, without your having even the slightest suspicion, the temperature shoots up ten, fifteen degrees in a single night. The days have come when the leaves on the few low crooked trees that divide one field from another flutter dully and listlessly on the branches, and the people grow just as dull and just as listless, until the temperature rises so high it hits you in the head, as they say around there. This lasts two, three weeks, and during that time you can walk into a pub any night and chances are two to one you'll see a fight you'd never see anywhere else. For no apparent reason, some guy who's been hunched over a table brooding the whole evening will suddenly jump up, lift a chair above his head and hurl himself at another guy. The owner of The Road to Amen, the pub where we always waited for the bus, once told us that you could be pretty sure that whatever they were fighting about probably dated from before the year dot. When the warm wind rises, men who are each other's best friends in the cold season suddenly remember that their great-great-grandfather was once refused right of way by the great-uncle of God-knows-who and that the insult has never been properly avenged.

When Friday came around again, the last day of the season and probably also our last in the area, it had been warm for three days running. On Tuesday morning I'd pushed aside the rag that covered the window next to my bed in the boarding house, and there, in the distance, I'd seen the Southeast wind rolling over the plain. That day, and the days that followed, it was warmer, dustier and stuffier than ever before. Now and then the wind died down and it was calm for several hours at a time, and when I looked up at the sky I'd see columns of dust and sand, as tall as cumulus clouds. Even if the wind were to drop immediately, it would still take a whole day and a whole night before the air was clear, and chances were that a fresh wind would rise and send the dust flying around all over again, so for at least a month, maybe even two, you'd be walking around in an atmosphere that felt like a blanket which hadn't been aired since time immemorial.

At seven-thirty the sorting machine squeaked and groaned into motion. On the conveyor belt, which ran from outside to inside through a hatch in the wall covered with rubber flaps, the first load of potatoes came crawling in. Though clayey and wet at the start of the season, they were now dry, sandy lumps that gave off dust as soon as they came in and filled the hall with a cloud of fine yellow-brown powder. By eight o'clock we all looked like croquettes that had been freshly rolled in breadcrumbs. Slowly, the gears and drive belts began creaking and whining. If you stood close enough you could hear the sand being ground between the cogwheels of the big diesel motor. Raph and I were in luck.

During the coffee break, when half the men stayed at the belt, which was kept running at half speed, and the rest stood outside unscrewing thermoses and digging into lunchboxes, Gillis and the foreman came to blows. The foreman – Raph and I hadn't ever heard anyone call him by his name – had one eye and never spoke. If you did something wrong, he came up behind you, unexpectedly, and grabbed you by the shoulder with an iron claw. Jonatan, the operator, had said that the foreman was Gillis's cousin. Jonatan had told us everything we needed to know about the plant, then went back to his machines and never spoke to us again. Gillis, who, at twenty-five, was half his cousin's age, was slightly retarded. He squinted like a Siamese cat and his eyebrows had grown together into a thick black bar. Maybe Lombrosian types didn't exist, but there were certainly a lot of people in those parts who came close.

I was sitting next to the foreman drinking my coffee, when Gillis leaped up and flung the contents of his cup into his cousin's face. At least, that's what he meant to do, but Gillis was not only retarded, he was also a lousy shot. I got drenched. His intention, however, was clear enough. The foreman jumped up, hauled back and punched Gillis in the nose with the full force of his calloused fist. Raph, who was still inside working, later swore he'd heard the bone crack. Gillis went sailing backwards like a water tower that had been blown up at the base: he soared into the air, came back down again, and fell slowly, but heavy and limp as a deadweight, into a heap of crates that were stacked up against the wall. Gillis was a big, burly guy with a pigeon breast which, with his build, was more of an elephant breast. He went crashing through the pile of crates and came to a halt somewhere in the middle of all that shattered wood. Before we could get him out he was back on his feet, a lump of wild flesh with shreds of clothing and splintered laths hanging off him. He ducked down and rammed his head into the foreman's stomach.

They rolled around on the ground, while everybody else just sat there chewing bread and drinking coffee, and then the whistle blew and they got up and went inside like the rest of us. The foreman had a lip the size of a bicycle tyre, Gillis's nose looked like a mushy plum.

Raph and I already had the wind and the dust and the heat in our favour, but with this fight, the ground was truly ready for planting. At a quarter past eleven Raph went off to the bog, and as he passed the machines, he tossed a handful of fine sand into the tank of diesel oil.

At eleven-thirty Raph looked outside. Way off in the distance, he saw a red dot appear on the horizon. Rika was late today. She wasn't the only one. Our timing had obviously been wrong too, because the machines were running the same as before. They were groaning, creaking and whining with dust, but that was only normal on days like this. Raph looked from the belt to the window, from the window to the belt. My stomach churned. And all of a sudden – the red Chevy was clearly visible by now, if you looked closely you could even see Rika's black hair – the belt jammed. First the machine sputtered, then there was a deafening crunch, and finally the conveyor belt hiccupped and the drive belt stopped. Potatoes went flying through the air. Smoke rose lazily from the greyish green cabinet that housed the motor. Jonatan shouted something, yanked down on the lever that was supposed to put the belt into neutral, and was shoved aside by the foreman, who pushed the black button with the white letters 'STOP'. Under the hood we heard the driving rods clanging against the pistons. The foreman looked at Jonatan and slammed his fist against the valve in the oil pipe. With a tremendous bang, a piece of iron burst through the steel motor housing.

I'd gone over to stand next to Raph, and saw the manager, who had left his office and was just on his way to the car. He slowed down, turned around and listened.

The motor didn't stop. The foreman looked at Jonatan, at us, at the machine. Raph stared at Jonatan. I opened my mouth, but before I could say a word a second piece of iron burst through the hood. It suddenly dawned on me that our handful of sand was laying the entire plant in ruins.

Raph gave me a nudge. I looked out again and saw the manager walking back, slowly, suspiciously, faster and faster, until he was running. Raph rushed to the door, threw it open and screamed something I couldn't understand.

Inside, the machine was busily demolishing itself. Fat clouds of smoke were rising from the motor. You could almost feel the damn thing overheating.

By the time the manager stumbled inside, it had become nearly impossible to see anything. The motor, now in its final throes, was spewing hunks of metal in every direction.

I went over to Raph, who was still standing by the door.

'Got everything?'

Raph nodded.

We stood in the doorway and beheld the fall of the plant. It had all gone very differently, and much further, than we had expected. Sure, we'd meant to jam the machine, but no more than it usually did when sand got in the motor. Then Jonatan would've had to take off the hood and clean it out. We'd even hoped a couple of the guys would get into a fight, which is what often happened when there was a jam. The fact that things had gone differently was very convenient for us, I just didn't understand it.

That fight, the major flaw in our (when I look back on it) rather shaky plan, was about to begin. The foreman was standing there roaring at Jonatan, who had pulled the disconnecting lever instead of turning off the inlet cock, and Jonatan listened in silence, but his face was red with anger. Even in the smoky hall, you could see that the veins in his neck were thick and full.

I saw Raph's gaze wander to Gillis, who was still standing in his usual spot at the belt, right next to the mouth of the machine. The manager looked from one to the other and kept shouting: 'Stop that thing, stop it!' But the hall had turned into a pressure cooker and no one was listening.

When Jonatan hauled off and punched the foreman in the jaw, and he staggered back, hitting the black button with the white letters 'STOP', the machine choked. The room fell silent, and in that sudden silence I saw Gillis heave himself over the belt with one gigantic swing, so powerful and menacing that I involuntarily stepped back into the sunlight. Raph did the same. In the dark smoky hall I saw somebody walking toward Gillis. The foreman picked himself up off the floor and shook his head. Jonatan drew back his fist for another wallop. The manager roared something unintelligible. Then everybody flew at each other's throats at more or less the same time, with the manager in the middle trying desperately to end the fight before it began. Raph and I turned and ran, in the direction of Rika's red Chevy.

We were careful to stay as long as possible under cover of one of the outer walls, but when we reached the car I heard a shout and when I looked back I saw the manager and a few of the other men standing in the doorway. One of them pointed at us. Just then, Rika began turning her car around.

'Run, Raph, run!' I shouted. Images of savage retribution flashed before my eyes, and somewhere in my head the voice of reason began to speak, the way it always does when you don't need it anymore.

Not such a great scheme after all, eh?

Christ, no, it sure wasn't.

You would've expected more from a couple of shrewd drifters than a lousy handful of sand in a machine and then running off to a ten-dollar whore and hoping for the best . . .

'Fucking hell!' I shouted, because Rika had turned the Chevy around and was steering that low-slung hulk of a car onto the road.

We reached the door just as the car was picking up speed. I grabbed the handle and yanked. The door was locked.

What exactly did you think would come of all this? Did you really expect them to stay in there fighting, while you screwed around in the car?

About thirty yards back a troop of running men was rapidly gaining on us.

'Open up!' I shouted. 'They'll kill us!'

Rika looked sideways. I could see she was scared.

'Open it, Rika! Open the goddamn door!'

I saw her pressing down harder and harder on the accelerator. I heard Raph behind me, out of breath.

'Oh God, oh God,' he panted.

I looked into the car. Rika's black eyes stared blankly into mine.

She has no idea what's going on, I suddenly realized. She just doesn't get it. As I was thinking this, the voice inside me started preaching again: *This is a fine mess you're in*. That's a record, I thought, that's a song I once heard.

'Rika!'

I looked around and saw the men from the factory about fifteen yards behind us.

Then Rika reached across the seat. She yanked at the door handle and the door flew open and I dived inside and Raph grabbed hold of my shirt and pulled himself in and the car drove off, at full speed. When I sat up on the wide leather seat of the

Chevy and looked back, I saw the men from the factory fading into the yellow dust that billowed up behind the car.

Rika let us out at the fork, where the long straight road comes out onto the canal and goes left into town and right into the fields, to villages we'd heard of, but never seen. She steered the car onto the shoulder, gave us one last, piercing look and told us to beat it. Raph opened the door and got out. I started to say something to Rika, a kind of explanation, an apology. She had her hands in her lap and was staring out the window, at the black water in the canal, the straight row of poplars, the endless fields. As I mumbled my lame excuses, Raph stuck his head back in. He looked at Rika.

'How'dya like to take part in our great scheme?' he asked.

'What scheme?' I cried. 'No more schemes! That was the last fucking scheme!'

I started getting all worked up. At the word 'scheme' I saw that troop of men running after us again.

Rika turned her head to the side. She looked past me at Raph, raising her eyebrows slightly. There was something young and alert about her face.

'Don't listen to him,' I said. 'He —'

'The reckoning,' Raph said to me. 'The final reckoning. We forgot that today's payday.'

I couldn't believe what I was hearing.

'It's payday, Sam. We'll lose a week's wages.'

'Oh no, Raph, no way.' I knew exactly what he wanted, I knew that note of resignation in his voice. Whenever he looked like someone who had given up all hope, he was at his most determined.

'Boys,' said Rika.

'I've been working all goddamn week in that filth!'

'So what!' I shouted.

'Boys, would you mind telling me what's going on? In case you're interested, I just lost my best client.'

'We're not going back,' I said.

'I want my money.'

'You wanna die!'

'Hey!' yelled Rika.

Raph leaned forward a bit more and looked into the car with that owlish face of his, at Rika, as if it no longer made any difference that I was still there and was against any new scheme whatsoever.

I sat there next to Rika on the big leather front seat, and Raph launched into some complicated argument, and as I looked out the windscreen at the black canal, I suddenly felt all my tension draining away. What am I doing here? I thought. My God, where am I? What's this all about? I suddenly saw that anonymous landscape where everything was flat and straight and I remembered the jobs we'd had to take in the past year, the haughty faces of farmers and police officers and housewives and pub owners who all shook their heads when we were hoping for a 'yes' and nodded when 'no' would've been a lot more convenient, and I thought: what was it we were trying to prove with this crazy trek through no-man's-land? What is this, our way of tempting fate? I turned around and stuck my legs out the door and crawled under Raph's arm and out of the car. He kept on talking. I took the road that went right, and walked, almost without thinking, along the strip of sand between the road and the shoulder, the narrow path between asphalt and grass. In the distance, tall sallow clouds drifted across the horizon, the water in the canal lay dead and black between its banks. I never looked back, not once, even though I didn't know for sure whether Raph would come after me or not. One thing I did know was that this was the end of his schemes. Chatting up a farmer's wife for a little cash was harmless enough, taking on all kinds of odd jobs, fine, wangling rides and meals, no problem, but that was about as far as my longing for adventure went. I didn't feel like being found in the tarwater of this canal, bobbing along the unmown bank like a bloated purple pig. The scheme had failed, and I wasn't about to take part in some act of revenge that was bound to lead to an even greater chase by even wilder locals. What this had been all about, I thought, lapsing into my old drifter's gait and walking almost mechanically along the road, what we'd wanted, what *Raph* had wanted, was a year of freedom, total freedom. After that we would do what everyone else did – maybe not everything, maybe not exactly the way most people did it, but we'd try to earn our own money and we'd rent a house and buy a table and a chair and a bed and a couple of books and we'd mind our own business. After all those years in foster homes, we would set ourselves free by having no more ties, no possessions, no money, no goals. That, I thought, had been our original intention.

But life along the road had turned out to be not much better than the monotonous regularity we had left behind. The two of us had been through a lot, that was true, we'd been free in the sense that nobody told us what time to go to bed and what school we'd be going to, but somehow I still had the feeling that I was caught on the same old treadmill. In our foster homes we'd been made to do things we hadn't thought up ourselves, at school we were forced into a rhythm that wasn't our own, but on these wanderings we'd had our asses kicked too, plenty of times, only now it was employers, police officers, farmers, hunger and thirst that held our fate in their hands. True freedom, I thought, was probably something else, but I didn't know quite what, or where to find it.

These were the things I thought, and I didn't look back. I shuffled along the sandy path between the asphalt and the grass, my head bowed slightly, and said to an imaginary Raph: If you try and get even now, you're going too far, it's no joke any more. And suddenly I realized that for Raph, it probably never had been a joke.

We were brothers and friends, and we knew each other better than anyone, but our reasons for hitting the road were completely different. I had followed Raph in order to get to know him, while he, it was becoming more and more clear to me, you could see it in the stubborn way he always insisted on carrying out his plans – he was just plain wild. Something inside him was searching for the limit, something that wanted to go further and further and further. He didn't really feel alive unless he was being chased by a herd of stampeding potato sorters, or wandering along the road for days on end, bedraggled, hungry, tired, chilled to the bone. I was willing to keep this up for a year, two if necessary, if that's what it took to get to know him, to become brothers again, but after that I was going to find a quiet spot and wait until real life began. I thought: we have two very different notions of what life is.

I heard his footsteps. He wasn't running, but he was in a hurry. When he'd caught up with me neither of us looked at each other, we just walked along, side by side, he on the asphalt, I on the sand, about two, three hundred yards. After a while he said: 'She wasn't interested. I almost talked her into it, you saw that, but all of a sudden it went wrong. I don't know why.'

'I wouldn't have gone with you anyway,' I said.

'Sure you would've,' he said.

I shook my head.

He began walking more slowly. He looked at me out of the corner of his eye. 'Seriously?'

I kept shaking my head.

We walked on, a couple of hundred yards, without the landscape changing much, without feeling like we were getting anywhere. In those parts you can walk for hours and still think you haven't covered a single mile.

'Why not?' he asked finally.

I stopped, and looked around me. Behind us, the land was empty. Ahead of us, in the distance, was a house with a sign. I pointed to it and said: 'Let's go over there and get something to eat and drink and then find a quiet place where we can talk.'

Raph nodded and I started heading toward the house. 'Hey,' he said as he tagged along, 'it must be pretty serious what you want to tell me, huh?'

'Depends,' I said. 'Depends what you mean by serious.'

For a moment I had the feeling that I was the older brother, the kind who commands the respect of the younger brother by vaguely referring to something important and then not saying anything for a while, until the time is ripe to lay down the law.

The house turned out to be a pub called The Copper Plough. I stood at the bar, in the clammy air that hangs in pubs in the morning, when the place still smells of stale beer and cheap cigarettes and wet shoes, and I asked the owner, who was wrapping a bottle of gin in a piece of brown paper while his wife made egg and cheese sandwiches, if he happened to know how the pub had got its name. I, for one, had never seen a copper plough before, and certainly not around here.

'Nope,' said the owner. He put down the bottle and waited until his wife was through.

'We haven't had the place all that long,' said his wife.

'How's business?'

The man shrugged.

'There's an old tale, about that copper plough,' I said.

The man stood behind the bar, his head bent slightly, and peered at me through narrowed eyelids, as if he thought I was about to make off with the till.

'About a farmer who used to own land here,' I said, 'in the very spot where this pub now stands.'

Oh God, I thought, here I go again with another one of my bullshit stories.

The woman broke an egg over a blackened frying pan and dropped it into the butter. Looking up at me, she broke a second egg, a third, a fourth. The butter crackled, the eggs glided into the pan and slowly turned glassy and then white.

'Break the yolks,' I said.

She picked up a piece of eggshell and pierced the membranes of the four yellow eyes.

'One day this farmer decided to chop down a hazel tree.'

I looked over at the woman, who was standing in front of the pan with a spatula in her hand and staring intently at the eggs.

'Hazels should never be chopped down. A hazel protects the land. But this farmer was a pretty stubborn guy, so one morning he walks into the field, an axe over his shoulder, his left hand in his pocket. He comes to the hazel, which is standing on a little mound in the middle of the bare field, and takes the axe off his shoulder. He sits down, lays the axe across his knee and starts unwrapping the blade. Then he stands up and turns around. He raises the axe, swings it back . . . and it just hangs there! He tries to swing it forward, but he can't. It's as if somebody's got hold of both his hands, as if his right arm is made of wood. Everything comes to a halt.'

'Salt?' asked the woman.

I nodded.

She stuck her hand in the stoneware pot next to the stove and took a pinch of salt between thumb and forefinger. Her hand moved in a slow arc over the pan.

'So anyway, he can't chop,' I said. 'He can't even move his arm. He's standing in front of the hazel with his axe in the air and a cramp in his shoulders, when suddenly he hears this lisping little voice. Farmer, farmer, how could you think of chopping me down? The farmer looks around, but there's nobody there. It's me, says the voice, what else is there to chop down around here? The farmer looks at the hazel. He tries to move his arm, but whatever he does, the axe just hangs there in mid-air. Listen, farmer, if you swear to leave me alone, I'll let your arm swing freely once more. I'll even reward you. The farmer nods. He feels his arm moving again.'

The woman slid the pan back and forth, the eggs glided over the bottom. She cut them apart with a knife and placed four thick slices of bread on a sheet of wax paper.

'The farmer lowers his axe to the ground. If you chop me down, says the tree, your land shall become barren and you shall lose your money and your home. Your wife's womb will be as dry as the fields you try to sow. But if you leave me alone, I'll reward you with a piece of sound agricultural advice. The farmer thinks this over for a while. Then he nods. Okay, he says. The wind rustles through the leaves of the hazel, and he hears the voice again. Forge a ploughshare out of copper and plough all the land you own, and your harvest shall be greater than that of all your neighbours. The farmer shrugs his shoulders and wraps up his axe. Then he turns around and walks home.'

The owner's wife had put the eggs on the bread and topped them with slices of cheese, just as I'd asked her to. I followed her movements, the folding of the paper, the string she tied around it.

'Then what?' asked the owner.

60

I looked up. He was standing behind the bar, leaning on his forearms. He eyed me suspiciously.

'What do you mean?'

'What happened to the farmer?'

I picked up the packet of sandwiches and placed it next to the bottle of gin wrapped in paper.

'Nothing,' I said.

The owner straightened up.

'Nothing?'

'Who'd be crazy enough to use a copper plough?'

'So why didn't he just chop down the hazel?'

I picked up the bottle and tucked it under my arm. Turning to go, I said: 'That copper plough was a load of crap, but suppose it really was true what the hazel said, that the land would become barren . . .'

I walked to the door and pressed down on the handle.

'You haven't paid!' shouted the owner.

I was hoping he'd forget. I turned around and walked back. I put the bottle on the bar and took some cash out of my pocket.

'Did that really happen?' asked the woman, who was vigorously scrubbing the pan.

'Why else would this pub be called The Copper Plough? Did you call it that?'

She shook her head.

'And the people who were here before you?'

She shrugged.

I counted out my money and watched as the owner re-counted it. Then I picked up the bottle, waved, and went outside. Raph was leaning against the wall of the pub, eyes closed, face in the sun. I handed him the gin and started walking.

We'd gone about fifty yards, when the door of the pub opened. I looked around and saw the owner's wife step outside. She came walking towards us. I slowed down.

'Here,' she said when she'd caught up with us. She handed me two big green apples. 'For the road.' She smiled, a bit awkwardly, and walked back. I called out a thank you and blinked my eyes. I thought: I'm getting too soft for this life.

After about half an hour of walking, we came to a spot where the canal curved right and lay in the land like a knee. Beyond the bend was a bicycle bridge made out of a couple of iron T-bars and some boards. On the opposite bank was a grove of young deciduous trees; a narrow path led inside, shaded by pale green leaves. I thought: whatever's at the end of that path, I want to follow it, so I pointed the bridge out to Raph and we turned left and walked across the clattering boards to the other side. The air smelled of peat and wet wood. We walked, half stooped, through the tunnel of branches, the earthy, rainy smells growing stronger and stronger, and then, after God knows how many twists and turns, we came out of the grove and found ourselves at a pond with patches of heather and moor grass around it and here and there a cluster of pines. The ground was spongy and wet. We had to balance and jump as we made our way around the pond, but finally we reached one of the clusters of trees and I found a dry spot under a broad Scots pine and sank down onto the fan of brown needles around the base. Raph sat down beside me and looked out over the pond.

Judging by the position of the sun, it was about two o'clock. The air, misty and damp, began to grow warmer, the fen released a heady mixture of smells, resin, wood, grass, heather, chalybeate water, and now and then the sweet lure of a flower. I leaned my back against the tree and felt the weariness rising from my legs. I took one last look at the unruffled water, and fell asleep.

When I woke up, Raph had disappeared and the sun was behind the treetops. A seagull floated on the grey water, every so often I heard the cry of a bird. I wondered where Raph was and what he was doing and how long he'd been gone. The bottle was still there, the packet of sandwiches was balanced on a few sticks that had been stuck in the earth in the shape of a tripod. I was still sleepy, drowsy in a contented kind of way. I slouched against the tree and looked out from under half-closed eyelids at the water, the tall grass on the other side, the reflection of the sinking sun on the smooth surface of the fen, and suddenly I thought of home, home with a capital H, and I missed everything that was there, which was nothing, because the house was gone and I could hardly remember a thing about the days when Raph and Lisa and I were still together and our parents were alive, but somehow it was still Home and I wanted to be there, between the walls that had heard our voices, the closets where my mother's dresses had hung, my father's dimly lit study, with the blackboard on the wall where he wrote his calculations. I missed the table in the room Raph and I shared, the scratches in the tabletop, the old radio on the shelf. I sat there with my back against the tree and my God, I loved everything that, up until that moment, I had forgotten. A lump came to my throat as the images welled up inside me like a slow tide. The vague, bowed figure of my father . . . The hair that fell in front of my mother's eyes as she sat reading . . . I loved the lock that cast a shadow over her brown eyes, over a face I could no longer remember. I shook my head, I kept on shaking my head, but it wouldn't go away. Why, I thought, looking at the fen, doesn't the seagull affect me like that? Why am I thinking about a house where nobody lives anymore, about all those half images, why am I thinking of that and why does it move me and why is that seagull, which is real and alive, which I can see perfectly clearly, why is that seagull nothing more to me than some bird on the water?

Then I saw Raph on the other side of the fen. He was standing in the tall grass and he held up his hand and suddenly I knew with such certainty that our ways would part here, I could feel it stinging behind my eyes. It was one thing knowing that Raph and I differed when it came to our motives for this year of wandering, but leaving him behind was another story. I saw him walking along the water's edge, head bent, serious, as only he could be serious, jumping over a gully, raising his arms slightly to catch his balance. It took him forever to get halfway around the pond. I sat against the tree and saw his every movement, in minute detail, and each time his hand went out to the side, or his head nodded, I knew why he had done it. When you've been on the road together for a whole year you know each other the way a man and a woman know each other. I mean: we'd stolen laundry together after falling into a stinking boghole, we'd fought in a pub with a couple of guys who tried to drag us away from a pinball machine, and afterwards Raph bought band-aids and patched up my torn eyebrow. He'd stood guard while I ducked into a barn with a farmer's daughter who'd been giving me the eye and screwed her with her back against an enormous threshing machine. And when Raph had got the flu, about a month ago, I'd spent all the money in my secretly saved reserve fund to rent a room where he could recover.

'Hey, little brother,' he said, when he was standing in front of me. 'Guess what.'

I shook my head.

'Come on, guess.'

'You've got the money.'

'Nope.'

'You went back to have a look at the plant and the whole fucking dump was burned to the ground.'

'Nope.'

He could keep me guessing for hours. After a while I'd begin suggesting the most bizarre possibilities – he liked that.

'I don't know, I have no idea.'

He picked up the bottle and the sandwiches and started unwrapping them. He opened the bottle, drank, then passed it to me. I raised it to my lips. My gums itched under the alcohol.

'If you follow that path, you come to a station.'

I took the sandwich he held out to me and frowned.

'I've already asked. We've got just enough for a one-way ticket home.'

I had the sandwich in my mouth, but didn't bite. I sat there looking at him, the smell of gin in my nostrils, the faint odour of cheese and fried eggs rising from the bread.

'One one-way ticket?'

'Two,' he said, with his mouth full. He chewed his bread and watched as the seagull flew up out of the water. He looked contented.

I took a bite and started to chew. Somehow this announcement didn't make me very happy. I thought: wait a minute, weren't you the one who wanted to travel on and on, weren't you the one who wanted to live from scheme to scheme? I grabbed the bottle and drank. As I threw back my head and tasted the gin, I saw the dark blue stripes of evening appear in the sky.

'Explain,' I said.

He turned around, his head slightly tilted, with the expression of someone who doesn't know what you're talking about.

I said: 'All of a sudden you want to go back? You've never even mentioned it before and now all of a sudden you want to go home?'

'Whaddaya mean, I never mentioned it? What about you? Have you ever mentioned it?'

'No, but that was obvious. You knew I wanted to go back, didn't you?'

'Of course not,' he said. 'You never told me.'

I chewed my bread and looked at him. I thought: how could I have been so wrong? I thought: I didn't tell him, I've been talking to myself the whole time and I just assumed he knew what was on my mind. Maybe it was the same with him, maybe we both wanted to go home, but didn't say it.

'How long have you been thinking about this?' I asked.

He rubbed his temple. He picked up the bottle and drank.

'Ever since I got sick,' he said, handing me the gin.

I could understand that.

'First I thought: hang in there. Because I figured you were only really . . . strong . . . if you could hang in there at a time like that. But maybe I was wrong. I mean, I wanted to hang in there, but I couldn't. I suddenly thought of home and all I wanted to do was crawl into a dark corner in my own house instead of lying in that shitty little room.'

'Jesus, Raph, I completely misread you.'

'No,' he said. 'We were just putting up a front, both of us.'

I drank.

'So what's next?'

He shrugged. He said: 'I thought, if we walk to the station tomorrow, we could maybe ride back.'

I looked at the water, growing dark beneath the gathering dusk. Insects buzzed around our heads, somewhere in the distance I heard the dry crackle of buckshot. I gave the gin to Raph and watched him drink, his head tipped back. His silhouette was black against the darkening trees. The liquor gurgled softly in the bottle. I took two cigarettes out of the pack I carried for both of us and lit one for him and one for me.

We sat together in the warmth of the evening, silently smoking, staring ahead. Lightning flashed on the horizon, but the storm was far away. The thunder was yet to come.

On the other side of the cellar, the lift started up and the cables in the shaft began to sing. My cigarette had gone out. I threw it onto the concrete, stamped on it, just to be sure, and shoved the butt under a rack. I scooped up the box of paper and headed for the lift.

Julius the Nightfly

At the end of June, when I had rounded off my last assignment and discovered that 'real life' didn't exist, I met the Norwegian. It was the night after a visit from Lisa.

She'd come over to see me and sat pushing her supper around with her fork. Her black eyes glowed, her reddish brown hair hung in dishevelled curls about her face. She smoked one cigarette after another. The thumb, index and middle finger of her right hand were stained with so many colours of ink, they looked as if somebody had bashed them with a hammer. She hung in the chair, her left arm along the back, the sputtering cigarette in her right hand. Every so often she glared at my plate. We didn't say much. Now and then she got up and went over to the radio. She spun the dial impatiently, so quickly that the stations flew by in bursts of static and half words. Perhaps it was because of that inexplicable nervousness that she didn't feel the wine. Whatever it was, I had to open a new bottle, even though I'd only had one glass.

Lisa and I know each other so well that we no longer ask about each other's worries. If either of us has something on our mind, we wait. I waited. I ate my supper and drank my wine and remained silent.

Just before midnight, when the table had been cleared and we were sitting drinking coffee, she said: 'I want to come live here for a while.'

She leaned forward and stubbed out a cigarette with great concentration.

'Okay,' I said.

Her head moved slowly up and down. I noticed that her

lips were slightly pursed, the way they always are when she's sceptical.

'I'm leaving Simon,' she said. 'You do realize that, don't you? When I ask you if I can stay here for a while, I mean I'm leaving him.'

'I know.'

'And that's it?'

'What do you want, Lisa? Do you want me to ask if you're leaving him when it's perfectly clear to me?'

She grabbed the crumpled pack and lit a fresh cigarette. I reached for the bottle and poured out the last of the wine.

'He doesn't do anything,' she said. 'He sits on the edge of the bed from morning till night, reading the encyclopedia.'

'The what?'

'The encyclopedia.'

'Which one?'

'What?'

'Which encyclopedia?'

'The *Encyclopedia Britannica*! Goddamnit, Sam, what difference does it make which encyclopedia he reads? He sits on the bed and reads. Something. An encyclopedia. The weather report, for all I care. Jesus.'

'Sorry.'

She groped for her wine glass and drained it in one gulp.

'It makes me furious,' she said. 'I come home to a stinking hole, a bed in the middle of the room, an ashtray overflowing with ashes and butts and this guy who just sits there reading the encyclopedia.'

I nodded my head, something between nodding and shaking.

'I can't stand it anymore. It's driving me crazy. I go out every morning to earn a little money and I'm up late every night trying to earn a little more, and all he does is laze around.'

'Maybe it's temporary. Maybe he just needs a push,' I said.

'Simon has never done anything. He's never seen anything through. Not that he doesn't have plans. He's got loads of plans. But he never does anything with them. I've told him: Take a chance for once, finish what you've started. You know he has

68

talent. Everybody knows. He could be anything he wanted to. But he always gives up. They're all just pipe dreams.'

'Listen,' I said. 'You have the key, you can get in whenever you want. I've told you before: my house is your house. I'd be more than happy to have you move in. You don't have to say when or how. It's up to you.'

She shook her head. She looked to one side, as if there was somebody sitting there with whom she could share her rage.

'He doesn't care,' she said. 'One of 'em reads the encyclopedia and the other one couldn't care less. Why me?'

'This is something between a man and a woman,' I said. 'I don't know what's going on with the two of you, I don't know anything about your relationship, and I don't want to pass judgement on Simon. What can I do? I'm a harbour, you sail in from time to time.'

'What?'

'Forget it.'

'A harbour. Jesus, has it ever occurred to you that I might have asked you this a lot sooner if you weren't so incredibly emotionless? So . . . so unmoved, so . . . phlegmatic. Don't you ever feel anything?'

I raised my eyebrows. She lowered her shoulders, sighing deeply.

'I can't stand it anymore. It's driving me crazy. I love him. At least, I did love him, but there's a limit to what I can take. This is the limit.'

Her eyes filled with tears.

'Lisa . . .' I said.

'Sam, I can't stand it anymore.'

I sat across from her and nodded. I wanted to say something, something comforting, but nothing came to mind. I laid my hand on hers and stroked her fingers.

She stood up and smiled. She took one last, deep drag on her cigarette and stubbed it out.

'I'll walk you part of the way,' I said. 'I need to clear my head.'

A few minutes later we were walking through the moonless night, arm in arm, my sister and I. It wasn't easy keeping up with her. Lisa isn't the kind of person you can take a stroll with. She moves from goal to goal, as quickly as possible. We walked past the houses on my block. The balmy warmth of the summer night lingered beneath the trees. We talked about the weather, why it seemed to be getting warmer every year and where all that yellow sand in the streets came from, why there were so many windswept old newspapers lying in the gutter, and then we reached the square where the city's night life is concentrated, where the pubs and discos chew up and spit out one mouthful of people after another. It lay between the buildings like a bowl full of light. The trees were strung with red, blue and yellow bulbs, and boys and girls in hip-hop gear, men in double-breasted suits and women in evening dress were parading down the asphalt road that divided the square into an inner area and a kind of outer strip. While Lisa hailed a cab, I looked around. I decided to go for a drink.

As I pressed her to me, I felt the tense wiriness of her body. The taxi stood at the kerb with its door open, ready to swallow her up.

'I need to think things over,' said Lisa. 'There's a lot I need to think over. If you don't see me for a while, don't start worrying.'

I tried to say something, but she disappeared into the cab.

The door slammed shut, the car drove off.

It was around two in the morning when I met the Norwegian. He was sitting at the bar of a pub that looked like a living room adorned with oak panels and brass rails. Racks of bottles and glasses hung between the bulky columns at either end of the bar. In the mirrors behind the sinks, the light from bulbs capped with little green shades bounced from bottle to glass and glass to bottle. When I came in there were about twenty people crowded into that one small space. The heat and noise were overwhelming.

I was standing behind the bar stools, one hand half-raised in an attempt to order something, when the man on the stool in front of me turned around and asked, in English, what I wanted to drink. I pointed to the tap, which was spouting a golden stream of beer. The man nodded, leaned across the bar and roared out a name. The woman behind the bar looked up. He stuck two fingers in the air and made a beer-tapping movement with his right hand. The barmaid took down two pint mugs and held them under the beer pump. Thirst shot through my gullet. The beer was set down on the bar. I held out a bank note. The man waved his hand.

'It's my treat.'

He spoke slowly, with pursed lips: Uts moy truut.

I emptied my mug in one gulp. When I put it down, I saw him grinning from ear to ear.

'We have another one, okay?'

I nodded. 'But this time the drinks are on me.'

He mimed another order of beer, she brought it, and we drank a toast.

'May we never get thirsty again,' he said.

I told him my name, he told me his. He was Julius Fleming, he came from Norway.

By three o'clock we had reached the state of camaraderie that I knew from other nights on the town. We'd left the pub after the second glass, and from then on I let the Norwegian be my guide. Everywhere we went, he knew the name of the man or woman behind the bar. His sign language worked every time. After a couple more pubs we left the square. We zigzagged down a broad shopping street, wandered through alleyways and across courtyards that reeked of urine and rotting vegetables. We swam in and out of the light of sodium lamps hanging from blank walls painted with words of Old Testament proportions, which were half covered over with other words, drawings, illegible scribbles and torn posters. We walked down a street where the asphalt was cracked and littered with paper cups and styrofoam clamshells with half-eaten hamburgers and greenish blobs of sauce, and all along the road, behind endless rows of parked cars with puddles of glass next to doors with smashed windows, were tall houses with red-lit display windows in which whores sat reading magazines. We walked past renovated mansions and on the stairs leading to one of the basements was a kid lying on top of a woman. She had her skirt hitched up, her white legs wrapped around his back. He was kneeling on a step, grinding his teeth, as he pumped his body up and down. At the foot of the stairs, among old newspapers and faded plastic bags, sat a girl in a miniskirt who was pushing a hypodermic needle into her nylon-stockinged leg.

We ordered drinks in a bar that looked like a 1930s Viennese cafe. All around us stood men in dark blue suits, with colourful ties in frenzied patterns, and young women in waisted jackets and short skirts. On the way to the men's room I caught snatches of conversation about money and houses. At the chrome-trimmed urinal I was joined briefly by an older gentleman, who then went over to the mirror, took a small metal-coloured box out of his jacket, brought it to his nose and sniffed.

'There was a guy in the toilet sniffing coke,' I said to my companion, after I'd pushed my way back through the crowd and was standing beside him.

Fleming shrugged. 'Life is tough.'

'People used to say that a man had to sell his soul in order to get what he wanted. Nowadays you have to offer your body as well,' I said.

Fleming smiled. 'It's the same at the university. Scoring. Zero points, zero possibilities. In the old days we could do studies on subjects that interested us, but now everything has to be applicable. How much will it bring in? That's what it's all about. Big business, no nonsense.'

'You know,' I said, looking around, 'these are the kind of guys I always see walking into their offices, and there'll be this beggar lying in front of the door and they just step right over him and look the other way. I once spent a couple of hours on a bench outside the office buildings near the station, and I counted how many of these types gave something to a beggar. How many do you think?'

Fleming raised his eyebrows.

'Not one. Not one. They all wear jackets that a bum could live off for three whole months, or a watch that you or I would have to work a year to be able to afford, but not one of them'll reach into his pocket and take out a guilder to give to a beggar.'

'You have to draw the line somewhere,' said Fleming.

I shook my head. 'That's not the point. What bothers me is . . . All these men were raised by parents who built a society on

72

thrift and humility, and what do they do? They stuff their faces, they appease their dissatisfaction with cars and design stuff and ridiculous drinks. And cocaine.'

'You're not some sort of minister, are you?'

'The point is, there's no modesty, no . . . no compassion. It's your fucking obligation to give somebody money if he asks for it.'

'Hey,' said Fleming, 'we're not saints.'

'You don't have to be a saint to . . .' What I was trying to explain was something greater, more complex than the notion that we all had to share our cloaks with the needy. 'Listen,' I said, 'you can't live in a world where everyone's only interested in filling his own belly. Guys like these, most of them wouldn't even be here if somebody hadn't looked after one of their ancestors. Life isn't some kind of room, you don't just stroll in and gorge yourself and gratify your senses the best you can and then stroll back out again.'

'I have nothing against gratifying the senses.'

'No, neither do I, as long as you give at least one guilder to a beggar, as long as you don't just step over a tramp as if he's a goddamn . . . a . . . a thing.'

'Some people fail and they simply can't be helped,' said Fleming.

'What the hell has that got to do with it?'

'I mean that sometimes there's nothing you can do except step over somebody.'

'No,' I said. 'It doesn't matter whether somebody can be helped or not, what matters is whether or not I help him, whether or not I take pity on him. I'm willing to accept that there are tramps, and beggars, and all kinds of psychotics wandering around the city, and maybe they can't be saved, but the important thing is that we don't abandon them, that we continue to see them as individuals, with the same human dignity as you or I. The fact that these bastards can afford a fucking gold nugget on their wrists tells me absolutely nothing about their intrinsic worth. Those watches just prove that their worth is inversely proportional to their wealth.'

I was waving my arms around. I felt my chest going up and down. My God, I thought, take it easy, you're supposed to be emotionless, didn't Lisa say you were emotionless? Why get all worked up over a couple of bums and beggars?

'You really are a minister,' said Fleming. 'We're out drinking, remember?'

'Right,' I said. 'We're out drinking.'

'So don't get all excited. You can't change things tonight anyway.'

'But that's the whole point,' I said resignedly. 'Everybody's always saying you can't change things tonight anyway.'

'Or are you just an old-fashioned Communist?' asked Fleming.

'I'm nothing. I just can't stand those smug, overfed faces all radiating what a success they are, but forgetting that they're up to their knees in shit.'

'Perhaps they do wonderful things in private.'

'They don't,' I said. 'Let's corner one of these guys and ask him what he plans to do when he gets where he wants to be, when he has time and money to spare. Half of them will say they're going to buy a new house and finally start enjoying life, the other half will start whining about a boat or a vintage car. Not one of them will say he's planning to use his money to help the poor, or that he's going to work as a volunteer in a crisis centre for drug-addicted prostitutes.'

'Probably not,' said Fleming. 'But on the other hand, they're the ones who earn the money that enables the government to do those things.'

'Bullshit. I don't give a fuck about what the government does with the tax money that these bastards are reluctant enough to hand over as it is. I'm talking about one's own personal responsibility for the world.'

'Bloody hell,' said Fleming. 'This would have to happen to me. I'm out drinking with Mother Teresa.'

'What I'd really like to know is whether they realize just how small a distance there is between themselves and that beggar, what a narrow tightrope they're walking on. I wonder why they're all so greedy.'

'Perhaps because they do realize how narrow the tightrope is?'

We looked at the knots of people scattered about the room. Laughter rose, humorous remarks were tossed back and forth in loud voices. I thought: this is the real world, men wearing the same suits, women in identical skirts.

'A saint,' I said. 'You think you're out with some minister or a rabid Communist, and my sister thinks I have no feelings.'

Fleming peered over the rim of his glass and raised his eyebrows.

'But I do feel something,' I said. 'I just don't trust love, that's all.'

Fleming shook his head.

'I think people overrate love. They fall for somebody and suddenly they all think they're Tristan and Isolde, when it's really just some misplaced longing for sex and Mama.'

'Oh God,' said Fleming.

'It's much more important to care about people who aren't beautiful and desirable. My sister doesn't love her husband any more, but she doesn't know that the reason she doesn't love him any more is because he's got weak and ugly. My sister thinks love has to be something that goes without saying, a great mystery, torrid nights, pelvic miracles and multiple orgasms.'

Fleming laughed.

I thought: when I hadn't seen them for nine years, Raph and Lisa, I could no longer love them as brother and sister. I had to learn how. The link between blood and love was gone and that's why I had to *want* to love them, and I was glad about that, I'm still glad about that.

'Love,' I said to Fleming, 'is an act of will.'

'No,' he said. 'It has to happen to you.'

'Love,' I said, 'is as much an act of will as victimhood.'

'Do you actually think that someone who is hit by a car wants to be a victim?'

I nodded. 'If he lets himself become a victim, that is. He can also decide to be injured and to heal, but if he chooses to think of himself as a victim instead, it's an act of will.'

Fleming gave a low whistle. 'Modern theology and utopian socialism. How's your sex life?'

'I don't fuck enough. Not nearly enough.'

By five o'clock we were back at the pub. The door was closed. Through the uneven glass we saw two vague figures. The Norwegian knocked on the door. One of the figures moved. We heard the sliding of bolts.

'Julius the Nightfly,' said the barmaid. She held the door open and let us in. Then she walked back to a stool behind the bar and listened to a young woman sitting opposite her, who resumed their interrupted conversation. We sat down, ordered beer and talked about our work. Julius Fleming was a physical geographer at the university. He ran a network of observation posts, men and women who were stationed at various points in the field and took measurements. 'There is a great shortage of people,' he said. 'It's lonely work, rather like being a fire lookout. In Canada you have these students who work as fire lookouts during the summer. Something like that. You spend the whole day sitting in the middle of nowhere, you write down figures, put them in an envelope, and then wait until the following day. It's badly paid, too. The conditions are lousy. The posts get provisions and technical help only once a week, when the envelopes are picked up.'

I asked what they did, the people at the observation posts.

'They record changes in the landscape, we measure this and that, we do soil research with hand drills.'

There was nothing particularly shocking about this study, said Fleming, but the interesting thing was that they were observing an area in which an entire drilling rig had disappeared, and which had been more or less forbidden territory ever since. The flora was overwhelming, it had turned into a kind of unrestrained experiment with unbridled nature. Perfect silence in a perfectly green world. I thought of Kopakker and told him about my report.

'But that's exactly the area where we're working! You've studied it?'

I explained that I was classifying and describing the archive material on the Kopakker accident.

76

He looked at me closely. 'With your knowledge of the material it might not be a bad idea if you were to spend some time out there. How would you like to do a few months' observation?'

I shook my head and said I did archival research, not field work. Besides, I wasn't a geographer. 'Actually,' I said, 'I'm nothing at all. The only thing I can do is classify material and arrange it into a well-ordered report, and then only if it's in files. I can't bring any order whatsoever into my own life.'

He nodded, and began telling me about a town near Kopakker where he and his students had spent some wild nights, and I looked at the two women at the bar.

I'd recognized the barmaid. She used to be my doctor's assistant. As a boy, I'd had visions of doctor's appointments at the wrong moment, the doctor off somewhere, she in her white coat. She was tall, about five foot ten, with blonde hair that hung way down below her shoulders. In my opinion, she was a classic beauty. The young woman she was talking to had curly red hair and wore a brightly coloured collection of curious garments. She looked like she had just stepped out of a folk dance.

'We will have champagne!' Fleming shouted suddenly. He banged his fist on the bar and laughed. 'Pink champagne!' He pointed to the two women, looking at them sternly. 'And you will join us.'

The tall blonde raised her eyebrows. Julius banged his fist on the bar again.

'Has he been drinking?' she asked me.

I shook my head. We hadn't drunk that much, a few glasses of beer, gallons of mineral water.

The blonde got off her stool and walked to the end of the bar. She opened a refrigerator and took out a bottle of champagne and a bag of ice cubes. She filled a bucket with ice, water and salt, put in the bottle and covered the neck with a napkin. As she worked at the cork, Fleming and I moved down to the stools next to the women. I shook hands with the redhead and introduced myself. The blonde, her hands still under the napkin, looked up at me.

'We know each other,' I said.

She squinted slightly. I told her my doctor's name. She slowly began to nod, while her hands made massaging movements under the napkin. Then the cork came out with a gentle 'plop'. She removed the napkin, took four champagne glasses out of a rack hanging over the bar and filled them. It wasn't 'pink champagne', it was straw-coloured sparkling wine, with a strong taste.

We sat and drank. It was warm in the pub. Soft, indefinable music floated past us, and Fleming told tall stories, half in English, half in slurred, round Dutch. The redhead leaned on the bar and listened to him. What was the barmaid's name? I watched her as she polished glasses and ran hot water over the rack under the faucet. Steam billowed up, her pale hair shimmered in the haze of vapour. Helen. Isabelle. Something like that. I was always a bit taken aback when I opened the door to her little office. I'd have just spent half an hour in the dreary waiting room, surrounded by people in greyish winter coats (winter . . . in my memory it was always winter when I went to the doctor) and then I'd open that door and stand before her desk. Sunlight would be streaming in through a big square window. There were brightly coloured posters on the walls, her red typewriter gleamed, her hair had a golden sheen. That slightly mocking gaze. Always a vague, teasing smile, watchful eyes. As if she knew exactly what I was thinking.

'Time to close, folks.'

She held her glass by the stem and looked at me knowingly, the way she used to do. Julius stood up and bowed to the redhead. He held out his arm. She laid one hand on his wrist and ran the other wearily across her forehead.

'Au revoir,' she said, to no one in particular.

As he was paying the bill, Fleming pulled a business card out of his wallet and put it down in front of me on the bar. I was just about to pick it up when he took it back again and scribbled down a phone number.

I put on my jacket and looked around, but Fleming and his lady were already outside, their vague forms rippling over the wavy glass.

I finished my drink and stood up. The barmaid turned out the light over the bar and walked with me to the door. As I held the door open, she switched on the alarm.

Outside it was still warm. The air smelled of bread and coffee. Above the buildings the sky was the colour of washed ink.

'Which way are you going?' asked the blonde.

I pointed to the right.

'I'll walk with you.'

She tried the door one last time and turned around.

It was quiet in town. Now and then the lights from a passing car flashed across the shopfronts, an air conditioner hummed in the distance. We walked through the streets, past a park, where I heard the sound of muffled voices. A minute or two from my house, she slowed down. We had barely spoken. I'd asked her if she'd been working in the bar long, whether she liked her job and how she'd ended up there, and her answers had been friendly, but measured.

'I go left here,' she said.

'I'll walk you part way. It's a nice night to be out.'

'It's pretty far.' She mentioned a street I'd never heard of. When I asked where it was, she explained that it was somewhere in the abandoned industrial estate, the industrial estate where Raph lived and Lisa had lodged.

'Then I'll walk you all the way. That's a dangerous journey.'

She shook her head.

'Listen,' I said. 'I've had an old-fashioned upbringing. I take ladies home. Otherwise I can't sleep.'

She shrugged her shoulders and began walking.

It wasn't even that far, but we had to walk along a wide, dark road, once the entrance to the industrial estate, now an asphalt river with gnarled roots and young birch trees poking through the cracks. About halfway down, a fire was blazing in an abandoned oil drum. The park itself was even darker than the road. We passed buildings with smashed windows and crooked doors. We had to walk through holes in burned-out barricades, across a large car park full of melted beer crates.

When we came to a corrugated-iron Nissen hut that lay on a piece of wasteland like a tube sawn lengthways, we stopped.

'That was educational,' I said.

'Haven't you ever been here before?'

'A long time ago. My brother has a studio here and my sister lived here for a while. But she moved out and I hardly ever visit him. He usually comes to me. My sister too. I seem to be the family meeting point.'

She smiled. Her full, perfect mouth traced lines in her cheeks. I held out my hand.

'I'll make coffee,' she said. She turned around and unlocked the door. As she stepped inside, she looked over her shoulder and beckoned to me.

The Quonset was divided into two parts. It was high in front, above us gleamed the metal roof. The rear section was hidden from view by an unpainted wooden wall. Along the arched walls were racks full of boxes, scrap metal and tools. The partition was covered with old rock concert posters and outdated theatre bills, many of them half painted over with red lead. Perforated iron plates had been wired together to make the floor. She unlocked a door in the wooden wall, switched on a light and let me into the back of the shed.

This was her home. A bedroom in the air, on an elevated platform made of scaffolding and pallet boards. Below that, against the curved wall, a tiny kitchen, no more than a sink, a chopping block and a couple of shelves.

She went over to the tap and filled a kettle with water.

'I don't know your name,' I said.

'Ellen.'

I walked around and looked at the tumbledown interior. Against the straight wall that formed the back of the Nissen were sloppily painted wooden racks full of books, dishes, boxes covered with shelf paper, towels, old LPs in battered cardboard sleeves, and bottles. In front of the racks was a sitting area: four plastic crates with a sheet of wired glass on top and three sagging chairs. I wondered how she'd ended up here.

There was a whooshing sound. I turned around. Ellen put an old enamel coffee pot down on the floor, next to a gas cylinder with a raging burner. I followed her movements. Years ago, when she worked for my doctor, everything on her desk had always been neatly arranged and bright and cheerful in colour. Well-groomed, that was the word that best described her then. Long blonde hair brushed the obligatory hundred strokes a day, silk blouses washed in salt water, manicured nails, a smile of polished ivory. Here, in this old shed, with no coffee maker, no cabinets, where the air smelled of rough wood and oil, she wasn't all that different. Somehow she seemed as much at home in this setting as she had been in that immaculate little office. Under the carefully darned red sweater, her body moved as smoothly and easily as in the elegant blouses she had worn in better times.

The smell of coffee rose. She came over to the table and set down a stubby candle in a rusty iron holder. She lit the candle and placed the coffee pot over the flame.

'You've got a strange house,' I said. 'If I hadn't stood here for a while, I would've thought you lived in pretty dismal surroundings, but that's not true. It's a house. Capital H.'

She went to the racks against the back wall and took out mugs and spoons. We sat down. The room was silent, except for the sound of coffee dripping through a filter.

'Maybe I should become an observer for Julius Fleming,' I said.

She leaned forward and poured the coffee.

'And maybe you shouldn't,' she said.

I wanted to ask what she meant, but when I turned my eyes toward her I suddenly saw her with the hunger of someone who has gone too long without eating. She seemed bigger, blonder, more beautiful and desirable than ever. It was as though I could see through her clothes to a body in the darkness, a pale glimmer of light along the slope of her waist, the slow curve of her breast. In the shadows rose the arc of her buttocks, the dotted line of her vertebrae. Her back was a stretch of sand with two pale dunes. I saw her turning around me in the darkness. A mysterious animal. The smell of her body enveloped me like a warm blanket. I felt her breath in my neck.

'Sugar?' she said.

I coughed up something that sounded like 'yes'.

As she leaned down to spoon sugar into a mug, the candlelight glided across her face. Her jawline, her nose, her cheekbones, her whole face grew soft and friendly. It was almost as if we'd known each other for years and now, in an old familiar gesture, she was leaning over to kiss me good night. Her eyes flashed violet, her long hair fell in front of her face. She put two level spoonfuls of sugar into my mug. I looked up, at the nest of shadows under the hollow roof. I closed my eyes and rubbed my forehead.

Behind my trembling eyelids I saw my tongue go from her ear, through the valley of her neck, to her breast, and up, along her nipple, a tiny circle, and down, the slow journey down her flank and in along her groin, to the inside of her thigh, to the borderline between thigh and buttock and then up and around and around, and down again, wriggling and searching, and teasing and tasting, and up and around and around and up and down . . .

Cold drops of sweat ran down my chest. I leaned over and picked up my coffee. I sat there with my hands around the mug, my teeth chattering.

Ellen got up. She went to the book rack and reached toward a high shelf. Against the lathing, long slender arms raised, back curved, her body was an arabesque in the half-light.

I put down my mug and stood up. 'Time to go,' I said.

She came back with a pack of cigarettes which she'd fished out of the book rack, pulled out a cigarette and held it to the flame below the coffee pot. I was having trouble seeing her as she really was. My fantasies kept sliding over the reality. It was like standing in a double exposure, a jumble of lines, light, objects. Bottles in the light, upturned tables, hands sticking out of walls, four-eyed faces, tilted floors, trees with their crowns on the horizon. Then she came up to me. She blew a puff of smoke past my face.

'Bye,' she said.

Obviously We Don't Know a Thing About Love

July was hot. Every morning the sun shot up to its zenith and stayed there for the rest of the day, a dazzling white disc that burned everything dry. The trees lost their leaves, the people shuffled slowly past the houses and the whole town smelled of tar and gas and dust. Every evening I'd lie on the bare wooden floor of my room, in the breath of wind that puffed out the net curtains like white ballgowns. One evening I was lying there, lost in thought, a saucer of butts on my stomach, a ring of empty beer bottles around my head, when suddenly there was a shadow standing over me. For a moment I thought the beast from the gardens had crept in through the open window.

'Sam?'

I gasped. The floorboards surged under my back.

'Simon. It's me, Simon. Where are you?'

'Here. On the floor. Jesus, couldn't you have knocked?'

He shrugged his black shoulders.

I closed my eyes and took a deep breath. 'Why don't you get yourself a beer from the fridge and join me, Simon.'

He turned around and went into the kitchen.

'There's no bottle opener,' I called out. 'You have to lay the cap against the edge of the counter and slam down on the bottle.'

There was some rummaging around, followed by a feeble tap. I got up and went into the kitchen. Simon was standing there with a bottle in his hand, looking at me with raised eyebrows. I took the bottle, opened it and walked ahead of him into the room.

'The door was open,' he said, when he was sitting opposite me on the floor 'the downstairs door too. I coughed, but you didn't answer. How are you?'

'Fine. And you?'

'The same.'

We drank beer. Stifled noises came from the floor below. My neighbour had a new girlfriend. They fucked every night. I was so used to it I knew exactly when they were about to reach their climax, and what they were doing to get there.

'It's French Night,' I said.

Simon leaned forward and stared at me. His mouth hung open.

'Downstairs,' I said. 'My neighbour. If they're just plain doing it, you can hear the bed banging against the wall. Tonight she gets to come for real.'

'Jesus,' he said.

Soft whimpers rose.

'That was her. If you're lucky, they might even fuck.'

It was still.

'So, what brings you here?'

Simon shifted uneasily back and forth. He lifted his bottle and drank. Downstairs, the bed started creaking.

'My God,' he said, 'are they always this noisy?'

I nodded. Then I tilted my head slightly, my hand half raised.

'Here he comes,' I said.

'Yes!' cried my neighbour.

Simon cleared his throat. The female voice below us shouted unintelligible words of encouragement and the banging of the bed grew louder and faster.

'Now,' I said.

There was a long rattling sound, then silence.

'The hunger has been stilled, the apple has been eaten. How's Lisa?'

'How's . . . Fine, fine. God . . .'

I looked at him. His face glowed blue in the twilight. He leaned back, on his elbows, and peered gravely in my direction.

'Your sister,' he said, 'is a tiger cat.'

I put my bottle down next to the others and got up to get a new one. When I returned, Simon was sitting on the other side of the room, leaning against the bed. He had his legs pulled up, his head back, the bottle of beer clasped to his chest. I walked across the empty room, and when I got to where he was I went over to the open window and looked out at the dark gardens. A couple of torches signalled with their flickering light. Shadows moved among the trees.

'Why are you here?' I asked. 'Did you finish the encyclopedia?'

I looked around and saw him peering at me again.

'What?'

'Lisa told me you were reading the encyclopedia, the *Encyclopedia Britannica*.'

He shook his head.

'I'm doing my PhD,' he said. 'I use the encyclopedia now and then, but mostly it's the Bible, Ovid and Plato and Homer and Joyce and . . .' He sighed. 'The *Britannica*. God, I wish I could afford it.'

'What are you studying?'

He took a swig and stared ahead for a long time.

'Lisa told you I was reading the encyclopedia? That's all she said?'

I nodded.

'I'm finishing my PhD, anthropology. I'm writing my dissertation on border-crossing as the underlying structure in religious and secular texts, oral and written.'

I was aware that my mouth had dropped open.

'In my opinion, most religious and . . . er . . . secular texts consist of two parts. Exodus and Odyssey. Have you ever heard of Isaac Deutscher?'

I shook my head.

'Stalin's and Trotsky's biographer. I once read a book of his in which he described how, ever since childhood, he'd been fascinated by the world outside the circle in which he grew up. He was born in Chrzanow. He was a Jew, and such a brilliant Talmud and Torah student that he had the privilege of waking the Rebbe every morning. Are you familiar with that world?'

I shook my head. He couldn't see me doing it, but he obviously assumed I was a layman in this area, because he went right on talking.

85

'The Hasidic Jews regard their Rebbes as holy men. Tzaddikim, the righteous. If you were allowed to wake up one of these Tzaddikim every morning, you were pretty special. Deutscher realized very early on that he was being pulled across the border. He writes something like . . .'

He leaned forward and placed his right hand on his forehead. From the gardens behind my house came the shouts of late-night drinkers. Glass tinkled, somebody cried: 'Get him!' and then laughter rose. I looked out at the dancing torch flames. I suddenly had the feeling that life was nothing more than this, that in the end, this was what it was all about – one night of running through the dark gardens.

'Like this,' said Simon. 'He writes something like this. When he was a child, he read a story that completely corresponded with his own longing for, let's say, the other world. It was the story of Rabbi Meir, a great saint and sage. The rabbi took lessons from a heretic, Elisha ben Abiyuh, who was called Akher, the Stranger. One Saturday Rabbi Meir was out with his teacher and they got involved in a deep discussion. The teacher was riding a donkey, and the rabbi, who wasn't allowed to ride on a Saturday, walked along beside him. He was listening so intently to his teacher that he didn't notice that they'd reached the ritual boundary, which the Jews weren't allowed to cross on the Sabbath. His teacher pointed this out to him. He said: This is where we must part, you may not accompany me any further, go back. So Rabbi Meir turned back, while his teacher rode on, beyond the boundaries of the Jewish community. That's basically what Deutscher wrote. I was fascinated by it. Deutscher himself, who broke out of that . . . er . . . super-religious environment, and made the transition, you might say, from wunderkind to secular socialist, and that rabbi who wasn't allowed over the boundary, with whom he so strongly identified. Border-crossing is a central theme in religious thought. At least in the Judeo-Christian tradition. But actually, the crossing of a border is not so much the cause, as the result. The cause is always desire, a deep longing for something, or someone else.'

'I didn't know you were a student,' I said.

86

Simon got up. The empty beer bottle dangled from his index finger. He looked at me questioningly. I nodded. He took my bottle and put both bottles in the ring on the floor, then went into the kitchen for more beer. I listened to his attempts to knock off the caps. He was in there for quite a while. When he finally came back into the room, he said: 'There's a French philosopher, Levinas, who wrote almost exclusively about the other, with a capital 'O', and the other. Rather . . . er . . . obscure. French philosophy isn't very lucid. They're too elegant, I think. He writes that the longing for the other is born in a person who has everything he needs, it's born over and above anything that this person might be lacking or that might satisfy him.'

He handed me a bottle which was oozing a slow head of foam, and then walked through the room, past the shrinking and swelling clouds of curtain. Now and then he disappeared completely in the white gauze.

'"In longing, the I moves toward the other," says Levinas. As a result, the identification of the I with itself, and this is the whole point, is jeopardized. Er . . . "The movement toward the other, instead of completing or contenting me, implicates me in a concurrence of circumstances which, in a way, did not concern me and ought to leave me indifferent: what in God's name was I looking for here? Where does this shock come from, each time I, indifferently, pass the other by? The relationship with the other calls me into question, strips me of myself, time and time again, by showing me ever new resources. I did not know I was so rich, yet I no longer have the right to keep anything for myself." That's what he says. Jesus, I've read it so many times I can quote it word for word. That's scary.'

I drank and looked at my sister's husband. I hardly knew him. Lisa had got married when Raph and I were still on the road, and after the wedding we had seen them together only a couple of times. I rarely saw Simon on his own. We just never hit it off, and I could never figure out why. He was a nice guy and he didn't seem to have anything against me, yet all those years we had kept our distance and remained awkward strangers.

'I'd like to add something to that,' he said. 'Levinas depicts responsibility as a movement towards the other. It may be done reluctantly, but there's always that sense of urgency. When Adam and Eve eat the apple and start longing for each other, they're forced to leave Paradise, and in doing so, they cross a border which has been placed under such strict surveillance that they can never return. You remember. The flaming sword outside the Garden of . . . er . . . Eden. That's the point at which they have to *make* their own life, create their own world. They have to work the land, actually make the world, in order to survive. They have to multiply, *make* man, in order to ensure that the human race doesn't end with them. They've changed, from creatures without longing or aspiration, to mortal beings who know nothing else, who are *compelled* to long for and aspire to each other and the other. Moses is continually crossing borders. He leaves his mother's house and journeys, in his basket of reeds, to the land of Pharaoh, returning only when his sense of justice, of concern for the other, compels him to do so: when a Hebrew slave is beaten by an Egyptian. He changes, at that moment, from someone who doesn't care about anything, into someone who has discovered *the other*. Suddenly he's no longer the Egyptian prince with an Egyptian name, but a man who sees that he's got brothers. In fact, it's the first time the word "kinsfolk" is actually used, even though Moses can't possibly know that these slaves truly are his kinsmen. Later, when he flees, he crosses yet another border, and for the first time he's taken into a community, the tribe of his wife. His life, up until the flight from Egypt, is a genesis, in which the longing for the other is, time and again, the motivating force.'

He was really into it now. He paced slowly up and down the room, with that slightly curved body of his, with the long neck that seemed to slide in and out as he spoke. I suddenly thought: he looks like a fucking giraffe. He went from one end of the room to the other, sixty feet there and sixty feet back, and when he was all the way down by the door, I could see nothing but hazy flecks, a hand with light falling on it, his face turning towards me now and then.

I had trouble following his argument. I've never got any farther than that passage by Pico della Mirandola, a couple of books by Giordano Bruno (another one of those Italian monks), and some stuff by Wittgenstein, who, as far as I was concerned, had the same rigid, monastic background. I saw these men not so much as philosophers, but as lonely explorers, astronauts of the soul. I had tried to emulate them, particularly after Raph and I returned from our journey, but not so much because I agreed with them. Wittgenstein was more of an example to me. This was how you should live, in constant search of purity, of honesty (starting with yourself), in a continuous, critical dialogue with your own soul. No more small talk about the weather, or soccer, or politics, all your energy had to be devoted to methodical, searching inquiry. Of course, this hadn't made it any easier to get to know other people. Someone who spends all his time striving for purity and univocality isn't the most appealing conversational partner. People are more interested in unintelligible mumbling than analytical dialogue. Whenever anybody said something, an ordinary remark, something like: good thing Eastern Europe's finally going to be free, I'd ask them what they actually meant by 'being free' and how they'd ever come up with the insane notion that what was happening was *good*. 'For two thousand years, people have been blindly chasing the craziest theories about Creation, the solar system, and chemistry, and each time something turns out not to be true, the next theory is embraced with equal enthusiasm.' I'd said this to Raph, who had been so thrilled for the poor Eastern Europeans. 'Why not be sceptical for a change,' I said, 'why not wait and watch? Who says our ideas about freedom won't turn out to be totally perfidious in a couple of centuries?' Raph had asked if that meant I was in favour of people not being allowed to leave their own country. 'No,' I'd said, 'but what makes you think we can leave ours? First you have to buy a passport, actually *pay* for it, and you only get one if you happen to have been born here, and then you just have to pray you've got a clean slate, because otherwise they'll arrest you. Of course, if you're unlucky enough to be from Sahel, or Vietnam, you can forget the whole thing. Or you can flee, and run the risk of being sent back after I don't know how many years. Do we really want the Eastern

Europeans to be allowed out of their country? Then why aren't we willing to take them in? They can't get political asylum, let alone a residence or work permit. What are they supposed to do with all that freedom to travel? Go on vacation?'

But that's not what Simon was talking about. Simon was concerned with a whole other way of thinking. He was talking about a world in which everything revolved around the movement from one to the other, and he didn't mean the way my downstairs neighbour was doing it.

'Three stories,' he said as he went rocking through the room: 'the tale of "Paradise Lost", Moses' *Bildungsgeschichte* and the story of Deutscher's life, all with the same basic pattern: first an exodus, then the odyssey. It's an Oedipal pattern: one leaves home to go out and discover the world, to become a complete person. There's hardly a book or a narrative, religious or secular, in which the story isn't told along the lines of the journey. Gilgamesh, the Bible, the *Iliad* and the *Odyssey*, *Le Morte d'Arthur*, Reynard the Fox, Ulysses, Orpheus – each and every one of them is based on the idea that man leaves the place where he is and goes out into the world around him.'

'Did you think all this up yourself?'

He stood in the dark, on the other side of the room. I thought he nodded, but I couldn't be sure.

'So what you're saying is that our lives are nothing more than leaving the home of our youth and travelling around, and that we do that because we're curious about something or somebody else?'

'Not curious,' he said. He came moving toward me through the darkness. His massive silhouette slowly changed into a figure with human features. 'Longing. That's what it all boils down to. A deep, inescapable longing, for another person, another thing, for the past, for Father and Mother, for violence or sex, but that's the same as Father and Mother, for food, for sleep. It's not a primary urge, like hunger, it's something spiritual. When all is said and done, it's the desire to find the peace you lost when you left home and set out on the odyssey.'

'I don't mean to be crude,' I said, 'but are you saying that every time that guy downstairs buggers his girlfriend, he's busy having regrets about his adulthood?'

A couple of nights earlier the bed had started banging and, just as they were nearing their climax, I heard my downstairs neighbour screaming hoarsely: 'I'm gonna shove it up your ass, goddamit! I'm gonna shove it up your ass!' My heart had skipped a beat. But then I heard his girlfriend: 'Do it, you bastard, do it!'

Simon was standing in front of me. I saw his mouth twist into a wry smile.

'When we leave the home we grew up in,' he said, 'when we say farewell to our youth, we begin to long for that home, for that youth, because during the odyssey one thing becomes clear: we've lost our innocence. Once we've taken a bite of the apple from the Tree of Knowledge, and that knowledge is the other, knowledge we don't yet possess . . . once we've taken that bite, we've left Paradise and we can never return. The blissful state of ignorance is gone forever. Before you can possess, you must first know loss.'

I sat on the windowsill and stared at the face of the man opposite me. I thought: it sounds insane, it sounds like stark raving bullshit, but he's probably right.

'What did you want to tell me about Lisa?' I asked.

He gave me a look of total incomprehension.

'You came here to talk about Lisa, right?'

'I . . . er . . . yes,' he said. 'How did you know that?'

I shrugged.

He sank down onto the edge of my bed and lowered his head. He sat there, hunched forward, the bottle of beer in one hand, the other hand over his mouth. He stared at his shoes. I thought: why does the whole world have to sit on my bed and tell me what's wrong?

'Have you got a cigarette?'

'I think so,' I said. 'You smoke?'

'Sometimes.'

I walked over to the ring of beer bottles on the floor and hunted around for cigarettes, which I finally found when I stepped on them. I went back to Simon and held out the pack. Simon drew

91

a cigarette from the crumpled paper and gazed sadly at the bent white rod between his fingers. I walked back to the spot where I'd found the cigarettes and started looking for the matches.

'It all began about a month ago,' said Simon. 'She came home very late, several nights in a row, then for a while at the usual time, and then one night she didn't come home at all.'

I sank down on my knees and groped around, over the floorboards. I didn't want to turn on the light, because then I'd have to close the windows to keep out the mosquitoes.

'Three days,' he said. 'She was gone three whole days. Then she came back as if nothing had happened. I was sitting at the table working, I'd hardly eaten a thing all that time, a little yogurt now and then, some tea, lots of vodka. I was a wreck. She comes in, looks around, throws a bundle of clothes on the table and says: I could use a glass of that. As though she's just been for a walk around the block.'

I couldn't find the matches. I stood up, went into the kitchen and got the big box lying next to the stove. When I came back Simon was sitting motionless on the bed, as if somebody had turned a knob and switched off his current. Three days, I thought, she was gone for three whole days. She spent one night here. What the hell is going on with that sister of mine?

'What did you say to her?'

He shrugged his shoulders, drawing deeply on his cigarette. 'Nothing,' he said, in a cloud of smoke. 'I thought: I'll act as if nothing has happened. I thought maybe she'd been to see you.'

I lit my own cigarette and sat down on the windowsill again, with my back to the gardens. I looked at the dark figure on my bed.

'A week later she disappeared again. For one night. She came home at six the next morning. I was asleep, and all of a sudden she was bending over me. She said: I wanna fuck.'

He raised his head and turned it slowly towards me. Here comes the tiger cat, I thought. He stood up and tottered into the room. The curtains glowed in the darkness. He walked past the billowing sails, slightly stooped, looking pensive.

'I . . . er . . . She was very . . . wild. The next night too, and

92

the night after that, and . . . God, she did things I'd never even heard of.'

He stopped somewhere on the other side of the room, a long way away from me. He turned around. I could tell he was looking at me, even though we couldn't see each other.

'If you don't want to hear this, I . . . er . . . I'll stop.'

'Go on, it's okay.'

'One day she wanted to go for a walk. Lisa, of all people. We took a bus to a village. I forget the name. Just outside of town. When we got to a bus stop in the middle of nowhere she said we had to get out. She had it all planned, she knew exactly what she was doing. We'd gone about half a mile and suddenly she started looking for something. The road we were walking on was a kind of lane. Trees on both sides. Hardly any traffic. She went up to one tree and looked that thing up and down and then she sat on the ground and leaned her back against the trunk. It was hot. The sun was directly above us. We were sitting there for a while and all of a sudden she . . . er . . . she started making love to me.' He drew his hand through his hair and shook his head. 'Jesus. I mean, it was quiet out there, but it was still a road. A car went by at least every ten minutes.'

His voice rustled through the darkness. Even though it was warm, a shiver ran down my spine.

'The next night she came home and said: I'm moving in with Sam for a while. I . . . was . . . I was stunned. I said: "But what's happened? Is there someone else, or . . ." No, no, there wasn't anybody else. The spark was gone, the . . . magic. Love has to be a mystery, she said, and there's no mystery between us anymore. It was no use talking to her. I just didn't know what to make of it. One minute she's a tigress, the next minute everything's gone.'

He walked towards me, in that slow, thoughtful way of his. For a moment I had the feeling I was being stalked. When he was standing in front of me he said: 'I think she means it, I think she really wants to go away.'

I took one last drag of my cigarette and threw the butt out the window. Simon flung his clumsily out after it.

'So now you've come here to slit my throat in revenge,' I said.

'Or are you going to punish me by making me memorize the collected works of that spacey French philosopher of yours?'

His face caught a glimmer of light from outside. I saw his eyes wandering. I turned around, and saw the dusty trail of a shooting star fading into the velvet night. I looked back at Simon.

'Did you see that?'

I nodded.

'Did you make a wish?'

I shook my head. 'I'm the son of an astrophysicist.'

Simon raised the bottle he was still holding and peered inside the neck.

'Let's have another one,' I said. 'Let's get drunk. Obviously we don't know a thing about love.'

'*We*?'

'*We*. *We*, because you've been reading too much of that encyclopedia, and I've been thinking too much and doing too little. *We*, because I don't understand Lisa any better than you do.'

That Was the Past

After she had announced that she was coming to live with me, I didn't see Lisa for two whole months, until one night in September when I came home and found her in my room. She was sitting in a wicker chair which she'd placed by the windows near the bed. At her feet was a pot of tea over a flame. Yellowy candle-light flickered through the holes in the metal tea warmer, distorted Christmas stars leaped about on the floor. I stood in the doorway, my jacket in one hand, the door handle in the other, and looked at my sister sitting there in the chair she'd brought down from upstairs, the thin eddy of cigarette smoke above her head, the bluish glow of the night behind her. As I was taking in this scene and trying to remember what the image reminded me of, she slowly turned around.

'Sam?'

I tossed my jacket on the table and went over to her. She was sprawled in the chair, head back, bare legs stretched out in front of her. There was an ashtray in her lap. I kissed her and looked at her face.

'I thought it was you,' she said. 'Want some tea?'

'I'll get a glass.'

When I came back, she'd pulled up my desk chair. I sat down beside her, let her fill my glass and looked out the window. It was a quiet night. Now and then a bird chimed, I didn't know what kind, but it was one that chimed. In the distance was the murmur of traffic. A high voice laughed, or cried, in the dark of the gardens.

'I've taken the attic room,' Lisa said. 'It was empty.'

'That's fine.'

'Is it okay if I store my painting stuff up there too?'

I nodded.

We sipped our tea in silence. Lisa lit a fresh cigarette.

'So you've left him.'

'Yes.'

'Does he know that?'

'Yes.'

I looked at her. She was still sprawled in her chair. She drew on her cigarette, blew out smoke, drank and looked outside, at the barely visible stars.

'Well?'

She shrugged her shoulders. I picked up my glass and drank down the last few drops.

'I'm going to get a beer,' I said. 'You want one?'

She shook her head.

I walked towards the kitchen, but when I got to the door I turned and said: 'First you accuse me of not caring, then I ask you all kinds of questions and you don't answer. Is there some sort of logic to that, or have I missed something?'

'I was enjoying the silence,' she said when I came back. As I raised the bottle to my lips and felt the cold beer flooding my chest, she told me what had happened, how she'd broken the news, and what he'd said, that he'd helped her pack, that, in the end, they'd both gone down together, he with a suitcase in each hand, she with cartons full of painting stuff. Then they'd loaded her things into the car and she'd driven away. I listened and drank and took a drag of her cigarette. Her eyes gleamed in the dim light. I laid my hand on her hair. She sucked in her lower lip and bit it.

'Right,' she said, 'that was the past.'

I looked outside. What must that be like? Telling someone, after so many years, that you're leaving, packing your bags, going out together into the street and driving away, while someone in the mirror stands and waves, someone who grows smaller and smaller and smaller, until all that's left is the memory of a raised hand? Lisa had presented it as a rather silent event, two people nodding sadly in the realization that there was no other way.

She sat up straight, my lonely sister, and took a deep breath. She tossed down her tea, stood up and went into the kitchen. I heard her opening the refrigerator. A minute later she came back with a bottle of beer. As we looked at each other and toasted, I heard the voice in the distance again. It was definitely laughter.

'Announcement number two,' said Lisa. She stared straight ahead. 'This is temporary. I want a place to stay until I can find something else. I have to be alone, I have to lead my own life.'

'I understand.'

She looked at me, her head slightly tilted, suspicious, almost. 'I don't know,' she said. 'I don't know if you understand anything about people and human relationships.'

'Maybe not.'

'Have you ever loved anyone? Besides Raph and me? A stranger?'

'I don't believe in love,' I said. 'In lust, maybe, in mutual dependence, in being together because it's convenient, in love as the name you give to the marketplace where two people trade services, love as a decision, but not as in Tristan and Isolde.'

She bit her lower lip again.

'And you?'

She nodded, with averted head. 'I used to love Simon. I really did. But you can only love another person if that other person makes it possible. He wanted me, but he didn't want the responsibility.' She pressed her lips together and shook her head. 'The advantages,' she said, 'but not the disadvantages.'

'Isn't that what everybody wants?' I asked. 'The advantages without the disadvantages? And who's to say you're not running away from the disadvantages?'

She was silent. From down in the gardens came the babylike squall of fighting cats.

'You don't know a damn thing about it,' she said.

'I love you both,' I said. 'You and Raph. And I loved Papa and Mama. I think. Not out of laziness. Because you were my family. I wanted you. I decided that I wanted to love you.'

'How romantic,' she said. 'What a sense of passion.' She sounded bitter.

That was the start of our joint household. Every morning we'd meet in the kitchen, where Lisa silently drank her black coffee and I spread out the newspaper and read the comics while I ate my toast. Every evening I made supper, and she'd sit on top of the little refrigerator and tell me all about stuff that had happened at work. During the day I sat at my table, worked on the Kopakker report and thought about all the things I had to do, would do, and wanted to do. I realized that, once again, my life had changed without my having meant it to, just as I had never actually meant, after my parents died, to take on another family, and another, and another, just as I had never actually looked for a job, but had allowed myself to be talked into one. I thought: If I don't want to go on being a victim of circumstance, I better do something.

This made me think of Raph, of his restiveness, that time when he sat in his room and told me he wanted to travel, get away, be alone. I began to understand that the journey we had made back then had been more than an escape: it was an attempt to appease the hunger of youth, the hunger that drove you to do something, anything, it didn't matter what, the hunger to live, to take life into your own hands, however pointless and primitive that might seem.

I'm a late bloomer, I thought, it's only now that I'm getting around to puberty, and only now, all these years after we set off, am I ready to go.

But I just sat there, surrounded by index cards and stacks of xeroxes, one hand on a blank sheet of paper, a pen in the other, and I gazed down at the gardens, waiting for the girl with the polka dots, who never came out anymore.

I rounded off the Kopakker report much too late, in October, a month after Lisa moved in. For a while it seemed as if autumn was going to do an about-face. The temperature rose, the trees stopped losing their leaves. When I put aside my work in the afternoon to take a stroll around the neighbourhood, I walked down the street without a jacket on, my hands in my trouser pockets. It was the season of autumn revels. Boys rode their bikes along the pavement, and when they were right behind you, they pulled a string that set off a rattle in the front wheel. Vrrrrrrt. In a barren park, where the bushes had died of thirst and maltreatment and lay across the hard grey earth like shrivelled tentacles, little children swarmed around marble holes and groups of skinny girls shot at each other with plastic guns.

I finished my work on a Thursday afternoon. I drew up a table of contents, looked over the index and slid the report into a large brown envelope. Then I grabbed my jacket, walked into town and shoved the envelope into the oil company letter box. After that I bought a newspaper and had tea in a cafe that looked like an ad for contemporary home furnishings.

When I got home, Lisa was lying in my bed. I tiptoed across the room. I sat down beside her and whispered her name. She moaned softly. Her forehead was beaded with tiny drops of sweat.

When she opened her eyes it was as if she were looking straight through me.

'I thought a word,' she said.

I nodded.

'It's like I'm a body floating through the universe, and the word is a pebble being lowered down on top of me on the end of a long, long rope.'

I got up and went into the kitchen. I found an empty wine bottle and filled it with water.

When I had sat down beside her again and offered her a drink ('Sweet,' she said, 'sweet'), she seemed to come around. She pushed herself up and leaned her back against the wall. It was wet between her breasts. Her skin glowed.

'It's really weird,' she said, 'I've been dreaming words.'

'What kind of words?'

'Knife. House. Water. Words like pebbles. A word as a weight, a thing. Slow. And for the rest, nothing.'

'Is everything all right?'

She nodded. 'I just had a bad dream. I got home and I was so tired I went to bed. What time is it?'

'Around seven,' I said.

'God, I haven't even slept an hour.' She blinked her eyes and frowned. 'I had very slow thoughts,' she said. 'A mind like molasses. I thought words and it was almost as if they were falling into me, like raindrops in a puddle. Pan. I thought that too. And rope. Panrope. And sand and God. And knife and house and water. Like pebbles coming out of the darkness and very, very slowly touching my stomach. A word like a pebble. A word as a weight. A word as a thing. And for the rest, perfect silence.'

She took the bottle and drank. Outside, a car alarm started bleating. Lisa raised her head and looked at me through narrowed eyes. 'I love him,' she said.

I smiled in such a way as to suggest that I knew what she was talking about. She's got a gift for obscurity, I thought. First she dreams 'pan', and then she says she loves 'him'. I put my hand on her arm. 'I'll fix us something to eat,' I said. 'You go back to sleep, I'll wake you in half an hour or so.'

She sank back into the pillow and closed her eyes.

I made a salad out of leftover pasta, lamb's lettuce, fried mushrooms and a handful of walnuts, sliced up some bread, piled everything onto a tray and went back into the room. We ate, Lisa propped up against the pillow, me sitting on the edge of the bed. She chewed mechanically, smiled politely once or twice and then dropped off to sleep again.

As I stood in the kitchen washing the dishes, the doorbell rang. I walked downstairs, opened the door and saw Raph. The light from the stairwell shone on the sandy pavement and hung like a haze under the chestnut tree with the battered trunk. The sky was dark. The night covered the street like a hood. For a moment I had the feeling that Raph and I were figures in an old-fashioned peep show, two little cardboard men next to a little cardboard tree, in the glow of a yellowy lamp, beneath the black, star-studded lid of the box.

We walked up the stairs. In the kitchen, I put my finger to my lips and said that Lisa was asleep in the other room.

He raised his eyebrows. 'This early?'

'She's pretty upset about leaving Simon.'

He glanced at me and shrugged. 'I don't get it. I never did think much of that asshole.'

100

That was more or less what he had said a week or two earlier, at our traditional 'Family Night'. Lisa had turned to him with a face of stone.

'She obviously feels differently,' I said.

'So why did she leave?'

'Raph,' I said, 'when you love somebody, do you ever get the feeling there are actually two people involved? The one you love, and the real person?'

'I think so. Yeah, sure. I guess you always fall in love with the illusion you have of somebody.'

'Not Lisa. For you, and for me, the person you're in love with is something very different than the woman herself. We fall in love with an image that's conjured up by our lust, a kind of . . . fata morgana. It's got more to do with will than reality. Those "love affairs" of yours, all those girls who stay the night, why don't they ever work out?'

'Because that's just the way it goes sometimes.'

'Or maybe because the illusion doesn't correspond with the reality, because each time you think you've found "the one" she turns out not to be the one and you can't accept that?'

He looked at me. His mouth dropped open.

'Lisa really loves Simon,' I said. 'Without delusions, without mutual attraction and romantic fantasies getting in the way. And that's her problem. At first I thought she didn't want to stay with him anymore because he's got a little strange. Lisa says he sits on the bed all day reading the encyclopedia.'

'Which one?'

'She said the *Encyclopedia Britannica*, but I don't know if she was being serious.'

'Maybe he's not so crazy after all,' said Raph.

'But she didn't leave him because he reads the *Britannica*. Actually, she says it's not possible to love anyone.'

Raph's eyes grew wider and wider.

'This is True Love, pal. This is The Real Thing. With suffering and melancholy and great longing and the whole bit. It's almost religious. She really loves him. She says so, too. She just doesn't know it yet.'

'Hold on. She says you can't love another person and at the same time she loves him? Am I crazy? Is there something wrong with me or what?'

'The point is,' I said, 'she's got all these vague feelings for him and he's letting her down. At least, that's what I think. And that must come as a shock. In the end, we all want to love someone who's kind and beautiful and healthy and good. We can't help it. We're only animals. I think it has a lot to do with surrender. It's like when people have a vocation. God comes along and says: Here I am, I want you, and you reject Him, because if you say yes you have to accept a whole lot of other things that go against your sense of reason.'

I heard the distant wail of a goods train as it thundered through the station.

'Maybe true love is only possible in religious terms,' I said. 'Maybe I've been wrong all along.'

'Don't tell me, Sam: you've joined the Pentecostal Church,' said Raph.

'Right. And from now on I want all women to wear white ankle socks in bed.'

We laughed.

'But why,' Raph asked, 'did she leave him when she says she loves him?'

'Who knows. Maybe it's because, deep down, you only want what's strong and healthy, because your genes are hoping to increase their chance of survival, because Lisa loves the real person and can no longer fall back on the illusion. Or even wants to.'

Raph nodded slowly.

I put the last few dishes back in the cupboard. He leaned against the table, lit a cigarette and followed my movements, so quietly, so intently, that I knew my muddled little speech had taken him by surprise. Usually Raph was the one who said things, and I listened. He was the older brother, a man of the world. He lived there in that old factory in the industrial park and went to all kinds of clubs where the city's swinging young elite danced and ate, and often he had his camera with him and he'd photograph these people. Now and then he'd take some listless young thing back to the studio, which was also his home. I once met one of these girls at his place, a skinny blonde who gave me a limp handshake without even taking out the earplugs of her Walkman, then tucked her legs under her and didn't look at Raph or me for the rest of the evening. When I asked him a couple days later what he talked about with girls like that, he shook his head. 'Not everybody's there to be talked to,' he said. 'Sometimes good sex is enough.'

I thought about this, and as I made tea and told Raph, in a low voice, what I was doing at the moment (which wasn't much, now that I'd finished Kopakker I was working on an inventory for a seismic company library, I didn't tell him I'd lost the oil company as a client) I saw him open and close his mouth a few times, as if he wanted to say something but kept changing his mind at the last minute.

As we stood there opposite each other, silently drinking our tea, the door opened and Lisa came in. She was wearing one of my T-shirts. She kissed Raph and asked for tea.

'How do you feel?' I asked.

She shrugged. 'Sleepy. And thirsty. Like I've been walking through a desert. Are you guys standing in here because you don't want to disturb me?'

'I'm not staying long,' said Raph. 'I just came by to see if he wanted to go into town, but we can do that some other time.'

I handed Lisa her tea.

'I'd just as soon be alone this evening,' she said. 'In fact I'd prefer it. I couldn't sleep knowing the two of you were tiptoeing around all over the place. Go into town, it's okay.'

'We'll go tomorrow,' I said.

'No,' she said. 'Go now. Do me a favour and go have a drink somewhere. I'll get some more sleep, and by the time you get back I'll be my old self again.'

Raph put down his glass of tea and looked at me, frowning.

'Promise to wake me when you get home?' Lisa asked.

*   *   *

'Where are we going?' asked Raph when we were outside and walking through the empty streets, sauntering, as usual, he, slightly stooped, shoulders forward, as if he was about to fall over, me at his side, hands in my pockets, my head turned so I could see his face, half visible in the light of a streetlamp, light and dark at the same time, the shadow of his nose slanting across his thin lips.

'No idea,' I said.

'Guess who I saw yesterday?' said Raph.

'Who did you see yesterday?' I asked.

'Guess,' he said.

I shrugged.

'That girl.'

'What girl?'

'The one who always sits in the garden, behind your house.'

'Where did you see her?'

'Guess.'

'Goddammit, Raph!'

He grinned. 'In the Circus.'

'The what?'

'The Circus, that new disco in the warehouse over by the harbour.'

'How do you know it was her?'

'It was her.'

A few months earlier I had caught him staring out of my window, and when I went and stood next to him and followed his gaze, outside, I saw the girl with the polka dots. She was lying in the grass, sunbathing. He asked who she was and I said I didn't know. I told him how long I'd been watching her. He wasn't surprised.

We walked along a row of galvanized steel fences that closed off a site where a couple of office buildings were under construction. Soft voices murmured above us, I heard metal echoing against metal and the faint, monotonous hum of a diesel engine. Under the brightly lit metal shed at the top of the building, men were walking back and forth.

'Wanna go' asked Raph, 'to the Circus?'

I nodded.

Behind the building site was a tram stop. There, on an island of pavingstones, we stood and waited as the traffic raced around us. I leaned against the glass shelter and looked up at the concrete walls, draped with trusses and scaffolding, veiled in the neon mist that steamed from under the metal shed. The mottled grey cliff was stuck with yellow tufts of rock wool. Thick bundles of cable dangled against the concrete, which was covered here and there with shiny blue-black tiles. The tram came, we got in at the back. Raph made his way down to the other end to buy tickets, I went and sat in the window. We turned right onto the wide street that I always regarded as the centre of town. On either side of the avenue, where tram rails had taken the place of water, tall modern buildings and 1930s' bombast were all jumbled together. Farther down was a square with honeycomb-shaped structures in dead chipboard colours, their roofs adorned with billboards and neon. One or two prefabs were so covered with graffiti, they looked like badly drawn boulders. Raph came swaying back up the aisle. In the middle of the tram, where a rubber accordion joined the two cars, somebody was slumped over in his seat. When Raph passed him, he lifted his head. He looked about our age. His face was purple, his mouth covered with a wide streak of foam. The tram veered left, the wheels scrunched in the rails, the bell clanged. We shot onto a highway where four lanes of cars were whizzing along the asphalt. Headlights hurtled through the darkness like meteorites, tall streetlamps flew towards us and toppled over behind the tram. 'Next stop,' said Raph, who had joined me on the windowseat. The tram turned right. We clung to a sticker-covered rail. The street was lined with beech trees, and behind that, mansions, old office buildings four or five storeys high. There was hardly any traffic. At a little square, under an awning of young chestnut trees, the tram came to a halt and we got out.

Raph led the way. He walked past the square and across a car park between two tall buildings, until we reached a small harbour. We strolled along the quay, in the glow of coloured lightbulbs strung between old oak trees. Below us, where rainbow-coloured oil slicks floated on the syrupy water, I heard the creaking of boats tugging on their hawsers. We crossed the street and turned into a dark road with long building fronts on either side that bore the names of former colonies, and warehouses called America, Africa and East Indies. The air smelled faintly of cinnamon and cloves. Between the buildings were pallets loaded with goods: tractors in crates, machinery under thick layers of foil, rusty tubes and pipes. Water sloshed in the distance. After a while we found ourselves on a quiet quay, at the back of a huge warehouse. On the reddish-brown wall, lit by a single bulb, was a garishly coloured mural: a diabolical-looking enchantress with her wand raised over a sailor, half man, half pig, who was crouched at her feet. Above the mural, in letters like tongues of flame, was the name of the disco: *Circe's*.

'Circe's,' I said. 'Not Circus: Circe's.'

Raph frowned and looked at the painted wall. 'I could've sworn it was called Circus,' he said.

'If it's called Circe's, it could just as easily have been called Circus,' I said.

Raph took a step forward, disappeared into the shadow of a doorway and knocked on what looked like the entrance to a dungeon. We stood there for a moment in the silence of the falling night, the faint gurgle of water behind us, the creaking of wood and rope, and then a panel slid open and reddish light fanned out over our faces.

'Two,' said Raph. He took a twenty-five guilder note out of his pocket and stuck it through the hatch. The money disappeared, the light went out. Raph stared at the closed door. He turned around and opened his mouth. Before he could say a word the door was unbolted and a wall of sound came crashing down on top of us.

We were drowning in a sewer of blood. The walls around us glowed red, laser beams scribbled jittery patterns in the rust-coloured smoke that filled the air. High above us, where smoke and light faded into the black of the roof, were huge screens that showed people dancing, Technicolor explosions, and naked bodies writhing like snakes in a basket. I had a hard time following Raph. The sea of bodies he was cleaving through closed immediately behind him. I held my arms in front of my chest and ploughed my way forward, head down. Every so often I had to make breaststroke movements to get the crowd to part. There was no air, just smoke and flesh and sound. Heavy bass notes covered my ears like hands and set my heart racing to the beat of the drums. When we reached a steel staircase that ran diagonally up a large wall, Raph stopped. He leaned against the side of the staircase and wiped his forehead with the back of his hand. I was standing right in front of him, so close I could feel his breath in my face. He lifted his eyes and moved them upward, toward the ceiling. Then he turned around and squeezed between the people and the railing and I followed him, up the stairs. The music played on and on. One track dissolved into the next. Now and then I heard familiar fragments below the feverish drumbeat: a line from a Bogart movie (*Here's looking at you, kid*), a distorted phrase from a minimal music composition that Raph sometimes played me, bits and pieces of a Strauss waltz. The stairs led to a bridge made of perforated metal that ran along the walls. Against each of the four walls were long bars. The first served only cocktails, but the second, which hung somewhere above the entrance, had beer. Raph pushed his way through the crowd and came back a little while later with two icy bottles of Corona. He handed one to me and held his up in the air, by way of a toast. We clinked bottles and I raised the beer to my lips. It tasted like piss.

'. . . even worse,' said Raph.

I shrugged my shoulders.

He brought his mouth right next to my ear. I could feel his words steaming in my neck. 'Upstairs. Even. Worse.' He drew back and looked at me. I nodded. We raised our bottles again, drank long and deep and then set them down on the edge of the bar. Once again, Raph took up his position as prow and began walking.

Somewhere in a corner, a second flight of stairs led up to the level which I'd mistaken for the roof. Here, the building merged with another. We elbowed our way back through the crowd, and when we reached the spot where the two warehouses met, we stood at a chrome railing and gazed down at a dance floor, some ten feet below us. In the roof above the pit were large racks of spotlights, operated by electromotors. Yellow, red, blue and green beams swept over the people dancing below, lighting up faces, blending to form new colours and occasionally picking out someone who was dancing better than the rest. As we stood there watching, the spots went out. The bluish light of a stroboscope flashed on and transformed the dancers into the black-and-white of an old movie at the wrong speed. An arm shot up and stiffened, a face turned jerkily to one side. In the midst of the jumble of petrified faces and glowing T-shirts, I saw the girl with the polka dots. At that same moment I felt Raph's elbow in my ribs. I looked at him. On his face, in the flashing light of the strobe, was a photographic grin.

She was dancing alone and looked practically naked. Her short black dress ran up in two wide bands across her breasts and shoulders and around her neck. In the strobelight, she seemed to be composed of separate parts. She drifted along in the whirlpool of dancers and now and then her face popped up in the white light and her bare shoulders froze. I thought of all the times I'd sat at the window in my room, forearms on the table, staring outside, as she lay in the grass in the sun.

The strobe went out. For about five seconds it was dark, then the pit filled up again with colour and smoke. I peered down, but couldn't see her anywhere. Beside me, Raph was also leaning over and peering down. He straightened up, looked at me and raised his eyebrows. We ran our eyes once more over the dancers, then turned around and leaned our backs against the railing. I gazed at the maelstrom of bodies before us and felt like a man without a soul. I tried to remember the route we had taken to get here, the tall buildings under construction, the floodlight along the web of scaffolding, the tram screeching around the bend, the cars whizzing by. I tried to picture all this, but when I shut my eyes all I could see was the after-image of darkness flecked with coloured light. A sweaty body, that's what I was, one of many bodies in the midst of other sweaty bodies, a part of a whole. Maybe it's finally happened, I thought, maybe all my life I've had the feeling that my soul was about to break out of my body and now it really has escaped and it's floating around here somewhere in the smoke and light, together with the souls of all these other people. But even as I thought this, I knew it wasn't true, I knew I was surrounded by more sound and light and people than ever before and that my soul was only doing what children do when you tell them a scary story, that it was hiding, in order to protect me from something too great, or too close, or, perhaps, too much like me. Raph shouted in my ear that he wanted another beer. I held up my hand and pointed to his feet: stay here, don't move, or we'll never find each other again. Then my gaze slid past him, and I saw her once more. She was standing in almost the same spot as a few minutes before, still dancing alone. I nudged Raph. He turned around. We leaned over and looked down. A guy was making his way towards her. He stood in front of her and beckoned. She turned around and went on dancing. It was as if she were moving in a total vacuum, a star at the centre of the Milky Way, surrounded by millions of other stars, but alone just the same, in her own orbit. She stood there in that mass of wriggling bodies, and somehow it seemed as if she could never be anything else *but* alone. Here I am, I thought, I feel like I'm dissolving into this crowd of people, I'm part of one large body. My soul has withdrawn so deeply into itself that it doesn't even seem to be there anymore, while she, who I only ever saw as an image, as something without a soul, is the opposite, completely cut off from all those other bodies, a soul that has withdrawn into a cage.

Raph grabbed my arm and pulled me towards him. 'The lady's inaccessible.' I looked at him, at his gently nodding head. My gaze slid down, to the white shoulders drifting through the melee. I thought of Circe, the enchantress who turned Ulysses' men into swine, who saw Picus, husband of the golden-voiced singer Canens, riding through the forest, and was so devastated by his beauty that she changed him into a woodpecker when he rejected her. I saw that black hair dancing on those shoulders, the hand sweeping the fringe off her forehead, and I wondered if she'd change me into a woodpecker or a pig.

I turned around and stepped into the bustle, in search of beer.

When I got back, Raph nodded his head toward the dance floor.

'She's gone again,' he said. 'Vanished into thin air.'

By the time we left the disco, the night was already melting into the hazy patch of light that hung in the east over the city. It was still dark, but within half, maybe three-quarters of an hour, the black clouds overhead would be so diluted by the watery light in the distance that the streetlamps would go out, and the dancers and drinkers would slink home through the dead light of morning and go to sleep and wait till evening came around once more. We walked back into town along the canals. Halfway across a small wooden bridge, we stopped and leaned over the railing to look down at the black water between the sloping banks and the bushes under and next to the bridge, the windblown newspapers and empty bottles on the grass. Raph stuck his hand in his jacket and pulled out a pack of Camels. I took a cigarette and felt around in my pockets for a light. When I'd found the matches I rattled the box and Raph leaned toward me. I drew a match across the flint. The sulphur hissed hoarsely. The flame shot up and light bounced off our faces. Shadows jumped back and forth. Raph's eyes flared briefly, then sunk back into their dark sockets. His nose twitched from left to right, his mouth was a frayed gash in a chiselled grey face. The face of a dead man, I thought, and I suddenly remembered a photograph of Frank Sinatra, a black-and-white snapshot taken in the Fifties after an all-night recording session. He's sitting on a bar stool, collar open, tie like a crumpled cord around his neck, hat pushed back on his head. In front of him is a stand with a microphone shaped like a fist, and next to that, an ashtray on a leg. He has a cigarette in his hand, and you expect, when you see the picture, that any moment he's going to bring the other hand up to his face and rub his eyes. The flame between us was almost out, and Raph turned away from me, dragging hard on his cigarette. I saw the tip glow and heard how he sucked in the smoke, greedily, hungrily. I lit my own cigarette with the last bit of flame, and Raph straightened his back and I

110

threw away the match and we walked on, to the other side of the bridge, and left, along the water's edge. We wandered down the brick road, under the trees along the canal. The streetlamps shed pale yellow light onto the pavement. In the distance, a watery slice of moon hung in a haze of blue and dirty white. The light above the houses on the other side slowly began to fade. At the end of the street we turned right, down a wide asphalt road, through a park, until we reached the centre of town.

'What time is it?' asked Raph.

'About three, I'd say.'

'We can still stop in at Kees' place.'

I shrugged my shoulders. Raph took a drag of his cigarette, the tip sizzled red, and then he threw it away. I followed the arc of the tiny orange light, until it shattered to pieces against the ground.

'Okay,' I said.

We went left, along a deserted shopping street, until we came to a kind of mall. We walked for a while through the darkness, surrounded by roll-down shutters covered with graffiti, past a butcher's, a greengrocer's, a place that sold prams, and stopped in front of a cast-iron gate that fenced off a flight of stairs leading down. Raph shook the gate.

'He's closed,' I said.

'No, he's just not in the mood for customers.'

At the foot of the stairs, a battered wooden door opened. A man poked his head out and looked up.

'Kees?'

The man stepped outside and came walking up the stairs. He took a key out of his pocket and opened the gate. We slipped inside and walked downstairs. Behind me, I heard the clinking of metal and the click of the lock. I opened the door and was engulfed by sound.

> *Night and day,*
> *You are the one,*
> *Only you 'neath the moon or under the sun.*
> *Whether near to me or far,*

It's no matter, darling, where you are,
I think of you,
Day and night.

We found ourselves in a small, cellar-like room, filled with music. A huge wooden bar loomed up in the shadows like a giant boomerang. Three men were sitting there drinking, at the end of the bar someone was asleep with his head buried in his arms. Here and there was a candle burning in a glass. Orange lights glowed on the bare brick wall.

The man who had let us in walked around to the other side of the bar, sat down on a stool behind the tap and began talking to the three men. Raph and I sat down at the corner. We opened our jackets and lit fresh cigarettes.

As we ordered coffee and smoked, I listened to the music booming all around us. In the dim light, the cellar was transformed into a long narrow room with high walls, the kind of bar I always picture when I hear Sinatra: here and there, the faint glow of a lamp, the silhouette of Coney Island on the dark windows, a rumpled tramp in the corner drinking sweet Spanish wine from a bottle in a paper bag. I could see us walking out, a little while from now, into the steaming dawn, through the clouds of vapour that plumed up out of manholes, two, three blocks, until we came to an early morning drugstore, where we'd drink coffee and eat doughnuts and . . .

'Hey.'

I looked up. The barman was standing across from us on the other side of the bar, grinning.

'I was just telling your brother, I've never seen you in here before.'

I nodded and held out my hand. He lifted his eyebrows, wiped his hand on a dishcloth and shook mine.

'That guy over there,' I said, nodding toward the man who was asleep with his head on the bar. 'Is he still alive?'

The barman weighed the dishcloth in his hand, glared at the sleeper and flung the wet rag into the face with the closed eyes.

The man jerked upright and looked around wildly.

112

'Every night,' said the barman, 'every damn night he's in here and every night he falls asleep. Go sleep in your own house, you stupid prick!' He turned back to us. 'So, where've you two been this evening?' he asked.

Raph began telling him about Circe's.

I sipped the bitter coffee, looking at the man who had been hit in the face with the dishcloth. He sat there, stiff as a board. His white hair stood on end, he was staring ahead with vacant eyes. The faded windbreaker he was wearing had slipped halfway down his shoulders.

'. . . a subterranean world,' said Raph, 'a genuine inferno, with flickering red light on the walls, TV screens all over the place with war videos . . .' Suddenly I heard Lisa's voice, Lisa saying that one day Simon had just 'stopped feeling like a lover', Lisa saying: 'Without the mystery, love is a series of motions'. What had she meant? She had sat opposite me, one hand in her reddish brown hair, her bloodshot eyes focused on a point in the distance, a burning cigarette in her other hand. 'Without the mystery, love is a series of motions.' What mystery? 'They've gutted the place,' said Raph. 'It looks like a hollowed-out block of stone, with bare walls, steel stairs and catwalks everywhere you look. I've been there twice now and both times I thought: this is a goddamn science fiction movie.' Lisa said: 'He just sits there on the bed and reads the encyclopedia. I can't stand it any more. I love him, but I can't stand it any more.' Hey, I said to an imaginary Fleming, you think love isn't an act of will? You should talk to my sister. Love *is* an act of will. You stop loving. It doesn't just happen to you. First you keep on loving someone, regardless. But when the 'regardless' lasts too long, you stop. Because you want to. 'You completely forget where you are,' said Raph. 'It's so fucking crowded, you feel like a slab of meat packed into a great big crate with lots of other slabs of meat. One night at Circe's and you're black and blue all over. And that kabunk-kabunk-kabunk makes mincemeat out of your brains. But there's something about it . . .' Echo, I thought, and this feeling I have that the world is slowly going under, that too many lives are seeping away and we just sit back and let it happen, let people go under, and we think, too

113

bad, better luck next time, but there isn't any goddamn next time, if you're not happy now you never will be . . . You've gotta be happy, said Raph, when we were on the road, you are happy, aren't you? Of course I'm happy, I'd said. Why did I say that? Never been happy in my life. No idea what it is. Taught myself to love Lisa and Raph because I wanted family, can't imagine you could make yourself feel that way about anyone else. Love nobody but my brother and sister and have transferred my compassion onto those less fortunate than myself. God, I thought, I've turned into a kind of monk who sublimates his lack of sex into charity. 'Great girls,' said Raph. 'Gorgeous babes in ve-ry hot outfits. But we're too old, they're for schoolboys.' What do I want out of life? If I know it'll never be what I expected it to be, then what do I want?

I squinted my eyes and saw the darkness of the bar melt into an orangy-black haze in which the candles glittered like six-point stars, pulsating, spreading, blurring into patches of light.

I looked to the side, at Raph. He was still telling his Indiana Jones version of our night out dancing. I'm so old, I thought, always have been. Born an old man. My heart shrank. My chest ached. I took a deep breath. My lungs filled with the smell of beer and tobacco. Laughter rose. Raph threw back his head and roared. The barman's mouth was open so wide it looked like someone had hit him in the face with an axe. I closed my eyes and searched the void inside my head. Where are you, memory beast, where? I opened my eyes and looked sideways. Raph turned his head towards me and smiled. I looked at the man with the white hair, sitting upright on his stool and staring straight ahead. One of the candles on the bar began to flicker, and suddenly I saw the bare shoulders of the girl with the polka dots gliding through the darkness, so sharp, so lifelike, I almost reached out my hand to touch her. It was then that I realized that, all these years after following my brother and staring at his back and wondering what it was that made him happy and yet unhappy, that after all this time, I'd finally arrived at the place he'd already left – a longing so great, I didn't even know what I was longing for.

The barman poured us more coffee and then went back to the

three men he'd been talking to earlier. Raph gazed at the curtain of sugar granules he was lowering into his cup.

Lisa had said I was heartless, when I told her I didn't believe a word of those Tristan and Isolde stories, when it turned out I didn't understand a thing about her tales of passion and longing, because she thought I regarded all those lovers around me as irresponsible egoists, who suffered under the rejection of the one they loved, but wouldn't think twice about stepping over a beggar.

Maybe she's right, maybe I have become a sour old moralist and I don't even know the difference any more between sex and socialism.

I stuck my hand in my trouser pocket, pulled out a wad of money and called to the barman. As I picked apart the crumpled bills, Raph looked at me closely. 'Are we leaving?' I nodded. We got up. At the door, as I waited for Raph to walk outside, I looked around. The man with the white hair was still staring into space.

We walked through the empty streets, towards the bus station. Raph wanted to take the bus back to the industrial estate. We sauntered down a long street lined with tall houses, pubs and shops. There were pale flecks of light between the buildings. Half an hour later we came to a viaduct. The bus station was underneath. A man lay sleeping on a bench in the burned-out waiting room. We crossed the street and walked onto the wasteland under the viaduct. About a hundred yards further on, the road above us dipped down. Grey sand lay between the pillars, a newspaper spun slowly on a current of air. We stumbled along through the sand under the sloping concrete roof. After twenty-five yards or so, Raph sat down at the foot of a pillar. He drew a pack of cigarettes out of his pocket and shook out two. He lit them both and gave one to me. He thrust his hands deep into his jacket pockets and held his cigarette in the corner of his mouth, one eye squeezed shut. I looked at a dark blue truck parked a bit farther down. A faint light burned in the cab. Now and then I heard the pedlar's cry of a gull. In the distance, a shed door rattled open. The truck's motor hummed softly.

'Hey,' said Raph.

I looked at him.

'Why didn't you go up to that girl?' he asked. 'Why didn't you give it a try?'

I shrugged.

We stared ahead in silence. The truck door opened. A man swung his legs out. He sat in the doorway and looked around, then raised a plastic cup to his lips.

'What's the matter, Sam?'

I frowned. Raph got up and walked to the middle of the viaduct, stopped, and peered up at the ceiling. I followed him. When I was standing next to him I saw that there was something painted on the concrete. I wondered how the hell they'd got up there, no pillar nearby, twelve, maybe fifteen feet high. 'Herman fucks Rita,' it said. I thought: who's Herman and who's Rita and who painted that on the concrete, and why? Was it Rita's boyfriend, who didn't have the nerve to fight Herman, but who had to get it off his chest, like in that fairy tale, and went and painted it in this impossible spot? How did that fairy tale go again? A barber cuts the king's hair and notices that he has horns and can't keep it to himself and shouts it into the reeds . . .

'Do you remember what supernovas are?' asked Raph. 'A star, a gaseous sphere in which the tension, the pressure, keeps building up, until it exceeds a certain limit and everything has to come out. You look through the telescope, year after year, and one day: Wham! It suddenly goes clear and bright, starts spreading like some kind of white ink.' He turned around and looked at me. 'You,' he said, 'are a supernova. You're saving something up, I don't know what, but I can see the tension growing in you and one of these days . . . Wham!'

'I lost my best client,' I said.

'The oil company?'

'Yes.'

'That sucks.'

I felt something stirring inside. 'I don't know the difference between sex and socialism,' I said.

Raph lifted his eyebrows and stared at me. I felt his gaze travelling over my cheekbones, to my mouth, upward. I shut my eyes. The music from the disco started playing in my head. I saw the girl with the polka dots gliding through the darkness, to a country road that was bathed in the low light of an autumn sun. Papa, I thought, Mama, Lisa, Raph, God, the mystery of love.

I ran my hand over my forehead and opened my eyes wide. I do want to touch her, I thought, but it's not really about her. It's about a person, a woman. I want to love someone. My mouth moved without my meaning it to and words came out which I only recognized as words when I listened to my voice. 'I miss them so much,' I said. 'I want them back, Raph. And I don't even know what they look like. And I can't even remember what love is. I've forgotten. Is that possible? Why hasn't the world become calm and clear?'

I turned around and looked at the man sitting in the doorway of his truck, drinking coffee out of a plastic cup. I noticed that I was gasping for breath. I looked up, at the grey concrete. Herman fucks Rita. I thought: I wish I was Herman.

'You left,' I said. 'You went roaming.'

'So did you,' said Raph.

I shook my head. 'I was following you.'

I felt Raph's hand on my shoulder. Where's that road, I thought, where's the road Lisa was talking about? I bowed my head and let the tears come.

Logical Processes in
a Chaotic Environment

A few days later I went into town, and when I got back, towards the end of the afternoon, Lisa was gone. I walked into the room, hung my jacket on the door and called out her name, but there was no answer. On the top floor I poked my head around the door, and the moment I saw the big table where her brushes and pencils lay, I knew she had left. There was a bunch of rust-coloured chrysanthemums in a vase I'd never seen before, a pale green spread on the bed. She'd brought the wicker chair up from downstairs, placed it in a corner and heaped it with brightly coloured cushions. The attic I'd always left empty because I preferred to live in one large space now looked like a perfect little house. And yet, there was a feeling of departure in the air. Someone had been here, but the question was whether or not they would ever return.

I was about to go downstairs when I saw the note, pinned to a beam. I pulled it off and sat down in the wicker chair. *Gone back to Simon, Lisa.* I held the piece of paper in my hand, and as I sat there, in the little house she had built in my house, I remembered something. It was a fragment, a sentence Lisa had written long ago: *The night is a mysterious phenomenon.* Twilight crept into the room, the corners disappeared, the sky behind the window in the roof turned dark blue. *The night is a mysterious phenomenon.* As these words rustled through my mind the walls of another house loomed up in the gathering dusk, and I saw myself stealing along those walls, a ghost, a smudge on the darkness. Over the stairs, past open and closed doors, up to the attic (where Ursa Major gazed in through the zinc-framed window), back downstairs, into the living room, to the sun lounge. I glided through the shadows like a knife through water and in the darkened sun lounge I saw my father's cigarette glowing. I stood in the dark and stared at his black silhouette. 'Go upstairs, Sam,' he said. Outside the door to my parents' bedroom, where my mother was combing her hair, light lay on the floor like a sheet of paper. I walked back down the stairs. I opened the door to the study and saw my father leaning back in his desk chair, his feet on the tabletop, his folded hands pressed to his lips. He had his eyes closed. Soft music came from the old record player in the bookcase. Four muffled voices, seeking and losing each other.

> *Dream beside me in the midnight glow,*
> *The lamp is low.*
> *Dream and watch the shadows come and go,*
> *The lamp is low.*
> *While you linger in my arms,*
> *My lips will sigh:*
> *I love you so.*
> *Dream the sweetest dreams we'll ever know,*
> *Tonight the moon is high,*
> *The lamp is low.*

'What is it, Sam?'
How could he possibly know I'd come in when I was invisible, inaudible, when he had his eyes closed?
'Are we gonna look at the stars?'
'Not tonight.'
I stood in the doorway and waited.
'I said: not tonight, Sam.'
'Why not?'
He took his feet off the desk, put his hands on his thighs and looked at me from under his eyebrows. 'Sometimes you have to be satisfied with the answer that someone gives you.'
I didn't move.
'All right, come in and close the door.'
I shut the door.

My father reached for the metal cigarette case that was lying on a pile of papers on his desk. He opened it. I followed the fleck of light across his face. He was impatient, I could tell by his gestures. They were going to a party. My father didn't like parties.

'Are you mad?' I asked.

'At you?'

I shook my head.

'At whom?'

'At Mama.'

He smiled.

'I'm not mad at anyone,' he said.

I walked over to the model of the Mercury capsule that stood in the bookcase. I thought of the record I'd heard as I watched my mother combing her hair.

> *Let me tell you 'bout*
> *the birds and the bees*
> *and the flowers and the trees . . .*

When I got back upstairs, to the room I shared with Raph, there was a note on our desk. *Sam. The night is a mysterious phenomenon: one side of the earth is dark, the other side is light. Lisa.*

My father had given a Demonstration with Flashlight and Two Oranges, to mark the occasion of the lunar eclipse. He switched off the lights in the living room and put a flashlight and two oranges tied up with string on the table.

'Long ago,' he said, 'an eclipse was a mysterious phenomenon. No one understood how the sun or the moon could just suddenly disappear.'

He handed the flashlight to Raph. Lisa had to dangle one orange in the air while I slowly turned the other one in front of it. As the orange ball moved into the beam of light, a slow shadow crept over Lisa's orange.

'That is an eclipse,' said my father. 'One heavenly body turns into the light of the sun and casts its shadow on the other. In a lunar eclipse, the earth casts its shadow on the moon. But if you happened to be standing on the moon, you would no longer see the sun, because the earth would be blocking it. On the moon, you'd have a solar eclipse.'

Shadows in space. I had always thought there was nothing in space. Stars, planets, suns, but no sound, no shadows, no wind blowing through your hair.

After I'd put away the note in the box I'd marked 'ARCHIVES', the door opened and Raph walked in. He went over to the desk, turned on the radio and set up the half-finished model we were working on. I got out the box of loose parts and glue. We had asked for a model of the Mercury capsule, just like the one our father had, but since he felt it would be better for us to start with aviation, we got a Dakota instead. Raph picked up a file and began smoothing part of the undercarriage.

We were sitting there, enveloped in a cloud of airplane glue and arguing about the elevator, when our mother came in with Lisa. She was carrying her jacket over one arm. She leaned down and kissed us.

'Promise to go to bed on time?'

'No,' said Raph.

My mother shook her head. 'Eleven o'clock,' she said, 'no later.'

'Kit!' my father shouted from downstairs.

He was standing at the foot of the stairs, we knew that, cigarette between the index and middle finger of his right hand, left hand in his trouser pocket, his hair already rumpled. We could hear him muttering under his breath.

'I've left a surprise in the fridge,' said my mother.

'Where are you going?' I asked. I already knew. It had been discussed the week before at the dinner table.

'To a prizegiving ceremony.'

'What kind of prize?' asked Raph.

My mother smiled. She knew we just wanted to keep her there a little bit longer. 'A prize from the university. For the –'

'Jesus.' Papa stood in the doorway. There were ashes on his lapel, his hair hung wildly about his head. 'Jesus, they're not babies. You don't have to goddamn tuck them in.'

Lisa dropped onto Raph's bed, shrieking with laughter. Raph and I laughed too. Our father scowled.

121

'Good God,' said my mother, 'I leave you alone for one minute and you look like you fell off the roof.' She smoothed his hair and brushed down his jacket. 'Let's go.' She turned to us again. 'You take care of each other,' she said. She looked at Raph.

They walked down the stairs. My father said he didn't want to stay long, my mother answered something I couldn't understand, but it sounded reassuring. We stood up and ran down the hall, to Lisa's room, where we pushed aside the curtain and looked out the window. Below us, the black car gleamed in the half-light of a streetlamp. My mother looked up and waved. She bent over and disappeared into the car. The headlights flashed on, the car veered quickly onto the road. Then all we saw were the red tail-lights dissolving into the black of the night.

I lay in bed and floated through the infinite darkness of the universe, in the void between two solar systems. I lay back in the seat of my capsule and looked at the instrument panel, at the red lights blinking on and off. The radio crackled and I heard a voice.

'Mercury, Mercury. This is Houston, ground control. Prepare for twenty-degree orbital adjustment.'

I raised my head and looked through the small square window above me. The earth hung like a veined marble in the black of the universe.

An hour later I got out of bed. The room still smelled faintly of airplane glue. Raph's breathing sounded like the rising and falling of the sea. I swam through the darkness, opened the door and went downstairs. Halfway down I saw the orange light from the streetlamp falling through the window in the front door. The hallway was the same orangy-black colour as the drawings of Winnetou's death.

Winnetou had died in the extinct crater of a volcano, where he'd been hit by a bullet from the gun of his pursuer. I hadn't been prepared for this. The comic book had arrived and I'd taken it upstairs and started to read. They were dark, shadowy pages, reddish-orange and black, and in that ominous darkness the unthinkable happened. Old Shatterhand knelt down beside his blood brother and laid his head in his lap, and the great Indian asked his friend to take care of his sister. I couldn't believe it. I read the pages over and over again. A ball of sadness swelled in my chest.

Downstairs, I went to my father's room. My eyes were used to the dark by now. I saw the bookcases and furniture as solid black shapes against a paler blackness. I stood there in the middle of the room, rubbing my thumb over the glue on my index finger.

Whenever we played Cowboys and Indians, Lisa was Winnetou and I was Old Shatterhand. I always wanted to be Winnetou, but I wasn't allowed to, because Lisa had long hair. We usually played indoors. The first floor didn't count, but the staircase and second floor and attic were the vast mountain ranges that we crossed in search of adventure, pursued by manhunters. Our horses climbed the steep mountain passes, rocks rolled down, pumas leered at us from huge boulders. After Winnetou's death we played for weeks on end in the attic which, as twilight set in, gradually turned into a crater. Time and again we lost sight of each other in the confusion of the fight, until the fatal shot rang out and the noble Winnetou collapsed and spoke his last words. 'Take care of my sister,' said Lisa, dying theatrically.

I sat down at my father's desk and stared into the darkness, peeling bits of glue off my index finger.

'What's death?' I asked my father one evening, as he stood at the blackboard that hung on the wall behind his desk.

He turned around, the chalk in his right hand, faint white stripes on his dark blue jacket.

'Why do you ask?'

'Winnetou's dead,' I said.

He raised his eyebrows and bowed his head slightly. 'Winnetou.'

'He can't just die, can he?' I asked.

My father put the chalk on his desk and beckoned to me. He scooped me up under the arms and set me down on the edge of the desk.

'Everyone dies,' said my father. 'Human beings don't live forever. You know that, don't you?'

I nodded.

'Is Winnetou an exception?'

I nodded again.

'The hardest thing,' he said, 'is when someone you love dies. You can't believe it. Even though you know that everybody dies sooner or later, you're sure that this one person is going to live forever.'

My father sat down in his desk chair and reached for his cigarette case. He took out a cigarette and lit it.

'Don't think about death, think about the people you know who are already dead. When somebody dies, it seems as if he's gone and everything's over, but as long as there's someone who remembers what that man was like and what he did, he's not really dead. He lives on in the thoughts of other people. That's what's important: that you live on in the thoughts of others. When there's nobody left who remembers you, then you're really dead.'

I gazed into the darkness of my father's study and thought of Winnetou and of the grandparents we no longer knew anything about and I wondered what kind of people they had been and what they had looked like, but when I tried to imagine faces above the greyish shapes they were in my mind, the image returned of Winnetou lying at the bottom of the crater, bathed in the sombre orangy-black of fate.

I was floating once more through the universe of my dreams, in my bed, when the silence exploded. Someone was ringing the doorbell, long and hard. I lay on my back, eyes wide open. The door moved. Lisa whispered our names. I sat up. Raph mumbled something and then woke with a start. He looked at us without recognition. The bell started buzzing again, and all three of us began to move, slowly, warily. No one said a word. We tiptoed out of the room, across the landing, until we came to the stairwell. The doorbell kept ringing. Now and then it stopped and we could hear the silence, but then it burst out again into that shrill, insistent rasping. Lisa nudged Raph in the back. He took a step forward and then stood still, his bare feet on the edge of the top step. He looked around, at Lisa and me. Lisa nudged him again. Raph pressed his lips together and began the descent, down the dark hole, to the hallway. We craned our necks and looked downstairs, where Raph was opening the front door. The orange light from the streetlamp fell across his pyjamas.

'Raph?' said a man's voice.

Raph nodded.

A woman stepped into the haze of light that hung in the doorway. 'May we come in?' she asked.

Raph said nothing.

'It's important,' she said. 'It's about your parents.'

I sat in the wicker chair and stared into the darkening room. Then I got up and looked at a sheet of watercolour paper that was lying on the table, on which a misty structure, a squat yellow tower in rickety scaffolding with tiny wooden sheds, had begun to take shape. All around the tower was a sandy plain, a weathered wasteland. Just as I was turning to go downstairs, something flashed in the corner of my eye. I took a closer look at the emptiness in front of the tower and saw a small watery figure standing in the sand, looking up at the building. The figure was dressed in indistinct scraps of fabric, its head wrapped in a cloth. I had the unpleasant feeling that Lisa was painting me.

That night I phoned Fleming. I found the business card he'd given me in the bar two months earlier, and dialled the number he'd scribbled down at the bottom.

'Don't you know what time it is?' he said, when I told him who was calling.

'Late,' I said. 'Early.'

'What's the matter?'

'Kopakker. Does the offer still hold?'

There was a long silence.

'Yes,' he said finally. 'You can start the day after tomorrow, if you like. But I thought you said that this wasn't in your line of work.'

'I say a lot of things.'

He told me where to meet him, a bar in a town near Kopakker, and listed the stuff I should bring (plenty of warm clothes, books, rubber boots) and the stuff (radio, liquor, companionship) I should not.

'Is there some special reason why you suddenly want to go to Kopakker?' asked Fleming.

'You pay, don't you?'

'Seven hundred fifty a month.'

'I can use the money.'

When I hung up the phone, my eye fell on the bits and pieces of paper tacked to the wall above my table. I looked at the xerox I'd made at the oil company which showed a listing derrick. I had found a book in the archives with pictures of a blowout, somewhere in America, the only spontaneous eruption ever to be photographed. Three greyish snapshots. In the first one you saw a small derrick, people were working on the drilling floor. The second picture was blurred, the rig had started shaking. The third showed a fountain of mud and oil gushing out of the top of the crooked rig and the drilling crew running in all directions.

God knows why I'd stuck that page on the wall. Usually I wasn't so enthusiastic about the reports I had to write.

Kopakker, I'd read in the accident reports, was one of the few cases in which an entire rig had sunk into the ground, completely disappeared, along with two Volkswagen vans, a container fixed up as an office and a truck full of measuring apparatus that just happened to be parked there.

At first there had been no sign of trouble. Seismic research had shown that the Eastern Field could be drilled to a depth of five thousand feet from the Kopakker location. Between the platform and the deposit were no obstacles to speak of, and the structure of the subsoil was similar to that of other locations. Kopakker was a routine job.

I had looked through the logs and read the supervisor's daily entries on the inspection of the cuttings, how much pipe had been used, what kind of fluids had been injected. It was a drilling like any other. The days went by with the same dull regularity as the pieces of pipe that disappeared, one after another, into the ground. Until one fine summer morning, when somebody smelled gas. The supervisor, who was standing about thirty yards away from the derrick, outside his container, saw the tip starting to tilt. A number of people had gone over to him, and as they looked up they felt a rippling in the earth. Moments later the platform had been cleared and the immense steel rig began to sink. 'It was like the ground turned into pudding,' one of the workers later told a journalist.

After the accident, the investigations began. Reports were written, pictures were taken. Eventually they closed off the area, and nature won back what was rightly hers. In the photographs, which were taken for up to ten years after the accident, the slab of asphalt surrounded by sand and grass was slowly transformed into a waving steppe, dotted with young birch trees, and later, as time went on, into luxuriant flora. Kopakker became a wilderness where plants and animals could live their lives in peace.

The next day I grabbed my knapsack, left a note on the table in case Lisa or Raph happened to stop by (*Be gone three – ! – months, Sam*), and headed for the station.

It was a dusty, shabby provincial town where I was to meet Fleming, a dismantled fairground by night, where seedy characters hung around waiting for God knows what. Outside the station I saw a long line of dilapidated taxis, and bums sleeping on their jackets. A wide main street led into the centre. At the end of the street hung an enormous orange moon.

I found the bar Fleming had mentioned, hidden away behind a red-lit wall, its name flashing on and off in yellow neon. The windows were boarded up with sheets of plywood, painted black. A broad-shouldered bouncer stood guard at the half-open door. It was eight o'clock, my appointment wasn't till nine.

At a sidewalk cafe I'd passed along the way, I drank lukewarm tea out of a glass clouded with lime. There was a blue skin floating on top. I leaned against the wall of the building, under the faded awning, and shut my eyes. I had the feeling that my thoughts were circling above my head, like vultures in a comic strip flying above a traveller lost in the desert. I didn't know what I was thinking, why my heart was fluttering in my chest. Everything inside me was in motion.

Soon I was walking down the dusty pavement again. A troop of men in baggy black suits passed me by, among them, a couple of hypnotic trumpet players. Taa. Tataa. Taa. Tataa. Shuffling feet. Sandy asphalt.

The moon rose over the end of the street, slow and round as a balloon. Sam, I thought, where are you going?

Cars cruised past, trailing the smell of warm iron and exhaust. Muffled bass notes drifted out of an open window. A girl in a miniskirt and bikini top leaned against a lamppost and smiled as I came near.

I got back to the bar where Fleming and I had arranged to meet, but since it was still too early, I kept on walking to the end of the street, where it looked as if the town had been ripped in two, so abrupt and out of place was the strip of night sky between the houses. The further I walked, the quieter it grew. Between the last few houses, where the street ended in sand and yellow grass, were barriers, red and white wooden beams on trestles. Beyond them lay wasteland, an endless, bumpy field under a network of greenish brown plants that looked like dead octopuses. I gazed out over the empty land, the moon hanging above it, the pale stars veiled in city light. With my head tipped back, knapsack between my shoulders, hands in my pockets, I waited for the silence.

After a quarter of an hour I decided I'd waited long enough: it was time for a beer. I turned around and walked back to the bar, where I paid my entrance and was shown into a room that was so dimly lit and so smoky, it was a while before I could see anything. I stood at the door and looked around. The outlines of a hall loomed up, tables, chairs, a patch of light. I turned toward the light and felt my heart slow down.

On a shabby stage, kneeling in a circle of burning candles, was a naked woman. She kneaded her heavy breasts, her eyes fixed on some indeterminate spot at the back of the hall. A little band played music that was much too loud and much too fast, a kind of square dance. Almost all the tables were full, men *and* women, but nobody was looking at the stage.

I was just about to leave when I felt a hand on my arm.

'So, you finally got here,' said Fleming. 'How was the train ride?'

As I was trying to tell him he dragged me over to the other side of the hall, to a little round table, where a young man and two girls looked at us impassively. 'This is Belinda,' said Fleming, 'and this is Tina and this is Tim, a colleague of yours.' I nodded and held out a hand that nobody shook. Fleming pulled up an extra chair. I put my knapsack on the floor and sat down. Fleming threw his arm around the one he called Tina, a girl who looked about seventeen. From the way he was grinning I gathered he'd had a lot to drink. My 'colleague' turned around and started whispering something into the other woman's hair. I looked down at the tabletop. Frayed scratches wavered under a liquid lens. *Schijtboys*, I read, and *Slasher*, *Zapp!*, *Prins Vailliant* and *Buddha Priest*, and lots of names of very old and very new groups: *Anthrax*, *Dead Kennedys*, *Joy Division*, *Killing Joke*, *This Mortal Coil*. Running under all these words were the lines of a vagina carved into the wood, a big tilted eye. The band struck up a new number. A couple of men were led onto the dance floor by bored-looking women. The girls at our table glanced at each other, shrugged, and took a sip of amber liquid.

They were a strange pair. I wondered where Fleming and my colleague had dug them up. Tina had such short black hair that you could see her scalp through the haze of bristles. She wore a black tank top, in which her narrow shoulders formed an improbable contrast to her enormous breasts. Belinda, who was leaning against my colleague, had hard features, masses of blonde hair and long narrow hands. She looked like someone who'd been put together out of the parts of three or four different people.

'What would you like to drink?' asked Fleming. 'You are my guest.' He looked tired. His eyes hung in their sockets.

'Beer,' I said.

Fleming called over a half-naked waitress and ordered Tuborg. The girl turned around and disappeared into the swirl of smoke and light. Fleming smiled at me. Two transvestites stepped into the circle of light on the stage, and the overwrought little band struck up a new number.

Where are you going? I'd asked myself out in the street. Here, in this cross between a village dance hall and a second-rate nightclub, I thought: the question isn't where you're going, but where you are.

The waitress came back and set our bottles down on the table. When she leaned over, her breast brushed against my shoulder.

I sat hunched in my chair, took swigs from the cold bottle and watched Fleming and his mate fumbling around with their women. The Norwegian caught me looking at him and leaned forward, grinning. 'You're my guest,' he whispered. 'Pick out something nice and enjoy yourself. The next three months, all you'll have is your hand.' His mouth stretched into a grin that scored lines from ear to ear. He turned to his companions, said something I couldn't understand, and then they all stood up, at more or less the same time. They went shuffling across the dusky dance floor and disappeared into the smoke. Onstage, the transvestites still hadn't got very far with their act. They were wearing tiny red G-strings and doing everything possible to postpone taking them off. I finished my beer and got up.

When I reached the exit I looked back, just in time to see one of the men kneel down before the other man and seize his G-string between his teeth. I turned around, pushed aside the heavy curtain in front of the door and left the hall.

Outside I headed in the direction of the moon. I hadn't gone far when the smell of charcoal and roasted meat came drifting along the street. A little boy wearing huge white sneakers was sitting with his back against a wall, keeping watch over a gridiron on a couple of stones. His right hand flapped about in the smoke like a bird. His left hand turned skewers of meat.

'What kind of meat is that?' I asked.

'Cow,' he said, waving his hand back and forth.

'Fresh?'

He turned the skewers. 'Ve-very f-fresh.'

He lifted his head. Eleven, twelve years old at most. A dirty brown face above a shirt that had been boiled so many times, the colour defied description.

'How much?'

'Three f-for two.'

'One order of three,' I said.

He turned the skewers again.

I stuck my hand in my pocket, took out some change, counted out the right amount and put it on the ground. Then I dropped an extra coin into the puddle of money.

The boy looked up.

'What's your name?' I asked, taking the three skewers he held out to me.

He shrugged his shoulders. It was like two sticks being poked up under his shirt.

I chewed on the tough, half-charred meat and stared at the wall behind the little vendor. *Wite Power*, it said, and *Rassists Out!* A car went screeching down the street in a cloud of music. I leaned forward, toward the boy. A tourist in a distant land, in search of young girls. 'You want fucky-fucky, I have nice sister. You want boys. I have small brother.'

'I'm looking for a hotel,' I said. 'Something quiet. Where I can get a drink. Maybe spend the night.'

The boy nodded. He got up, stamped out his fire, took the last few skewers off the gridiron and stuck them in a can. He hooked a piece of wire around the gridiron, picked up a grubby little bundle and then walked ahead of me, between two houses, into an alleyway that smelled of sand and piss.

Behind the main street was a row of ochre yellow houses, their walls covered with chalk drawings and painted-on words. Clotheslines hung along the windows, huge cartons full of rubbish stood against the front wall. The road was so bad that half the time we were walking through sand instead of on pavement. We turned down a side street, and another side street, crossed a courtyard, where people sat drinking in the doorways of their houses, and then we came to a large field of trampled grass and beyond that field was a sprawling hotel with a white verandah. We walked across the grass, climbed the stairs to the verandah and sat down in weather-beaten wicker chairs in front of an open window. The boy put his can, gridiron and bundle of dubious bits and pieces under the table, next to my knapsack, and peered in through the window. He held up his hand and called out a name. Moments later a man came out carrying a tray. He winked at the boy and, with a practised gesture, wiped a filthy rag across the glass tabletop.

By the time we'd drunk our second bottle, the street had livened up. The other tables on the verandah were full. The boy sat wiggling his legs, and now and then he'd say something. I sprawled in my chair, stared into space and drank beer. In the hotel the radio went on, soft music floated out the window.

The moon was a huge speckled lightbulb.

I looked at the boy sitting beside me, drinking his Coke and studying the starry sky.

'Do you know the stars?' I asked.

He shook his head.

I pointed to a spot just above the treetops. 'That square, with those two hooks behind it, that's Pegasus. That's the name of a horse.' I told him the tale of the winged horse, born of the blood of the beheaded Medusa, whose hooves were so hard that wherever they struck, crystal fountains sprang up. As I spoke, I wondered why there were no peaceful stories about the universe. We sat there, side by side, heads back, and gazed up at the blue-black canopy of stars and planets and interstellar space, at the vast emptiness between all those dots. And then I remembered what our early ancestors used to think about those tiny lights.

'Long, long ago,' I said to my little companion, 'people didn't even know those were stars, up there in the sky. That was back in the days when people still hunted reindeer and trekked across the land, from cave to cave. Sometimes they'd sleep out in the open field, and when they sat around the campfire and looked up at the sky, they thought they could see the campfires of other hunters, far, far away, and that the other hunters could see their campfires too. Then they didn't feel so alone.'

The boy looked at me and smiled. I laid my head on the back of my chair. My chest filled. This is practically Pico, I thought, the hunter who can find no place to rest his soul knows that he's not alone when he sees the stars. I pictured myself wandering over a steppe with nothing but waving grass, not a tree, not a bush in sight. Alone, year after year. At night, by the fire, a clumsy attempt to talk to an imaginary companion and, finally, a song to the stars, to the other hunters.

I was glad I'd been able to think of a peaceful story about the stars, but it didn't make me feel any calmer. My thoughts kept wheeling around my head. One moment I felt my heart sink, a few seconds later it was fluttering around again.

I thought of Kopakker and of my night with Raph, of the girl with the polka dots, who appeared and disappeared like she was Circe herself, of the attic room where Lisa's stuff was still on display. Over that slid a room in the home of my last foster family, people who had lost their little girl to some disease and never cleared out her bedroom. My foster father had opened the door and let me look inside. Everything was just as it had been five years before, when she died: teddy bears on the bed, dolls on a shelf along the wall, a dent in the crocheted bedspread. I wasn't surprised. In those days I, too, still believed that my parents would come back.

I felt like a television. The sinking derrick danced on the inside of my eyelids, the girl in the garden stretched her arms and gazed into the moonlight. An oil- and rubber-stained street. Echo's face. I sat at the bar with Julius Fleming and drank champagne. Lisa opened her eyes and looked at me as if she didn't recognize me. Fleming and the woman in the brightly coloured clothes rippling over the windowpanes. Ellen's silky hair, the red typewriter in her office, the glimmer of her body under the thin white uniform, the gentle curve of her breasts. The glowing tip of my father's cigarette in the dark of the sun lounge.

The boy began fidgeting in his chair. He finished his bottle of Coke and shoved it aside. 'What's wrong?' I asked. He shrugged. I thought about the question I had asked myself (where are you going?) and the answer I'd given: no answer. The boy jumped up. His boiled shirt hung down over his pants like a dress. He glanced around, nodded, grabbed his belongings and raced across

133

the field. The white of his sneakers flashed in the darkness and slowly faded away. I drank the rest of my beer, picked up my things and walked off the verandah.

Out on the main street, I passed places that were starting to look familiar to me. I headed towards the moon, to the wasteland at the end of the street, walked past the barrier and onto the field. I waded through the dry stalks until the buildings behind me were a strip of flickering lights. Somewhere in the middle of nowhere, on a rusty oil drum lying among the withered tentacles, I sat down to watch the stars twinkling. Where are you going? I thought again. To Kopakker, I answered this time. What are you going to do? In my mind, I heard what Fleming had said when I phoned him: 'There are people who find Kopakker terrifying, because that rig disappeared, sank right into the ground, and nobody ever goes there any more, hasn't been a soul in ten, fifteen years, so there's something unreal about the place, as though it has a grudge against people. But you'll be fine. Just keep reminding yourself that you're there to record logical processes.' I'd laughed: 'Logical processes in a chaotic environment.' I peered into the darkness and remembered how one night, long ago, I was walking through the industrial estate on my way to Raph's, and I found an old porno magazine. I'd picked it up and looked at it by the light of the moon. The sallow flesh colours, the grainy photographs of copulating models in unimaginative poses, had hit me like a blow to the jaw. I had stood there in the wasteland, my head bowed, the magazine turned toward the pale moonlight, and I felt an immense sadness welling up inside.

There was a photo of a woman lying spread-eagled on top of a man, while another man screwed her in the ass. All three faces were turned towards the camera, eyes wide, mouths contorted. Someone had taken great pains over the visibility of the penetration. Why? I'd wondered, what for? It was as if, there in the industrial estate, I could hear the shouts of my downstairs neighbour, his heavy groans, and the whimpering of the woman lying under him, and I thought of Raph, who'd said that sometimes that was all it was, just plain old fucking, and of what I'd wanted to say to him, that there had to be more, yet at the same time realizing that I didn't love anyone, couldn't even remember what it was like to be in love. As the moonlight glided over the photograph I had asked myself why I rejected one and didn't know what the other was. Perhaps, I thought now, in this other wasteland, right near Kopakker, perhaps you have to have a lot of faith to sleep with someone and you need just as much faith to fall in love, and maybe I haven't got that faith anymore, just compassion.

I walked back to the bar where I'd met Fleming. I still didn't have a bed for the night. The hotel that the boy had shown me had looked too expensive, but I hadn't found anything cheaper. I was hoping Fleming could help me out.

It was quiet in the bar. Two dancing couples were shuffling among the empty tables. The stage was bare. The waitress who had been walking around all evening stripped to the waist was now sitting at the refreshment bar in the corner of the hall, wearing a high-necked blouse and long trousers. There was no sign of Fleming. I sat down at an empty table, ordered beer and tipped my chair against the wall. On the dance floor, the women, shoulders drooping, hung in their partners' arms. The little band that, earlier on, had kept trying to catch up with itself, had finally run out of steam, and all you heard now was a vague plucking of strings.

A dark figure rose up beside the glare of a spotlight.

'All alone in the big city?'

I looked up, squinting.

'Far from home?'

It was a woman's voice, veiled in static.

I nodded.

'Where to?'

'Listen,' I said, 'I'd really like to offer you a drink, but . . .'

She stepped to the side, the star of light slid behind her, the smoke cleared. Her hair turned blonde. The face took on familiar features.

I opened my mouth. She leaned forward slightly.

'Ellen?'

She straightened up.

135

'Is that you, Ellen?'

She shook her head. She turned halfway around, twisting her fingers. I stood up.

'May I offer you a drink?'

She looked into the hall. A fat man in a tight dinner jacket was coming our way.

'I'm going to Kopakker,' I said.

Why did I say that, what did that have to do with anything?

The man went and stood next to her. He looked at me out of the corner of his eye. 'Everything okay?' he asked.

She nodded. He started walking away. She did the same.

I stepped forward and grabbed her arm. 'Ellen,' I said. 'You're Ellen. I brought you home. In the industrial estate.'

She jerked her head away. As I let go of her arm and took another step towards her, something flew out of the shadows and grew bigger and bigger. The ceiling tilted, the lights went out. A diesel engine started rumbling inside my head.

In Your Mind Real Life is Always Somewhere Else

Sand flew up along the tracks, bony cows walked here and there in barren fields. In the distance, behind the empty land, glimmered the bluish contours of a mountain range. The locomotive wailed. Sooty grey smoke blew past the open window, the smell of charcoal and half-burnt wood billowed in. I tried to change position, but couldn't stretch my legs. There were seven, maybe eight people in the compartment, their feet up on tattered cardboard suitcases, blanket rolls and bundles of clothes. I felt an elbow in my side. I turned around and looked into the sweaty face of Raph. He wiped the back of his hand across his eyebrows. 'I wish I'd brought my encyclopedia,' he said.

I shook my head. 'Thirty-two volumes? You wanted to bring all that?'

He nodded.

'Just be glad you could bring yourself,' I said. 'Just be glad you're here.'

I let my head drop back and closed my eyes. The train rumbled through my body. Far, far away I heard the wind sighing, and farther still, voices calling.

'God,' said Lisa, 'here we are, walking beneath the trees, and everything smells so good, they're burning off the ditches. Here we are and everything is lovely and green and it's warm and it looks like we've got shiny new pennies all over our clothes, here beneath the trees, and we won't remember any of this. In three years I'll say to you and Raph: remember when we walked beneath the trees, down that lane, and how it seemed as though we were going to keep on walking for the rest of our lives, until we just faded away, vanished into thin air? In three years I'll say that to you and you'll say: trees . . . I don't know what you're talking about.'

'Whatever gave you that idea?' I asked. I looked at the two rows of oak trees, the sunlight glittering on the new wheat, the grass-green stalks swaying in the breeze like hair. 'I see this too, don't I? And, besides, this *is* the memory, isn't it?'

'The memory?' she said. 'This is the event. The memory is yet to come. You're trying to think about something that hasn't happened yet.'

She laughed and ran on ahead of us. Raph looked at me and raised his eyebrows. We turned to watch Lisa, who was racing down the path and suddenly looked like a little girl. I turned to Raph and said: 'But it's true. This is the memory. She just doesn't know it yet, and she also doesn't know that in the end, it's not a very nice memory.'

There was muffled music in the distance. I tried to sit up, but my head was heavy and dull. I sank back against the cushioned seat and looked out. An enormous orange moon lay on the empty field and cast a strange pale light through the window. I turned my head to the left and saw, through the opening between the front seats, the small green light of the car radio. Next to it, my father was draped over the steering wheel. He looked sideways and smiled. His forehead was covered with a web of dark curlicues.

'Papa,' I said.

He didn't move. A husky woman's voice rose from the radio.

I leaned forward slightly. Against the right-hand door, halfway off her seat, with her cheek on the dashboard, was my mother. I heard voices. Somebody was pounding on the door of the car, shouting something I couldn't understand.

I opened my eyes and looked into Ellen's face. She smiled.

'It's eleven o'clock,' she said. 'I'll come back in a quarter of an hour.'

She got up and walked away. I sat up. I was lying in a double bed. Against the whitewashed wall, next to the bed, was a veneered table, on top of which lay a green book and my glasses. My clothes were lying on the other side of the room, on an old kitchen chair, and next to that, on a kind of divan, lay my knapsack. I got up and put on my glasses. In the corner, a door stood ajar. I pushed it open and saw a bathroom with a toilet, a sink and a shower.

Under the spray nozzle, as the greyish brown concrete floor slowly darkened, I had to do my best to stay awake. Now and then hazy images glided through the film of water in front of my eyes, but each time I thought I saw something, my head went foggy again.

I shaved with a disposable razor and shaving cream out of a tube that said: *At your service, Hotel Atlanta*. The razor made tracks in the lathery landscape of my face. The memory of a Sinatra tune came to mind.

> *By the time I get to Phoenix*
> *She'll be rising,*
> *She'll find the note*
> *I left hanging on her door . . .*
> *Time and time I tried to tell her so,*
> *She just didn't know*
> *I really would go . . .*

Lisa and Raph would be getting up somewhere too, and they didn't know where I was either. I didn't even know.

When I walked out of the bathroom, Ellen was sitting on the edge of the bed. She was dressed in a dark blue Nehru jacket, loose-fitting white trousers with blue flowers and dark blue suede pumps. Her long blonde hair streamed down over her shoulders.

'What took you so long?' she asked.

I grabbed at the towel around my waist.

'Won't be a minute,' I said. I snatched my clothes off the chair and rushed back into the bathroom.

Half an hour later I was swimming through an ocean of sound and image and smell, through a world that was new to me. I smelled asphalt and burnt diesel oil and the tang of bodies that had been out on the street since early morning. We walked among stalls that sold T-shirts, cassettes, fruit and spices. Horns squawked, mopeds shrieked, voices praised their wares and shouted names, booming basses pounded against the speakers of ghettoblasters, a harmonica strewed notes left and right. The knapsack dangled from my shoulder and banged into passers-by. I had to keep jumping back and forth and dodging people so as not to lose sight of Ellen. I felt around in my trouser pocket and pulled out a pack of cigarettes. Slowing down, speeding up, steering a course through the crowd, I lit a match, my eyes fixed on the straight back in the dark blue jacket with the stand-up collar.

In an empty side street, where shadows hung from the beech trees and the world was calm and clear, the air still stuffy, but without that confusing mixture of smells, we walked up a path to a tall brick house with a small stoop. Ellen climbed the three steps and beckoned.

I followed her through the front door, into a cool, vaulted foyer with black and white tiles. In the middle was a melon-coloured sofa, curved around an agave in a huge porcelain pot. Ellen opened a door on the right side of the foyer and we walked into a long room, where rush mats hanging in front of the windows cast tiger-stripes of sunlight on the floor. I put my knapsack on a table and sat down in the chair she offered me.

'Coffee?'

I nodded.

She walked out of the room.

I laid my arms on the armrests. It was a spacious room. Where I sat there were two small chairs facing each other. At the back of the room, one corner was partitioned off by a black settee and a pair of low bookcases. Footsteps echoed in the foyer. I heard somebody saying something, and then another voice, Ellen's, I thought, laughing. I leaned back and looked up at the moulded ceiling. A few crumbled images shot through my mind, a floor rising, something black flying towards my face, Ellen turning away from me, and later, only now it seemed like everything was happening at once, bending over me. I shook my head. She had been standing next to my table, back at the bar, that much I remembered. She had stood there with the bored air of a woman who hires herself out as a companion and, for a few overpriced drinks, puts up with the hands of hungry dance partners. She'd acted as if she didn't know me. I shut my eyes and saw that black thing coming at me again. Out of the darkness shot a fist. Involuntarily, I jerked back my head. Suddenly I knew for certain that I'd been punched, and that she'd been there. What had happened? Who'd hit me?

There was a knock. I went to the door and pushed down the handle. Ellen was standing there holding two white mugs. Balanced on one of the mugs was a plate of thick sandwiches.

'Breakfast,' she said.

I took the plate and a mug of coffee and walked back to my chair. I put the plate on the armrest and sat down.

'I'd like to explain something,' said Ellen. She sank down in the chair facing mine and began stirring her coffee. 'I wasn't very sociable yesterday. That's because I don't like running into people I know when I'm at work.'

People she knew. First she didn't recognize me, and now I was a person she knew.

'What kind of work is that?'

She shifted slightly. 'I dance, at Fata Morgana.'

Fata Morgana. I remembered Fleming mentioning the name that night when I'd phoned him, and then pausing, as if he expected me to say: That sounds pretty hot, Julius.

'A dancer,' I said. 'You're a dancer . . .'

She looked at me and sipped her coffee.

'I dance with men,' she said. 'I keep them company.'

'I didn't even know that existed.'

'It does. It's called taxi dancing.'

'To that wedding music?'

She smiled thinly.

I looked at her. Somehow I couldn't connect the image of the polished blonde who used to work for my doctor with the woman sitting opposite me, who said she danced with men for money.

I wanted to ask her what she said to these men and what they said to her, what kind of music she liked and what she thought about while she was dancing, but the questions never made it to my mouth, they were crowded out by totally different questions. Why had she pretended not to recognize me? Why had somebody punched me? Why wasn't she saying anything? I ate my sandwich and drank my coffee and felt the tension returning to my muscles. I was strong and keen. It was a familiar feeling. Sometimes, after a night of drinking, I'd wake up with an enormous appetite, with a huge craving for fried eggs and black coffee, with the unshakeable conviction that I could hold the world in my hands and toss it in the air like a rubber ball. I put my plate on the floor and lit a cigarette. 'Got any more coffee?'

Ellen stood up and took my mug.

When she got back, I sipped the hot coffee and asked her what she was doing here.

'I rent this house with a couple of other girls.'

'I mean in that bar, in this town. I thought you worked in that other bar, what was the name of it . . . I thought you lived in the industrial estate.'

'I left. The boss couldn't keep his hands off me.'

'Well you've sure found an original solution to that problem.'

She shrugged her shoulders.

'Here, nobody can keep their hands off you.'

She sighed wearily. 'It's one thing when they know that you're willing to dance with them for money, but when some guy thinks he has the right to pinch your bum just because he pays your wages once a month, that's another story.' She looked at me with a frown. 'I'm not saying it's the best job I've ever had, but at least here I can decide what I want and what I don't want. And it's just dancing, nothing else.'

'What happened, yesterday?'

The bouncer, she said, had thought I was giving her a hard time. Company policy was: punch 'em in the chin and carry 'em out, before it turned into a brawl that involved half the customers. Ellen managed to keep them from dumping me out in the street, and she and the bouncer had brought me to a hotel.

We sat there drinking our coffee. I looked at her, and went on looking at her, saying nothing, even when she returned my gaze. I saw her eyes gleam. I saw the soft lines of her powdered face, her mouth, the vein pulsing in her neck.

'Why did you act as if you didn't know me?'

'What . . .'

'You came over to me and you asked where I was from, or where I was going, and when you recognized me you turned away.'

'I just didn't recognize you, that's all,' she said after a while.

'The light,' I said, and once again I saw the spot behind her, a harsh white star in the mist of cigarette smoke. 'The light was shining right in my face.'

Her jaws were clenched. But not out of nervousness, it was more like determination. Her chest rose and fell, I could hear her breathing. She gave no reply. I went on looking at her. The blue of her eyes grew lighter, her pupils larger. Then she looked away. She picked up her mug and took a sip of coffee.

'Were you ashamed? Would you rather not be seen with a guy who hangs around cheap dance halls and drinks beer and wears a knapsack? Did you think: hey, that asshole has turned into a tramp?'

She looked back at me. 'Can't you understand that maybe I'd rather not be seen in Fata Morgana?'

'What makes you think I'd condemn that?'

Her eyes no longer avoided mine. Her lips parted slightly, as if she was about to burst out laughing. 'I know what men are like. Give them a woman in trouble and they jump on their white horses and start playing the noble knight.' She sat bolt upright in her chair, eyes glittering, face of granite. 'I'm my own person. I don't need anyone, anyone's pity. I do what I want, what has to be done. I don't have time for men who drool over whorish madonnas or . . . or madonna-type whores. And I don't need to be saved!'

My bated breath slowly ebbed away. Jesus, I said to myself, and you thought *you* had problems.

'Saving you has never entered my mind. It's never seemed necessary. Besides, I wouldn't even know how.'

She sighed. There was a long silence. 'How do you feel?' she asked at last.

143

'Fine,' I said. 'Better than ever. The knight has fallen, but he's back on his feet.'

She raised an eyebrow.

'So, how do you like this job of yours?'

She averted her head. 'They're lonely men,' she said. 'They walk in dreaming of a woman and all that happens is that they get to hire a girl to dance with. You create the illusion that you're wild about them, that is, if you can work up the enthusiasm, and at the end of the night you go home and take a shower and by then you've forgotten everything. Sometimes their hands start wandering, but if you put up a fight the bouncer comes along, so it's never really a problem. Actually, it's very sad. They're not even buying love. They're buying the illusion of companionship. It's the same everywhere. I once met a girl who worked in a nightclub and did sleep with the customers, but she thought most of them didn't come for that. They buy access. They think if they can just get near you, something wonderful will happen. Most of them are looking for true love.'

'True love . . .' I said, in a tone of voice as if I'd seen it all.

She gave me a wry smile.

I stood up.

'Where are you going?'

I shrugged my shoulders. 'For a walk. I'm leaving tonight.'

'Fleming's van isn't leaving till tomorrow. I just saw him yesterday. He was looking for you. Something about a repair job.'

I nodded.

'Why don't we meet up later on?' she asked.

As I looked at her and nodded, I wondered why she had asked me that. Guilt? Friendship? Politeness? I had no idea. What's more: I was almost certain I'd never find out, not even if I got to know her better, and this time it wouldn't be my fault that I didn't understand something or somebody. The woman sitting opposite me couldn't be understood by anyone.

'Around five, here? We can have a drink and then go out for supper.'

*   *   *

'Where's Orion?' Ellen asked me that night, as we walked through a park filled with old trees. We stopped at a clearing, a meadow of deer and sheep, and looked up at the sky. I had told her that the universe was a kind of boneyard for Greek heroes, and I'd spoken of all the times that Lisa and Raph and I had sat in the sun lounge and looked up at the stars, but the one constellation she asked me to show her, I was unable to find. I couldn't remember where Orion was or whether you could even see it yet.

She had taken me to the hotel where I'd spent the previous evening sitting on the verandah. She had chosen a bottle of wine and ordered two dinners and entertained me with anecdotes from the bar where she worked. The perfect hostess. I, in turn, had talked about Raph, about his photographs, about Lisa, her paintings, my faulty memory, Winnetou's death. As I was speaking I heard another voice in the background, faintly murmuring, reminding me of the things I'd dreamed about the night before in my hotel bed.

'How can you say you don't know anything about your youth,' asked Ellen, 'when you're telling me all these stories?'

'Because I've heard them from Lisa.'

'But how do you know they're true? Hasn't it ever occurred to you that the things you supposedly remember wrongly, or not at all, could just as easily be proof of your good memory? It's all pretty subjective, don't you think?'

Perhaps, I thought, but if Lisa's stories aren't true and my memory is empty, what's left?

We had gone outside, and as we stood on the pavement wondering how to bring the evening to a close, Ellen suggested we take a walk through the park behind the hotel.

It was a beautiful night. The sky was velvety black, and it was so dark that for a moment I thought that if I lifted my hand and ran my fingers along the firmament, I could touch the stars.

'When I was little,' I said, 'I used to lie awake at night wondering how space could be infinite. I always pictured a kind of sphere, probably because I couldn't imagine the universe not having any shape at all. Sometimes I had the feeling we were living in an aquarium, as if man was the pet of some inconceivably larger being. I'd think: fish don't know there's another life, do they? To a veiltail, the world outside the aquarium is the universe, just as everything outside the atmosphere is the universe to us. We live in an aquarium and we look out, but since we can never look from the outside in, it's impossible to know exactly what our position is, and that's why we'll always think we're seeing things the way they really are.'

'Listen,' she said, 'about this afternoon, or yesterday evening. I'm sorry.'

I shrugged my shoulders. 'We've already talked about that.'

'I know, but I still wanted to say I was sorry.' She paused. 'I'd already seen you, earlier on, with those whores,' she said.

'Whores?'

'The ones Fleming had with him. And then I saw you leaving. I wanted to call you over, but I was occupied.'

I saw her there in the darkness, in wisps of smoke and coloured light, in the arms of a fat slob who stunk of sweat and drink: Isolde and King Marc.

She sat down on a bench in front of a pen of deer. Her blonde hair caught the moonlight. I longed to run my fingers through it. If I can't touch the stars, I thought, at least that hair. Somehow these two things seemed, in much the same way, to be both very near and very far. I looked up at the zodiac, at the chaos of constellations. 'In astronomy you always calculate back to the Big Bang,' I said. 'Nobody ever talks about what happened before that. A world in which everything revolves around cause and effect and no one ever asks themselves what there was before everything was.'

'In the beginning,' she said.

In the beginning, I thought, we're talking about the beginning of everything when I don't even know my own history.

'I want to be your zodiac sign,' I said.

She turned slowly toward me, staring at me in amazement. I pressed my lips together and shut my eyes. Why don't I touch her? On the cheek. She stroked my cheek, that time in the Nissen hut.

She stood up. I followed her. We shivered, it was a chilly night.

She buried her hands in the sleeves of her sweater, I held the collar of my jacket closed.

'How about a drink at my place?' she said.

I nodded.

We walked on, enveloped in the vapour we exhaled.

At her house we sat opposite each other, once again. We drank Jack Daniels out of wine glasses.

'How do I get to the hotel from here?' I asked.

'Why do you ask?'

'I have to spend the night somewhere, and I didn't pay the bill this morning.'

'I've already taken care of that,' she said. 'It's my fault you got in trouble. You can stay here tonight, if you don't mind sleeping on a mattress on the floor.'

We drained our glasses and I helped her make my bed. She moved the chairs out of the way, then took a rolled-up mattress out of a cupboard and laid it in a corner of the room. She gave me a towel and a toothbrush still in its wrapping and led me to the bathroom, at the back of the house. When I returned she was standing in the living room in a long flowered nightgown.

'Good night,' she said. She turned around and drew back a curtain, revealing a small space with a bed.

I held up my hand.

That night, for the first time since my childhood, I dreamed I was travelling through the universe.

The Grain of Sand that
Makes the Desert

The next morning I sat and waited in the yellow light of the arc lamps outside the station. Wild curtains of rain tore across the road. I sat on a Van Gend and Loos loading platform, my knees raised, my back against an up-and-over door, a concrete pillar beside me. A bit further down was a pile of rags, curled up under a soggy sheet of cardboard. I lit a cigarette and stared out at the broom of water that was sweeping the city clean. Now and then a car crawled by, a black beast snuffling along the wet asphalt in search of prey, headlights groping, motor softly growling. In the puddles lay red and yellow patches of light. Each time the wind swept across the road, they seemed to shiver in the dark water.

Half an hour later a van drove up and trapped me in the glare of its headlights. The heap of cardboard on the platform stirred, a face slid out, peered into the light and then disappeared again. I ran through the rain to the van, yanked open the door and climbed inside. A thick, clammy warmth hung in the cab. My glasses steamed up, I felt my damp clothes sticking to my skin. I said hello to the courier, wiped off my glasses and leaned back.

The courier was a silent man in a corduroy jacket who stared sullenly ahead and gave curt replies to the questions I asked. No, Fleming wasn't coming along. Had to bring 'the other guy' to his post. How often did he go to Kopakker? Once a week. Picked up print-outs and lists, brought provisions. Yeah, a few of 'em got nervous, wanted to go back with him. Couldn't. Hit one guy over the head. Tried to sneak into the car. Nuts.

We drove over roads of water. The windscreen looked like it was covered with jelly. After half an hour the courier asked if I needed booze. I shrugged. 'Behind my seat,' he said. I leaned over. Under a grubby horse blanket was a crate. I pulled out a bottle of vodka and held it up to show him. It cost twice the retail price. I dug a few banknotes out of my trouser pocket and stuck them in the glove compartment. The diesel engine rumbled, the cab filled with more and more condensation.

Somewhere in the middle of nowhere, surrounded by water and rain-drenched fields, we turned onto a path that must have at some time been a lazy dirt road, but was now a churning muddy river. The car ploughed ahead, moaning and groaning. After a few hundred yards I had to get out to open a gate. The moment my feet touched the ground, I was soaked. I shut the gate behind the van and climbed back inside. We swam on, into the wilderness. Through the cascading curtains of water I saw young birch trees on either side of the path. Here and there they gave way to clearings of flattened reeds and withered grass.

The van stopped where the path dipped down, into a pond. Poking through the water's surface were the remains of dead trees. They looked like the petrified fingers of drowned giants who had clawed desperately at the air as they went under. On the other side of the pond was an egg-shaped trailer and a little white box on stilts.

The courier opened his door and jumped out. The rear doors opened, he jumped onto the floor of the van and kicked out a box of provisions and a box of paper. I climbed out of the van, grabbed hold of the sheet of plastic he threw me and pulled it over the boxes. The courier held up a key, shouted 'The trailer!' and threw it to me. He waved and pulled the loading doors shut. Behind the panes I could see him climbing over the driver's seat.

The wind scudded across the surface of the pond and tugged at the yellow grass. I turned up my collar and staggered toward my observation post, the plastic-wrapped boxes clasped tightly against my chest, my knapsack hanging like a soggy counter-weight between my shoulderblades. Each time I stopped to catch my breath (twice I missed the huge tussocks of grass surrounding the pond and my shoes sank deep into the black water) I saw the wind sweeping dingy grey clouds together and ripping them to shreds. An exuberant seagull tumbled through the tatters of rain like a windtossed newspaper. The trailer rocked gently on the squalls of wind. In the wildly surging grass, it looked like a houseboat that had been torn from its anchor and was drifting, hopelessly lost, on the sea.

Inside the trailer I took dry clothes out of my knapsack. I pulled off my wet things, got dressed and sat down on the edge of the bed. I was beat. Before I could even think about what I was going to do first, I fell asleep.

A few hours later I woke up with a sore throat and a pounding headache. There was a heavy stench in the little trailer. The air was thick and sweet as syrup. I opened the door and stuck my head into the fan of misty rain that swept past. It was as if I were standing on a ship, in the spray of waves crashing against the bow. Behind the pond, the grey sky was marbled with blackish-blue streaks.

When I shut the door again, the stuffiness came rushing back. I sat down on the ground, next to the boxes, and inspected the contents. The first contained a bulky package of printer paper. In the second, under the tins of vegetables, meat, butter and coffee, I found a large green book, with 'LOG' written on the cover in block letters. I got up to make coffee. As the water sighed in the kettle, I went through the logbook. From the handwriting, I could make out four predecessors. All of them had kept careful records of when they'd checked the probes and where and when they'd taken samples. Three men and a woman, assuming that men didn't dot their i's with a circle.

When the coffee was ready I sat down with my mug on the foam rubber bed.

'What do you plan to do there?' Ellen had asked when we were sitting in her room, an hour before my departure, plates of sandwiches on our laps, large mugs of coffee on the arms of our chairs. 'What are you hoping to find out in Kopakker?'

I didn't have to give that much thought: 'Peace of mind. Time for myself, emptiness. Insight, understanding. The things other people find in sects.'

'Why do you need emptiness?'

'Why do you need Fata Morgana?'

'You mean Fata Morgana is the same thing for me as Kopakker is for you?'

'Maybe.'

'And what's that?'

A Fata Morgana, I wanted to say, but I kept it to myself.

My head pounded. I leaned back against the cold wall of the trailer.

'What's this?'

'A sailor suit,' says my mother. 'Why?'

On a high cutting table. Feet buried in scraps of fabric, basting thread and buttons. I'm wearing a blue sailor suit with red-trimmed pants that end at the knee. The blouse has straight, wide sleeves and a kind of flap that covers my shoulders. Around my neck the tailor has hung a braided cord with a silver whistle.

I grab the whistle and hold it up. 'May I blow this?'

My mother nods.

Hoo hoo. The cry of an owl.

I took a sip of coffee and rubbed my eyes. This is one of Lisa's memories, I thought. I've so strongly identified myself with her memories, I don't even see Lisa any more. I'm looking at the images from her point of view.

'Sam,' Lisa said to Simon, when they were over one night, 'Sam doesn't remember a thing about the past. Whenever I tell him a story about our old neighbourhood, he raises his eyebrows. I can remember long expeditions across the roofs of the sheds, all the way to the stonecutter's yard, but he doesn't remember a thing. And what about that guy who came after us with an axe, I'll say, remember him? We walked across the roofs, to the Spanish Chestnut, and we threw sticks at the tree, and all of a sudden this guy leaped onto the roof and started running after us, still holding his axe, and we squealed like pigs and raced across the roofs, all the way around, until we got to the end and you screamed: Jump! and you kept right on running, you went sailing through the air and landed in the bushes, and I came sailing after you. We were

151

covered with scratches, from head to toe. He doesn't remember a thing. I could tell him whatever I wanted.'

She had observed me closely during these last few sentences, as if she were waiting for a sign, a flicker in my eye, a vague smile of recognition, as if I were a person in a coma who might suddenly move a finger. But I hadn't reacted. I'd let her gaze go right through me, without so much as batting an eyelid. I was too busy registering. I thought: if this is my life, for God's sake let me remember this story.

She'd turned her head away, that night, and stared through the corona of the candle into space and said: 'But it doesn't really matter if you don't remember anything. Knowledge is a burden.'

My sister: painter and mnemonic wonder.

'I don't remember a thing,' I had said to Ellen, in the restaurant next to the park, 'and yet, my whole life is memory. I'm the biggest adherent of the memory cult you're ever going to meet. I'm not afraid of getting older. What an opportunity to collect memories! I remember nothing about my youth, but at least when I'm old I'll have memories about life after my youth. And even after my death, there'll be something left. I'll be a figure in crumpled photographs, a name on yellowed paper, a number in the archives, the grain of sand that makes the desert.'

'Desert?'

'It's just an example.'

'The difference between desert and fertile land is not one single grain,' said Ellen.

I said: 'It's those grains, exactly that number of grains, that shape, that colour, that size, that make the desert. The point isn't whether or not one is missing. The point is that they're all there and make up that particular desert at that particular moment.

'The liquid in a glass,' I'd gone on to explain, 'would probably do just fine without a drop or two, yet it's these drops that make this glass. This glass is this number of drops, no more, no less. That's why it matters that I'm alive. I am the grain. I am the drop.'

I raised the glass of wine I was holding and drank it down.

'For somebody who thinks love doesn't exist, you sure sound like a romantic,' said Ellen.

I drank the last cold dregs of coffee from the mug. I am the drop. The prophet speaks. Echo. Another drop. But the glass hadn't disappeared. World keeps on turning. A romantic: I am the drop. For somebody who doesn't believe in love . . .

I said to Ellen: 'Isn't it strange, the overwhelming feeling of liberation you get when you leave the person you've loved for years?'

I'd been thinking of Lisa when I said this, though the subject had its roots in what Ellen had told me earlier, that all those men in Fata Morgana really came for 'true love'.

I said: 'I've broken off a couple of relationships, and each time I've been amazed at the lucidity, the feeling of immense relief. Apparently you tend to choose for yourself in critical situations and you're ultimately much more of an individual than you thought. The other person remains an abstraction. You've known him for years, but when it comes to the crunch you stand there looking at each other and you think: why does he do these things, and why in that way, how strange. All of a sudden he's no longer the person we loved so much.'

Ellen had looked at me blankly.

'We've extricated ourselves from the labyrinth of our emotions and we see the ordinary in what was once the extraordinary,' I said.

She shrugged her shoulders.

'Why is everyone so desperate for this great, all-consuming passion?' I'd said. 'Why do they all believe in Tristan and Isolde and forget that history has shown that it's the rule rather than the exception that people get sick of each other? What is love? Could it be nothing more than a very primitive drive that we make too much fuss about, a kind of etherealized mating urge, sublimated rut? What's the difference between the love you feel for your family and the way lovers feel about each other? What's the difference between compassion, charity and sex?'

Ellen had shaken her head. 'Have you ever loved anyone?' she asked.

I frowned.

'All I know is this,' said Ellen. 'Sometimes you meet someone and the only thing you want is to be with him, and at the same time you don't want that, because it would change your whole life, because . . . because maybe you're scared. And all the same, you're drawn to him. What do you call that? Mother Teresa sympathizing with the poor?'

'There's something very erotic in the way nuns surrender to God.'

'And some people are crazy about horses. Being in love is different.'

By which she merely wanted to say that I wouldn't know love if it was rammed down my throat with a baseball bat.

And not only love.

The calor gas light lay on my retina like sand. My throat was dry. I went to the sink, rinsed out the mug, filled it with water, drank, filled it again, glugged it down and filled it once more. My thirst was barely quenched. I put the mug down next to the bed, turned out the light and crawled under the blankets. Outside the little window the sky was as blue as ink. Inside the trailer hung the dull grey twilight of a wet autumn day.

When I leaned over to take another sip, it was dark. I groped about for the mug, found it and brought it hesitantly to my lips. Halfway there I saw my hands. They were soft and huge. I closed my eyes and felt a dry, feverish heat gliding over my face. As I drained the mug it slowly dawned on me that I'd caught a cold and had been asleep for quite some time. At that moment, I sank back onto the bed. My field of vision narrowed to a long black tube and I tumbled over backwards and went falling, slowly somersaulting, towards the bottom.

When I had fallen deeper than I could ever imagine, I looked down. There, all the way at the end of the immense tube, I saw the massive black shape of the beast from the gardens. It opened its jaws. I fell and fell, grey specks shooting past the corners of my eyes, and as the beast came closer I heard its roar. Then there was nothing but emptiness and silence.

The Memory Beast

High in the blue-black sky, above the dense crown of the oak with the nose of the car wrapped around it, like the jaws of an animal that bites and can't let go, high above the tree and the small green light of the radio and the gentle creaking of metal and wood, there, in the infinite sky: Gemini. And lower down, half hidden by the trees: Orion, and below that a bare black field, a moon as big as a house.

> *You must remember this,*
> *A kiss is just a kiss,*
> *A sigh is just a sigh,*
> *The fundamental things apply*
> *As time goes by.*

'Which vessel launched the Space Age?'
  'The Sputnik, in 1957.'
  'Who was the first human in space?'
  'Yuri Gagarin in the Vostok I.'
  'And the first American?'
  'John Glenn in the Mercury 7.'
  'And the first man on the moon?'
  'Armstrong, July 20, 1969. This year. That was easy.'
  'Sam, you're brilliant.'
We drive down a country road with tall oak trees on either side. Papa's favourite route. 'Like riding through a tunnel,' he said one night when the five of us were driving through and the headlights turned the trees and the road and the crowns into a tube.

Mama sits up front, looking out at the flashing greenery. The car careens around the bend and shoots into the green hole ahead of us.

'This is Houston, ground control,' says Papa. 'Prepare for twenty-degree orbital adjustment!'

I lean my head against the cushions of the back seat. The car pulls out of the bend the way Baron Münchhausen once pulled himself out of a swamp. To the right is the moon, lying on a field, the moon where a man walked this year and left footprints that will last forever, a moon you can step right onto. You just walk across the field till you reach the trees, then climb up along the huge orange ball.

'Look out!' says Mama.

Darkness.

'China,' says Papa. He looks at us, first Lisa, then me. 'China.' He looks at Raph, sitting on the chair opposite us. Lisa and I have already got our pyjamas on. Papa opens *The Young People's Encyclopedia* and begins reading aloud, and as he reads the dim light of the table lamps changes and the Yellow River starts flowing across the wall. A junk bobs about on the slow muddy water. Behind the secretaire, a small yellow man with a long black pigtail is selling candied apples.

A typical Chinese delicacy.

'Look out!'

We're all dressed up in our best clothes and we're sitting next to Mama on the bus, side by side, wiggling our legs, and Mama looks at us, first at me, then at Lisa. She smiles. We walk around the market (fish and cheese and onions and flowers and fabric) and then through a covered street, a kind of house built across the road, and at the back of that house is a door we walk through, into an oval tearoom, where platters of pastries turn round and round in large glass display cases. At a table by the window we have tea and petits fours. Mama keeps her hat on. She smokes a long menthol cigarette. Then we go to the photographer. We wait in a little grey room. After a few minutes the photographer comes in. 'My my, what beautiful children,' he says. He strokes our hair. I pull away. He takes us into a big dark room with lights on iron legs and long black curtains pushed into a corner. As he arranges us behind a table with a kind of bench on top he chats with Mama and he tells us to lay our arms on that bench. We fold our hands on the plush and look up at Mama. 'I can see you've had your picture taken before,' says the photographer. Raph has a box camera, it's all he ever does. The photographer crawls under a piece of cloth hanging from a square black box and tells us to smile, just like Mona Lisa.

Lisa, who always laughs, stares straight ahead. I, always serious, smile.

An enormous orange moon. Through the opening between the front seats, the small green light of the car radio. Papa is draped over the steering wheel like an old jacket. I can see the side of his face. A smile beneath a net of blood-red cracks. Like a veined marble.

A husky woman's voice on the radio.

Against the right-hand door, halfway off the seat, her cheek on the dashboard: Mama.

Sound of voices.

'Anybody there?'

No.

'Hello!'

I am invisible.

'Nothing.'

A drop.

'And, yes, yes, yes,' said Mama, 'the sun sank into the earth, as if it was being pushed into the sand and the sun said: yes, yes, and the earth blazed and the sky was red and yellow and blue and everything spun, the world tilted and the earth whirled like a pebble through the evening sky, no above and no below, no east, no west, nothing, and darkness slid over the world like a blanket, Mama's here, here is Mam-ma, sleep little one, sleep my little one, you're so warm, you're so small, my sweet little one, here's Mama, here, always, here, yes, yes, yesyesyes . . . I'll tell you a story, there now, hush, one day, one night, like Lilith who comes to you in your dreams at night, yes, yes, one night . . . time is a beast, time is made of beasts tonight, bees for the days, quails for the months, horses for the night, this is the night, hold my hand, take my hand, here we go my little one, hush, hush . . .'

What's this? A sailor suit, says Mama, why? Feet buried in scraps of fabric, basting thread and buttons. In a blue sailor suit with red-trimmed pants and a shirt with straight wide sleeves. Around the neck, a white braided cord with a silver whistle. The cry of an owl in the whistle. Do I have to wear this? Of course, says Mama, what's wrong with it?

In the distance I see the green trucks from the refuse department, silent beetles with curved backs that slide over the bumpy cobblestones, spraying a fan of water out of their mouths that evaporates in the hesitant warmth of the August morning and curls through the gutters like a sparkling fishbone. We follow Mama, follow the streaming water. Steps are being scrubbed, doors are open. The greengrocer sets out his crates of apples, lettuce and cucumbers, the owner of the coffee shop polishes the doorknob, a waitress does the windows, there's shouting and laughter. Outside the tailor's shop is Frits, the son, a roll of fabric under each arm. Mama asks Frits if his father is there. He points to the back of the shop. We walk past the counter, past the tall rolls of linen that nearly block the entrance to the stockroom. Behind the rolls the air is humid and warm. In the stockroom, among piles and piles of fabric, two young girls are laying out patterns with Frits' father. Frits' father looks up. He nods to Mama and puts down his pencil. Good day, Ma'am, how can I be of service? A sailor suit for this gentleman. Frits' father goes over to the tin coffee pot standing on the hot plate, next to a huge wedge of a steam iron. He pours coffee. Mama is offered a chair. Lisa and I sit down on a bale of cotton wrapped in burlap that's standing against the wall. Frits' father talks to Mama, they drink coffee. We wiggle our legs. Then I have to get up. Frits' father helps me into my new clothes. Muffled by the bales of fabric, the sewing machine rattles and the big shears click.

What's this?

A sailor suit, why?

'You used to think that everything was two,' says Lisa. 'Papa once said: in the universe, matter is always clumping, everything wants to be together, but once it is together, decay sets in and then everything's helpless, then it's only a question of time before it falls apart again. That evening, the man next door played *Il Silenzio* and you went outside and walked through the gardens until you were behind his house, and you stood there listening to the trumpet until Papa found you, and when you came home you told me that it was as if the trumpet was all alone in the universe, and was wailing. *Il Silenzio*, that was your universe. You said: Everything wants to be two. You walked through the gardens and the trumpet melted into the night and you smelled the scent of honeysuckle and under the open windows you heard people talking, the tinkling of glasses, a distant radio. You told me all that. Really.'

The notes of *Il Silenzio* drifted up towards the stratosphere, through the atmosphere, past the moon, past Mars, the planetoids, Jupiter, Saturn, Uranus, Neptune, Pluto. Until they were floating in deep space.

'You've always been a yearner. A chronically underfed heart.'

Like a knife through water. Orion and Gemini. The tip of my father's cigarette.

'I can't do any more than this,' he says. 'This is it. This is all I have to give.'

'I . . . never . . . you . . .'

'Kit, I'm no god, I'm as mortal as they come. My love for you has never diminished. If that's what you think, then it's because that's what you think, not because it's true.'

Mama looks outside, at the stars.

'It's gone,' she says. 'There's nothing left.'

Papa's face in the darkness.

'Go to sleep, Sam,' he says.

We're lying on a thick pile of Persian rugs. 'I hope they buy this whole pile. These are desert rugs,' says Lisa. 'In the Sahara people live in tents and they have rugs like this.' I turn over on my stomach and bury my face in the bristly wool. There's no sand left in the rug, not even deep down, where the tufts of wool are knotted, but I can still smell camels and horses. A salesman picks Lisa up and says we have to move out of the way. He wants to show a few carpets to a lady and a gentleman. He puts her down. We go over to the corner where the chairs are. I'm rocking away in a rocking chair when Papa and Mama come up to us with another salesman. 'The young Kennedy,' says the salesman.

'I look at your faces. They're burning off ditches in the distance. Smoke drifts across the path between the trees and we pass through the smoke and I turn my head and your face disappears and comes back again and you open your mouth.'

The house is dark. We wander around the room in our pyjamas. We're going to make breakfast. Lisa gets the newspaper, I climb up on the kitchen counter and fill the kettle. We butter bread, boil eggs and make tea, and then, when everything's ready, we pile it onto a tray. I pick up the newspaper and lay it on top of the eggs and the cups. It falls open to a thick black bar of letters: KENNEDY MURDERED IN DALLAS. A blurred photograph of a gleaming open limousine below it. A woman in a hat is bending over something greyish that's sagging against her. On the rear bumper of the car a man in a dark suit is climbing inside.

High in the blue-black sky, above the dense crown of the oak with the nose of the car wrapped around it, like the jaws of an animal that bites and can't let go, high above the tree and the small green light of the radio and the gentle creaking of metal and wood, there, in the infinite sky: Gemini. And lower down, half hidden by the trees: Orion, a bare black field, a towering orange moon.

A Feeling of Long, Long Ago

'This much I know,' I said, as I sat on the edge of my bed after three days of fever, drinking weak tea. Outside, a pale sun shone across the pond. It was a clear autumn day. The yellow grass around the unruffled water was a fuzzy blanket. 'This much I know. They weren't happy. They drove away on an evening when they were having a fight. The car had turned the corner before we could even wave.'

We looked down at the shiny dark car and at almost the very same moment the red taillights disappeared into the blackness.

Why did they fight?

My father had sounded like someone who had abandoned all hope. 'I can't do any more than this. This is it. This is all I have to give.'

And my mother: 'I . . . never . . . you . . .'

(I never loved you? I never get anything from you in return? I never hear you say: I love you?)

He'd said that his love for her had never diminished. Apparently, she'd thought it had. He worked hard. Not home much, and when he was home: very far away.

A tall, slender man in a blue double-breasted suit, supple white shirt and narrow silk tie, small round glasses, hair combed back. I thought he looked like a detective. He walked with a slight stoop, so that there was a hollow where his stomach should've been. Long, well-manicured hands, clasped behind his back, or in front of his face, on their way to his glasses or his nose. An intellectual, someone who sat in his chair in the living room and read, one long leg over the other long leg, a book held high in his left hand, a cigarette in his right. He had long telephone

161

conversations, leaning slightly over the phone, listening attentively, nodding understandingly.

His face . . .

No idea.

In the morning when we showed up at the breakfast table, he was always just about to leave. The radio sang. Lisa buttered rusks. I drank down the little bit of liquid at the bottom of his cup, every morning. I thought I derived exceptional strength from those few last drops of cold amber tea with the tiny black leaves floating in it. Mama and Lisa thought it was a bad habit.

'It's not a good idea,' said Mama, 'you might catch a disease from somebody.'

As if I could catch a disease from my father.

For a long time Lisa and I also drank tea with butter. I had read a book about a Tibetan boy which said that his people drank tea with yak butter. I pictured the rigorous treks over the high mountain passes, the piercing, snowy wind in your face, the heavy yak-skin coat wrapped around your body, and at night, by a small fire, the strong tea with rancid butter. Then Lisa read the book too and we decided to live that way, so every morning we dipped in our spoons and ruined our tea with a mush of melting butter. It wasn't very tasty.

'It's gone,' my mother had said. 'There's nothing left.'

'You know what's gone,' said Lisa, 'Papa and Mama and God and the mystery of love.'

But Lisa couldn't have heard what they said to each other, that night in the sun lounge, the night of the accident.

Had my father been driving too fast? It wasn't winter, there was no ice. Never heard anything about him drinking. But who would've had an accident in that gentle curve unless he'd been driving too fast? Who's a victim unless he decides to be one?

Wittgenstein, my guide, my example, wrote: 'Suppose I had such a good memory that I could remember all my sense impressions. In that case, there would, *prima facie*, be nothing to prevent me from describing them. This would be a biography. And why shouldn't I be able to leave everything hypothetical out of this description?'

162

Because memory has little to do with sense impressions?

Elsewhere he asks himself what it would be like for someone to remember for the first time in his life: 'Does he know that it is memory because it is caused by something past? And how does he know what the past is? Man learns the concept of the past by remembering.'

'Perhaps,' he says finally, in parentheses, as if he weren't sure either, 'perhaps one can speak of a feeling of "Long, long ago":
. . . for there is a tone, a gesture, which goes with certain narratives of past times.'

In the first case, the word 'remember' isn't right. Someone who doesn't forget any of his sense impressions isn't remembering. He's registering. Someone like that is a tape recorder, a camera. The characteristic feature of remembering, the concept that Wittgenstein plays around with in the second *gedankenexperiment*, is more of a feeling (of 'Long, long ago').

A man remembers nothing. That is to say: nothing but trivial details, a sound, a bird flying up, half a newspaper report, a name he's not even sure is right. The past, that which people who can remember call the past is, for him, an island in the mist. What does somebody like that do?

That man is me, a man with a distinct feeling of long, long ago, a feeling so vague and unreliable that I'm like a stranger in a foreign land: I see trees, mountains, rivers, but I don't know what the proportions are, how big the forest is, whether the river bounds it, or runs through it.

I ripped paper out of the printer in the little white hut next to the trailer. I checked the probes, drove the hand drill into the black peat, brought the log up to date and stared out the plastic window. I got up late, went to bed late, spent entire days sitting on the foam rubber mattress, behind the fold-out formica table. Apart from drilling and checking probes, there wasn't much to do. The work that Fleming had assigned me, there was a schedule in the log, took so little time that I was finished in about four days. That was my own fault. I'd screwed together the hand drill and gone at the spots he'd indicated like a madman. Since I hadn't brought any books with me, I'd had to resort to the labels on the cans of food. Once I'd read those, all that was left was the landscape.

After a week had gone by I began a letter to Lisa. I opened the box of printer paper and placed my pen at the top of the endless white streamer.

Welcome to another land. I once saw a documentary at Raph's house about the history of space travel, in which they talked about the death of Yuri Gagarin. He was killed in a plane crash, somewhere in the vast woodlands of Russia. It took ages for them to locate the wreck, and when they finally found it they had to call in somebody who had known him very well, because identification of the remains was almost impossible. Gagarin had a good friend, a fellow cosmonaut. A few days before the accident they were both at the barber's. When it was Gagarin's turn and the barber was about to shave the back of his neck, his friend said: 'Careful, dear barber, he's got a birthmark there, and we wouldn't want to damage the Hero of the Soviet Union, now would we?' They'd all laughed about that. Next came the journey to the scene of the accident. Gagarin's friend walked up to the wreckage, bowed over the body and saw the birthmark.

'Imagine,' he said to his interviewer, 'I had warned the barber about that birthmark and now I had to identify my friend Gagarin by that very same mark.'

He was a hefty man in military dress, a cap with a huge visor, a collar with red and gold decorations. He sat there, stiff and uncomfortable, in an army tunic that looked like it was made out of concrete. He told that story, and you could tell by his frozen face that he'd loved Gagarin. And he wasn't the only one. Everyone had loved him. The first man in space was a very nice person. (Just like John Glenn. Everybody likes him. When Glenn had an accident, slipped in the bathtub and almost ended up half paralysed, it was world news.)

An army man, you know the type, with a bull neck and a fat Siberian face, smiling mechanically as he tells that story. Somehow it's hard to imagine him having very deep feelings of love. Obviously, something inside us thinks that such feelings are reserved for Young Werthers, Emma Bovarys, Tristans and Isoldes.

Papa and Mama, for me, were part of the decor. You're a child, so you inevitably have a father and a mother. Okay, they're dead, but they're not really gone. Only: how can you love what isn't there? I can't remember them. Here, in my trailer, I've dreamed about them, and when I woke up I could even see Papa, his suit, the way he walked, the long thin hands, the dishevelled hair. But no face.

Does that mean that what you really love is a dark blue suit, the way somebody sits in his chair, legs crossed, reading a book? Can you love a memory without a face?

We (you, Raph and I) didn't see each other for years after the accident. During that time I couldn't remember who you were. When I think back on that period of my life I see myself performing deaf-and-dumb mechanical acts. I walk, look, sit, stand, fall asleep and wake up. A clockwork toy. If they take the key out of my back and the spring winds down, I'll never move again. No experiences. No feelings. Wake up! I get out of bed. Breakfast! I eat. Time for school! I grab my satchel and head out the door. Don't be late! I run.

Then, after all that time in 'the underworld', I was free again, and I went to Raph and I saw him in that bare room of his, making tea the way he still does – bag in a cup and up and down – and I thought: this is my brother. I decided to love him.

If you haven't seen each other for such a long time, love is a decision, I thought. Later I became convinced that love was always a decision.

But who decided to love Yuri Gagarin? I loved Gagarin. Never knew the man, a few blurred photos here and there, for the rest just stories, but I loved him.

165

Was it because he went tumbling about through the universe, all alone, the Hero of the Soviet Union?

You say you shouldn't think so much about love, that you should just do it, but why don't people ever talk that way about hate? Nobody ever says: hate? don't worry about it, just do it. Hate is a serious emotion, one you have to think very deeply about in order to understand why you actually hate somebody so much. I believe the same is true of love.

I'm living in a trailer in a sea of grass, pond out front (didn't used to be there, appeared when they stopped drainage), forest behind me. Twice a day I go to the little white hut on stilts next to the trailer and check the instruments. I put new paper in the printer, drill a hole, empty the rain meter. Read the ingredients on a can of peas. I didn't come here to find anything. I just needed to do something. Get out of the city. Stop thinking. Change of scene.

If you feel like writing back, leave your letter at the Physical Geography department, at the university, For the Attention of J. Fleming. He'll make sure everything gets to me.

Take care. Say hi to Raph.

I folded the paper in four, taped it closed and wrote down Lisa's name and address. When the courier arrived I gave him the letter, plus ten guilders for shipping and handling.

The rest of my stay in Kopakker went rippling by. It grew colder. Every evening I lit the paraffin stove, even though I knew I'd wake up the next morning with a pounding headache. The week before I left, the first snow fell. The big clumps of grass around the lake turned white. I sat at the oval window of my trailer, brought the log up to date, sorted out the piles of printer paper and blew on my hands.

On my last day Fleming came by, in person. I watched him get out of the van and undertake the arduous journey around the

166

pond. When he reached the trailer he gave me a limp handshake and followed me inside, where he flopped down on the little bed. I poured him a mug of coffee and looked at him sitting there, legs apart, shivering in his coat, the mug clasped in his hands.

I picked up my own mug and sat down opposite him, on the box of printer paper.

'When you get back,' he said, 'could you drop in at the university? We've been given permission to see the file.'

I looked at him blankly.

'When we met I suddenly thought: I must see this report you're talking about. I phoned . . . What's that man's –'

'Huizinga.'

'. . . Huizinga. I mentioned your name and he arranged everything. We'll pay. Hourly rate. I'm sure Mr What's-his-name would appreciate it if you helped us out.' Fleming stood up. He put his mug in the sink and buttoned up his coat.

'Poor guy,' he said, nodding out the window, towards the water. 'He doesn't know how cold it can get out here.'

I followed his gaze.

'Your successor. He's waiting in the van.'

'Who was here before me?' I asked. 'When I arrived, there was nobody here.'

'Your predecessor couldn't stand the silence. Gave him the creeps. One day he just took off. That was the reason you were able to start right away. Fucking students.'

I picked up my knapsack and the pile of print-outs from the past week and opened the door. Outside, I breathed in the crisp frosty air. The dew lay like shattered glass on the field. Two seagulls sat motionless on the icy lake.

In town, the driver dropped us off at the station. Fleming stamped his feet and blew on his hands. He stuck his hand in his coat pocket and pulled out an envelope. 'Money for the trip back, and expenses. Everything as we agreed. You just sign the receipt.'

I took the envelope and wrote my name on the slip of paper he gave me.

'What are you going to do now?'

'I think I'll drop in on somebody I know and then catch a train.'

Fleming nodded. 'I haven't seen you since that night in Fata Morgana.'

'Ah.'

'There was a tall blonde who said you had gone to a hotel, that broad we saw in the bar where we drank champagne.'

'Yes.'

His face disappeared now and again behind the thin clouds of steam he exhaled. 'Is she this person you know?'

I nodded.

He looked at me for a while, impassively. 'I've got to go,' he said. 'Do we have a deal?'

'I'll call you.'

He held up his hand and walked, shoulders hunched and legs stiff, into the station.

When I rang the bell at Ellen's house, a girl with short black hair answered the door. She was wearing jeans and a baggy workshirt covered with paint stains. Her face was oval, verging on round, her eyes were made up with lots of black.

'I'm here to see Ellen.'

'She doesn't live here anymore.'

'Oh.'

'Are you Sam?' she asked. 'The Sam she used to know?'

'More or less.'

Her name was Veronica, she lived on the top floor. 'Weren't you out in the wilderness?' she said, hugging her arms, shivering in the wind.

'Something like that.'

'Don't you wanna come in?'

I stepped into the hallway. Veronica opened the door to the kitchen and went over to the sink. She filled a kettle with water and lit the stove.

'Do you know where she went, Ellen I mean?'

She shook her head. 'Just packed up and moved out. She left

168

behind a note and an extra month's rent, and for the rest . . .' She made a vaguely dismissive gesture with her right hand. 'Did you come here specially for her?'

I shrugged. 'I'm on my way home. I just wanted to see how she was.'

'She's free, in any case, she doesn't have to go back to that dive. I got fired because of the work those girls do. Well, not exactly fired. They just told me they preferred that I left. I kept coming in late. But it was killing me. I'm the only one around here with an office job. *Was*. The other girls lead such an erratic life . . . They come home at four in the morning, get up at four in the afternoon. After a while I had the feeling I was living in another world. I used to wake up every single night when they came in, and the next day I'd be a zombie.'

The kettle slowly began to sing. She took it off the flame and filled the teapot, dangling a tea ball in the stream of boiling water.

'And now?' I asked. 'What do you do now?'

She shrugged. 'At the moment I'm painting my room.' She picked up the teapot and nodded toward the cupboard. 'Could you get the glasses? And the sugar, and there's a blue biscuit tin, bring that too.'

Her room smelled faintly of ammonia. The furniture was covered with large sheets of clear plastic, there were newspapers all over the floor. She cleared a table and put down the teapot. I walked across the crackling newspapers and set out the glasses and the sugar bowl and the biscuit tin.

'We'll just have to sit on the couch,' she said. 'Give me a hand, will you?'

We grabbed hold of the sheet of plastic covering the sofa and pulled it off. Then she sank down into the cushions and laid back her head.

'God,' she groaned, 'painting is hell. There's no end in sight. The walls were so dark, they're gonna need at least three more coats. This could take years.'

I picked up the teapot and poured. I handed her a glass, picked up mine and sat down beside her.

Veronica rested the tea on her thigh and laid her head on the

169

back of the sofa again. I looked at the curve of her throat, tendons running down, collarbones just visible.

'So . . .' she said, 'what are you going to do, now that you've finished your work in the wilderness?' She curled her fingers around her glass, straightened up and turned to me. She folded her right leg on the sofa, between us.

'No idea,' I said. 'Take the train back, I guess, spend a couple of days doing nothing. Somebody's offered me a job. Think I'll go by next week and check it out.'

She smiled. The smooth black bows of her eyebrows went up. She raised the glass to her lips and drank. Steam billowed around her face, a long lock of hair fell in front of her eyes.

'What time's your train?'

'Towards the end of the afternoon. I don't want to be home too late.'

Veronica put her glass on the table. She pulled the biscuit tin towards her, pried off the lid and held it out. I took a sandy yellow biscuit with a heart of jam.

'Can I help you paint?' I asked.

'Oh no,' she said. 'You're free. I don't want to have you slaving away all afternoon.'

'I love painting. It clears the mind.'

She pursed her lips.

'Really,' I said.

She nodded slowly. We looked at each other for a long time. I wanted to lower my eyes, but I went on gazing into her pupils, on and on, until I felt something stirring in my chest. I leaned forward, drank up my tea and put down my glass.

'Right,' I said, 'let's get to work.'

Veronica started covering up the sofa again. I inspected the tins of paint. When she was finished she came and stood next to me and explained what she'd done and what she thought still needed to be painted. She went over to a cabinet and took out a small blue bundle.

'This is a boiler suit one of the girls gave me, but it's way too big. Maybe it'll fit you.'

I took the boiler suit and tried it on in a corner of the room.

170

I could only get it on if I took off my jeans and sweater. When I was ready, I picked up a brush and started painting the surface that Veronica had told me to paint.

We worked all morning, to the accompaniment of a pop station that played music with no DJs butting in. Now and then we sang along, when a song came on that we knew. At one o'clock we stopped for lunch. Then I climbed the wobbly stepladder we'd brought up from downstairs and painted the ceiling, while Veronica painted the skirting boards black. By four o'clock, we were finished. We pulled the plastic off the chairs and gathered up the newspapers, and when that was done, Veronica looked around the room, grinning.

'God, that was fast,' she said.

I looked around me, at the white walls, the white roof. I thought: I should paint my own house. But at that moment I saw the crumbling ceilings, the remains of pipes and tubes sticking out of the bare brick walls. It's not even a house, I thought, it's a cave made habitable, a shoebox of stone and wood.

'A shower,' said Veronica. 'I wanna shower. How about you?'

I nodded.

'Okay, you first.'

In the bathroom, as the air slowly filled with steam, I once again saw the hotel where Ellen had left me after I'd been knocked out cold. I heard the voice that penetrated my sleep, saw the water streaming over the grey-brown concrete and staining it dark, the clear patch of glass in the steamed-up mirror, my face, grey and white, the razor blade making pink tracks in the lather. That's where it all began, I thought, that's where I forgot that everything crumbles and falls apart, that's where I came to life, under that shower, that was the moment when I realized that I no longer believed, not in the least, that we're all trapped in some kind of whirlpool, as if somebody's washed their grimy hands over a cracked sink and then pulled out the plug and, shhhh, the dirty water full of sand and mud and bits of soap tilts to the left and goes swirling down the drain. The water flowed through my hair, washed over my body. I lifted my face, into the stream, and felt calm and empty. I thought: it's taken me a long time to learn what everyone learns, I was young late, but now I've shed my first skin, I've grown up, and I know that some people are worse off than others, that the world isn't fair and that it's just pure chance if the axe falls left or right, and I accept that, I want to accept that.

I drew my hands through my hair and swept it back. I'm not happy, I thought, but I don't have to be. Happiness is something you remember.

When I came out from under the shower I realized that my clothes were still in the living room. All I had here was my boiler suit and boxer shorts. I opened the door and peered around the edge.

'Hello?' I said. 'Veronica? Are you there?'

No answer.

'Vee?'

I pushed the door open a bit further. She wasn't there. I pulled on my shorts, walked into the living room and went over to the little pile of clothes lying behind the sofa. I picked up my jeans, and just as I was putting on the right leg, Veronica's head appeared above the sofa. She looked at me sleepily. I stepped backwards, onto the empty trouser leg, slipped and fell.

As I was struggling to my feet, Veronica came and stood next to me.

'Oh God,' she said, laughing, 'you didn't hurt yourself, did you?'

She put out her hand to help me up, and as I grasped it and tried, at the same time, to put on the other leg, I went crashing over backwards again. Veronica collapsed on top of me and began howling with laughter. She tried to push herself up, but fell to her knees, gasping for breath. I lay on the floor with my trousers around my ankles and couldn't do a thing. The tears ran down my cheeks.

When our laughter had died away and Veronica sat up and looked at me with shining eyes, I said: 'I thought you were gone. My clothes were still here. That wasn't an assault, at least, not of you.'

She laughed. 'You couldn't assault anybody even if you wanted to. You'd break your leg.'

172

She stood up and held out her hand. When I was back on my feet and had pulled up my jeans and buttoned them and looked back up again, her face was right next to mine. She looked at me from under her dark eyebrows.

'I fell asleep,' she said.

The baggy shirt was crooked. Her right shoulder was bare. I lifted my hand and touched the curve of her collarbone. She looked into my eyes. My hand lay on her skin and I looked at her collarbone. I stroked her throat. Her head fell back slightly. I took a step forward and leaned towards her. When I felt the warmth of her face on my skin I closed my eyes and kissed her. I had forgotten that lips could be so warm. Veronica wrapped her arms around me. I felt a hand on my neck, her fingers in my wet hair, her other hand in the hollow of my back, where the back flows into the buttocks. Just like Lisa says it does, I thought. In my head, something snapped. I pressed her to me. Her hands glided over my back. Inside my head it began to rain. Then she bent over, her mouth left mine. She started unbuttoning my jeans.

'Vee . . .' I said.

'Shhh.'

I stepped out of the ring of denim lying around my ankles. She looked at me, then pulled the stained shirt over her head. I loosened her belt, pulled down the zip and helped her out of her jeans. She took my hand and led me to the sofa. She stripped off my shorts. My hand glided over her breast, down, over the rippling of her ribs, to her waist. I slid my fingers over her hips, into her panties, and as she raised herself slightly, I pushed them down. She freed them from her ankles with her left hand. Then she flung an arm around my neck and pulled me down beside her, on the sofa. I kissed her throat, her breastbone. She stretched out like a cat. My tongue travelled over her nipple and down her belly, across her groin, along the inside of her thigh. Veronica sighed, almost inaudibly. I put my right hand under her buttock and my left hand on her waist and as my tongue crept slowly upward along her thigh, leaving a silvery trail across her skin, I heard her whisper 'No'. When my lips were resting on her vagina and my tongue traced gentle circles, she went limp. I stroked her waist and her belly and I closed my eyes and all the time the same words kept running through my mind: I want you to forget everything, forget, forget everything, I want you to forget, let everything, drift, away. Her stomach began to shake, her legs spread farther apart. Veronica whispered something I couldn't hear. And then it began, the slow explosion of the supernova.

I stretched out beside her and held her tightly. She had her eyes closed.

'Come,' she said after a while. She slid under me and pulled me up. My lips went over her throat, her hands caressed my back and buttocks. I felt myself slowly gliding away. Suddenly she grabbed hold of my arms and tried to push me off.

'Get up.'

'What's wrong?'

She sat up on her knees and leaned over the back of the sofa. I put my hands on her hips, and as she guided me inside her I cupped her breasts in my hands and fondled them. She straightened up slightly. She laid her head on her arms and arched her back. I laid my left hand on the back of her head and as I stroked her hair my hand became a claw and I shut my eyes and everything turned white. Then I heard Veronica's voice. She said: 'I'm not in love.'

'So what's next?' I asked when she came out of the shower, her dripping hair wrapped in a towel. She looked at me as if she didn't know what I was talking about.

'What do you mean?'

She came over and sat down next to me on the sofa.

'You smell like rain,' I said.

She laughed. 'What do you mean: what's next? I wanted it, you wanted it. Isn't that enough?'

I shrugged my shoulders. 'I don't know,' I said.

She laughed again. As she hid herself, bit by bit, in clothes, and I started aching for her all over again, she said: 'Besides, you're after Ellen, right?'

'Ellen? Jesus, I've only seen her two, three times. I don't know

174

where she lives, I don't even know her last name. What makes you think there's anything between us? I just came to say goodbye.'

'And that's just what you've done,' she said.

I picked up my clothes and started getting dressed. Veronica went into the bathroom and put on her make-up, saying something now and again through the open door, in a slightly teasing voice. When I was ready I went in and stood behind her and watched as she drew black lines around her eyes. I put a hand on her shoulder and said: 'But how can you be so sure I'm not in love with you?' The pencil hovered briefly in front of her face. She opened her right eye a bit wider and touched up a line. She put the pencil in the little cabinet next to the mirror and took another look at herself. Then the eyes of our reflections met.

'You haven't said you're in love with me. That's the first thing. The second thing is: if that's the case, you'll have to find a solution, because I'm not in love with you.'

Five minutes earlier I'd known for sure that I wanted her then and there, on the couch, without thinking of anything other than sex, but now I suddenly felt a pang in my chest, as though, even if I didn't happen to love her, I wanted her to love me.

She turned around and nudged me aside. She walked into the living room and picked up her bag. I was still standing in the bathroom. I looked at my reflection. Slow drops of condensation were trickling down the face that stared back.

'Come on,' said Veronica. 'We've got to go to the station.'

The Man Who Forgot Everything

'This is what happens. Someone goes looking for the most important thing in his life, but doesn't find it until he has lost it.'

A smile stole over Raph's face.

'That's how she always began,' said Lisa, 'and then she'd close her eyes and raise her head. As if she was thinking, which she wasn't, because she knew the story by heart. She'd told it a hundred times and heard it a thousand more, from her mother, who had heard it from her mother. At least, that's what she said.'

Our shadows danced on the walls, shreds of smoke hung in the air around us. We sat at the table, Lisa, Raph and I, and we listened. That is to say: Raph and I listened. Lisa talked.

I was back home after a train ride that hadn't taken more than a minute, or so it had seemed, after which I'd walked through the centre of town and turned into my street. Sand crunched under my feet, light poured through the cast-iron windows on the ground floor of the warehouse where I live. Above me, behind the haze of light that hung over the city, I saw Castor and Pollux and, very faintly, Gemini, and below that, Betelgeuse and Orion's Belt. I thought: in Kopakker this would be a great night to see the Milky Way. I climbed the stairs to my flat, and from behind the doors I passed I heard snatches of music, quarrelling voices, a cartoon character shouting 'Surprise, surprise, surprise!' I slung my knapsack to one side, stuck my hand in the front pocket and felt around for my keys. Before I could find them the door swung open and light fanned out over the stairs. Raph stood in the doorway.

'The prodigal brother,' he said. 'Just in time for Family Night.'

He took my knapsack from me and walked ahead of me into

the room, where Lisa was waiting in the restless flicker of a pair of candles. Raph brought out beer, and when everything was ready, we sat down, and Lisa began to tell a story. She chose 'The Man Who Forgot Everything'.

'When King Solomon's days were numbered and the time drew near for him to join his fathers, a servant appeared at his bedside one night. He cooled his master's brow and brought him a fresh jug of water. The old king followed the young man with his eyes and bade him come closer.

'Why are you crying, David?' asked the king.

The servant bowed his head. 'Oh my Lord,' he sighed, 'what will become of me when you are gone?'

The king smiled and stroked the servant's hair.

'You shall roam the land,' he said, 'and you shall tell the people about me, and they shall reward you well. Do not be afraid, have faith.'

The servant kissed his master's hand and thanked him.

When the king was dead and the days of mourning were past, David packed his knapsack. He said farewell to those who were staying behind and set off on his journey.

Everywhere he went he told stories about his old master. Rich and poor alike invited him to their table, but never was he as handsomely rewarded as the old king had predicted on his deathbed. David, however, was a patient man, and he continued to roam about and tell his stories, even though he wasn't getting any wealthier. On the contrary: the longer his journey lasted, the more remote the regions he travelled, the less generous his listeners proved to be. Until, after seven years, on a cold winter's day, he came to a town in the north, and discovered that he had neither money nor bread. The wind tore at his ragged cloak, his boots absorbed more water than they kept out and his stomach churned restlessly in his belly.'

This was Lisa at her best. Usually she told her stories in telegram style, but now we got the unabridged version – as flowery as she could make it. She sat across from us and stared into the dancing candlelight, her paint- and ink-stained hands in front of her on the tabletop, her eyes large and unseeing.

'Evening fell,' said Lisa, 'just as he reached the market square. The merchants were clearing out their stalls, the last few customers were haggling over unsold onions and peppers. David walked through the market and realised that it was too late for him to find anyone to invite him in. As his feet squelched in the sodden boots and the wind tightened its icy fingers around his neck, he suddenly saw, not onions and peppers in the half empty stalls, but steaming plates of the most delectable dishes. The stalls turned into tables, laden with food. He saw a huge stuffed turkey on a silver platter, dripping with fat, and hot roast potatoes, nearly bursting out of their skins, and a plump, juicy carp basking on a bed of glistening vegetables. The hungry storyteller's head began to spin. Then he felt a hand on his shoulder.

'Stranger in these parts, eh?' roared the merchant who stood before him.

He nodded.

'Hungry too,' I can tell.

David bit his lips.

'What's your trade?' asked the man.

He told him what he did for a living, and that things hadn't been going too well lately and that it was so cold here and . . .

'I know just where you should go,' said the merchant. 'There's an old admirer of the king's, a rich man. Tell him the pickle man sent you, and he'll let you in.'

David thanked the pickle man and went off to the address he had been given.

It was just as the pickle man had said. He explained who had sent him and why he had come and was immediately shown into the private chambers of his wealthy host, where a splendid sight met his eyes. There was a long table spread with the most sumptuous dishes imaginable, and wine sparkling in crystal glasses. Men in richly embellished garments and women in silk and damask gowns ate and talked and laughed. The host, who was sitting at the head of the table, stood up and invited the storyteller to sit down in the chair beside him. He urged him to eat and drink his fill, so that, fed and refreshed, he could tell his story. David washed his hands and sat down.

'Now,' said his host, when the meal was over and everyone leaned back contentedly in their chairs, 'tell us about the great Solomon.'

David stood up and opened his mouth. His mind was empty.

For seven long years he had told stories about his master, and now, now that it was more important than ever, he couldn't remember a single one. He searched the darkest corners of his mind, but his head was like a granary after a famine, nothing but vague shadows and empty spaces. His host, seeing the storyteller's distress, shook his head and told him not to worry. After all, he had a rough journey behind him, and the wine was heady (at this he turned to his table companions: The wine was heady, don't you agree? They laughed heartily. It was heady all right! Kicked like a mule!), so perhaps it would be better to hear the stories about King Solomon tomorrow. Contented, the guests went off to bed. David too. For the first time in months he had a real feather pillow, and he lay between sheets so soft, it reminded him of the days when he was a child and slept between his mother's breasts.'

I knew the story, Lisa had told it before, but somehow it seemed more significant than usual. It was as if I knew the winter cold and the empty stomach and the visions of food. And not only that. The desperate searching through the catacombs of the mind, the impossible memory of 'the days when he was a child and slept between his mother's breasts' . . . that was my search, the memory I wanted above all else. Had she told this story exactly the same way in the past? I looked at my sister. She was farther away than ever. That's not concentration, I thought, that's a trance. She didn't blink once. Her pupils were large and black. I looked at Raph. He was staring at Lisa in amazement.

'The next morning, David stood beside the breakfast table, dressed in clothes he had received from his host. He opened his mouth to begin telling about the great, wise Solomon, but once again, nothing came out. He stuttered, he gasped for breath, he searched the farthest corners of his memory, but his head was as empty as a cask of wine after a wedding. His host patted him on the back. Come come, he said, tonight is a much better time. It's too early. Tonight you can tell us your story.'

Lisa turned towards me and gazed at a point somewhere behind my head. Her eyes were two holes that absorbed what little light there was in the room.

'David began to fear that he would never be able to tell stories again,' she said. 'All that morning and all that afternoon he paced his host's walled garden, but he couldn't think of a thing. Finally he sank down in the grass, and as the sun played upon his face and the gentle fragrance of the earth rose up around him, he closed his eyes and thought: you can serve a wise king, live in his castle, and not even be aware of your happiness, and later, if you set off and tell stories about him, you lose him, and you long for him more than you ever did when you were still with him.

He opened his eyes and looked up at the passing clouds. Oh my Lord, he said, why have you left me?

Then he fell asleep.

David dreamed that he was a young shepherd. He walked through the fields, keeping watch over his flock. Now and then he would stand at the top of a hill and he'd see his father in the valley with the older flock. If they both saw each other, they'd wave their caps. One day he asked his father when he would be allowed to go with him to the prayer house. When you know the prayers, his father replied. But the young shepherd couldn't read, and there was no one in the fields who could teach him. A week later he asked the same question, and was given the same answer. But he kept asking, and six months later his father agreed to take him along, on condition that he keep his mouth shut and do nothing but listen, particularly because that day was a day of mourning.

So off they went. Soon they came to the village. They entered a dark building, where men in ragged clothes were mumbling prayers. The young shepherd did as his father did and listened patiently to the singsong of the words, but after an hour he said: Father, I want to play my pipe. His father's eyes flashed. He leaned over and hissed in his ear: Keep quiet, do you hear me? Not a sound! The praying went on and on, bobbing along on a current of drowsy voices. The boy turned to his father once again and said: I want to play my pipe. Furious, his father grabbed the pipe that was hanging around his son's neck and put it in his lap. The praying continued. The young shepherd sank away in a sea of words. His eyelids fell shut. He felt the sentences gliding past him. All of a sudden he woke from his slumber and opened his eyes. He was seized with an irrepressible desire to grab his pipe and play it. Turning his head, he looked around the room. He counted the men, he gazed at the windows. Suddenly he snatched the pipe out of his father's lap, jumped to his feet and blew. A long, shrill note echoed in the little prayer house. The mumbling ceased, and all heads turned to the young shepherd. There was a silence so hollow, it seemed to him he had never heard silence before. Then the first angry voices rose. At that moment, the old man who had been leading the others in prayer stepped forward and resumed his chanting, only this time it went quickly, faster and faster, until the words seemed to go swirling up into the air.

When the final prayer had been said and the young shepherd and his shamefaced father were stopped by the old man and a group had formed around them, the man shook his head. He laid his hand on the boy's head and said: All this time, it has been as if our prayers were not rising, but falling, and gathering in a pile on the floor, but when you blew your pipe, the doors of heaven opened and our prayers soared upward. You did a good thing, for you did what your heart told you to do.'

This was a completely new story. I saw Raph shaking his head. I thought: she's adding something to the family story. Why? What's she trying to say? She gazed into the flames. I saw the tiny lights dancing in the black of her eyes. And at that moment, she returned to the story we knew.

'David awoke just as the sun was setting. He shivered. He thought: I've just been telling my stories about the old king, without any longing, like those old men in the prayer house, and that's why I've lost everything. I lost the longing, and when that was gone, I lost the memory as well. I have to blow the pipe. He got up and went back to his host's house. Brimming with confidence, he opened the door and walked inside.

That evening, once again, the table was richly laden. Everyone ate and drank. When the last course was finished, David stood up and told a story about his old master that he had never told before. In fact, it wasn't until he'd opened his mouth that the story even came to mind.

Once upon a time there was a poor man, he said, who dreamt that there was a treasure hidden under a bridge in the town. He packed his knapsack and set off, and after several days he reached his destination. He stood there on the bridge, while all around him, people rushed to and fro. The man hesitated. Surely he couldn't start looking for the treasure in broad daylight? Then a soldier appeared, and spoke to the treasure seeker. 'What're you hanging around here for?' he demanded.

The treasure seeker thought it best simply to explain what he had dreamt. Perhaps the soldier would help him search, and then they could share the treasure.

'You stupid peasant!' cried the soldier, when the poor man had finished. 'You came all the way to town because of some dream you had about a hidden treasure? I once dreamed there was a treasure buried under the stove in a house in a village, but do you think I'd be stupid enough to go there and look for it?'

The village the soldier was speaking of and the house he described were the treasure seeker's own. He hurried home, broke open the floor under the stove and found a chest of gold. A man, he said, may have a treasure in his very own house, but he must seek it elsewhere, or he'll never know it's there.

'This story,' David said to his listeners, 'was told to me by my king one night, when he had returned from his travels and I asked him what he'd seen.'

'This story,' said his host, who had risen from his chair, 'is about me.'

There was great consternation among the other guests. Everyone cried: But when? and: Why?

'It wasn't a soldier I met in town,' said the host, 'but an old beggar, who laughed at me and told me what he'd dreamt. When I got home and dug up my treasure, I realized that the old beggar must have been King Solomon, for the very same night I dreamt that he received me at his court and said that I was the finder and could keep my treasure, but I must also be willing to relinquish what had simply dropped into my lap.' He turned to David. 'That moment has come,' said the rich man. 'My treasure is yours.'

And so it happened. The host gave everything he owned to the storyteller and retired to a little house in the country, where he devoted the rest of his days to study and prayer.'

Lisa blinked her eyes. 'That was the story of The Man Who Forgot Everything,' she said.

Raph raised his eyebrows and looked at me.

'And you,' he said, 'have you found what you lost?' He pressed his lips together, tipping his head back slightly, and then turned to Lisa. 'That was the point, right? Somebody goes looking for the most important thing in his life and doesn't find it till he's lost it?'

She nodded.

'Maybe,' I said.

I leaned across the table, supporting myself on my forearms, and looked at my sister. She was sitting straight up in her chair, almost like someone who felt too good for such idle chatter. I thought: the story of The Man Who Forgot Everything, is that supposed to be my story? Is this some kind of ritual apology?

'You know everything, Lisa. You're the collective memory,' I said. 'You even know how it was before we were born. Tell me what happened the night they drove away.'

Raph's eyes darted back and forth, from Lisa to me and me to Lisa.

'Haven't I told you all that?'

'You've also told me the story of The Man Who Forgot Everything, but differently than tonight. What else can you tell me differently? That's what I'd like to know.'

Below us I heard the soft murmur of voices and the clumping of boots across a wooden floor.

'They just left, that's all,' said Lisa.

'No,' I said.

'We were home and we'd already gone to bed, we were asleep.'

'No.'

'Yes.'

'From the beginning,' I said, 'from the very beginning.'

I said: 'From the moment they started fighting.'

Lisa shot up. Her chair toppled backwards and crashed against the floor. Raph sat at the table with his head bowed. His hands lay on the tabletop and he was staring at those hands as if he was seeing them for the first time.

'They didn't fight. They never fought. It was the best marriage I've ever seen.'

'You're not exactly the one to judge a good marriage,' I said.

Raph lifted his head. There wasn't a trace of emotion on his face. 'Sam,' he said. 'This isn't going to get you anywhere. What's the point of digging up something that's so far behind us that not one of us can remember it clearly?'

I grabbed the pack of cigarettes lying next to Lisa's wine glass and pulled one out. As I leaned toward a candle and sucked in the flame, I said: 'The point is, that you've always treated me like the handicapped little brother, that you've kept me believing in an idyll which was no idyll, that somebody around here has gone to an awful lot of trouble to perpetuate the notion that stupid Sam doesn't remember a fucking thing, even though I knew,' I looked at Raph and saw him squeeze his eyes shut, 'I knew they had a fight that night. I saw it.'

Lisa hid her face in her hands and started shaking her head 'no'.

'It was evening,' I said, looking back at Raph.

Suddenly I saw the connection. I thought: if I trust myself, I've got to listen to the voice inside my head. I've got to be a shepherd's son and blow my flute.

'It was evening,' I said again, 'and I saw Papa sitting in the sun lounge and I went back upstairs and when I went past the door to their room Mama was sitting on the edge of the bed. She was combing her hair. No, she had the comb in her hair, but it wasn't moving. She'd stopped halfway. She looked like a bronze statue of a mermaid, a siren who lures ships and sits out on a rock somewhere combing her long hair. I stood at the half-open door and looked at Mama and I knew something was wrong, because she didn't see me, not even when I pushed the door open a little further and stood in the doorway. And then I went back downstairs, through the dark house. All the lights were out. The staircase was dark and the hall and the living room and I saw that the sun lounge was empty and then I got to the hallway and I walked to the study and there was Papa sitting behind his desk and I wanted to ask him why he was sitting here, because they had to leave, and why Mama was sitting upstairs on the edge of her bed and combing her hair and the comb wasn't moving, but I didn't know how to ask that. I said Winnetou was dead.'

I saw Lisa look up. Her cheeks were wet. She looked like a doll whose eyes had been knocked out.

'They had a fight . . . They had a fight. I could never quite remember the car driving away. We were upstairs watching from the window, but before we could really and truly see them getting in, the car was gone. He was driving like a lunatic.'

'Nooooo . . .' said Lisa.

Raph put his hand on her shoulder. He said: 'You're wrong. They didn't have a fight. Or maybe they did, but that's not the point.'

'Why,' I asked, 'did you call me?'

His eyebrows plunged.

'When we were both living somewhere else. I was about . . . fifteen. Why?'

'I think because I wanted to know how you were. I don't know.'

I shook my head. 'Or because you wanted to keep me from remembering what really happened? Why have you both gone to so much trouble to make me believe that we lived in Paradise and that we were kicked out because of a senseless accident? When it was nothing but a shitty argument?'

Lisa bit at the air, once, twice, then bowed her head. Raph slowly got to his feet. He picked up the fallen chair and pushed Lisa onto it. She stared down at the tabletop. Her shoulders shook gently. Raph looked at her for a long time. Then he fixed his eyes on me. He shrugged, as if he were apologizing.

'The truth is,' he said, as Lisa raised her head, mouth open, eyes open, her head shaking almost imperceptibly, 'the truth is not that they had a fight. You were in the car.'

Where Are We Going?

It was a broiling hot summer. The warmest warm summer of the century? Warm. Warm enough to drive our mother into the cool shade of her mother's cellar. She'd sit on a stool among the shelves of mason jars, reading trashy novels (*Compassion Isn't Love*) and drinking glass after glass of lemonade. She could hear her parents' footsteps overhead, and the high-pitched voice of her son Raph, who sat under the table with the long tablecloth and played hide-and-seek with everyone who passed by. They'd got married four years before and had lived on the top floor of her parents' house ever since. They didn't have much money. He earned practically nothing as a teaching assistant and she'd had to quit her job as an executive secretary when her belly got too round. Every evening the four of them would sit in the big garden behind the house and follow Papa's finger as he pointed out the constellations: Aquarius, Pegasus, Andromeda, Cassiopeia in the east, Corona Borealis, Bootes (the herdsman), Hercules in the west and, all the way at the edge of the northern hemisphere, Ursa Major fleeing from Canes Venatici, the hunting dogs. They drank lemonade. Sometimes, if it was really hot and they were feeling festive, Grandpa would pour himself and his son-in-law a beer. Upstairs, at the foot of the secondhand wooden bed, in the room with the slanting roof, Raph lay asleep in his wooden crib.

September came and summer began to fade. The leaves on the trees stopped gleaming, the grass grew dark, the flowerbeds in the garden behind the house slowly lost their colour. Mama came out of the cellar and folded the tiny socks, shirts and bibs into neat piles, for the six hundredth time. She ironed the nappies and sterilized the bottles, again, and she cried at the least little thing.

Not because she was happy or sad. She just cried, she didn't know why. Over a late butterfly. Because somebody had startled her. About the sun, that shone on the garden every morning and made all those wilting flowers seem so soft and defenceless.

By mid-September she was nine months' pregnant, but still no sign of labour pains. Her feet swelled, her fingers tingled when she tried to bend them in the morning. It became harder and harder to get out of a chair or put on her shoes. The doctor came, tapped her on the belly and said: 'Wake up! Time to be born!', but although she laughed, she was worried. What kind of child was this that refused to leave her stomach?

On September twenty-ninth she had a contraction. One. That night, the doctor felt her stomach, frowned, and called the hospital. Five days later, as the Sputnik was leaving the atmosphere, Lisa and I were delivered by Caesarean section, and as the Sputnik orbited the earth, sending out its lonely bleeps (you could hear them over the radio, for years afterward Papa talked about the sad, lonely cries of that small metal ball), we, the Gemini, screamed our lungs full of air and were launched into the world we had avoided for so long.

Our grandparents died one after the other, before we had the chance to get to know them well enough to be able to remember them. The house was remodelled. Our father's telescope was moved to the sun lounge, workmen turned the front room into a study. We grew up, went to school, learned the alphabet and the times table, the constellations and the composition of salt and water and that the earth's crust was made up of shifting plates that renewed themselves in a perpetual process of melting and solidifying. Raph and I began building airplanes, in preparation for our first space flight. Lisa drew on every scrap of paper she could find, on walls and doors and pavingstones, once even on the unpainted wooden staircase leading to the attic, and everyone stood and stared and wondered how a girl of seven or eight could think up such desolate, crumbling buildings. If anyone asked where she'd seen things like that, she said all she had to do was close her eyes and she saw a whole different world.

And then it was 1969, Autumn 1969, just after our twelfth

birthday, a few months after the first man had walked on the moon and left his footprints in dust that would never be blown about in the wind. Lisa and I played Old Shatterhand and Winnetou and I glided through the darkness like a knife through water. Gemini and Orion twinkled on the windows of the sun lounge. Below them glowed the tip of the cigarette that dangled from my father's fingers. I hid behind a chair that was really a boulder and looked at the inky blue on the windowpanes. My father's voice dragged hoarsely through the silence.

'I can't do any more than this,' he said. 'This is it. This is all I have to give.'

My mother said something unintelligible.

'Kit, I'm no god, I'm as mortal as they come. My love for you has never diminished. If that's what you think, then it's because that's what you think, not because it's true.'

My mother coughed.

There was a long silence. I slid along the ground, until I could see past the chair. I saw my mother, she was standing with her back to my father, looking out. At the stars, I thought.

'It's gone,' she said. 'There's nothing left.'

My father's chair creaked. My mother turned around and walked out of the sun lounge. I heard her gentle footsteps fading away. I lay on the floor and waited, without even knowing what I was waiting for. Then I crept carefully upward, up along the boulder. When I looked into the sun lounge, I saw my father, his face dyed blue and black in the night shadows. 'Go to sleep, Sam,' he said. I stood up. 'You too,' he said. Lisa's crouching shadow unfurled beside the sun lounge door.

I went upstairs and as I went past the door to my parents' room I saw my mother sitting on the foot of the bed, the comb in her hair, frozen in motion. When she didn't see me I knew I was finally invisible, that I could now go anywhere I wanted and nobody would know. I glided through the shadows, no longer a knife, but a ghost, the ghost of an Indian. I floated down the stairs, through the living room, into the empty sun lounge, and back again, until I was standing outside the door to the study. A soft bar of light gleamed along the edge. I laid my hand on the

189

wood and pushed the door open a bit further. My father was leaning back in his chair, feet on the desk, hands behind his head. A damp autumn breeze wafted in through the open windows, but he didn't seem to notice that the papers on his desk were sliding together and sailing to the floor.

And then I went back upstairs and Raph came in and we got out the Dakota and later Lisa and Mama walked in and we heard our father's voice from downstairs and when he was upstairs too, he said to me: 'Are you ready?' I looked up and said: 'Ready?' And he said: 'Yes, you can come with us. Raph came along to the opening of the observatory, now it's your turn.'

And three days later, when they had placed us in a temporary foster home, when I'd just come back from the hospital, Lisa disappeared. Raph and I went looking for her, the people whose house we were living in went looking for her, finally even the police set off, but nobody knew where she was, except Raph and me, and when the house was empty and everyone was running around like blind mice trying to find her, we slipped out. We took the tram to the terminus and from there we walked to the edge of town, until we came to the road we always drove down, the road that looked like a tunnel of leaves, and halfway there, the sun was shining, but the vapours of autumn lay like hazy fingers between the two rows of trees, halfway there we saw a little blue dot at the foot of a tall oak tree and when we got closer we saw that it was Lisa. She was wearing her new jacket. We sat down beside her, against the trunk, which was damaged all the way to the wood, the bark in shreds, a puddle of glass among the roots, and all around the tree, the grass flattened and torn. And as we sat there, knees raised, arms around our legs, chins on our knees, as we sat there Lisa said: This is where it happened, and I looked around and thought: what happened?

Towards the end of the afternoon, the autumn light shone low over the fields, we stood up, all three at the same time, as though we had planned it, and we took each other by the hand, Lisa in the middle, Raph and I on either side, and we walked back into town. The light filtered through the trees, here and there the first evening mist seeped through to the road and now and then we'd

190

disappear in one of these banks of fog and we could barely see each other's faces and then we'd squeeze each other's hands and we knew that we were still there, and all that time, as we walked between the trees, in the low, golden light of autumn, in and out of the mist, all that time I thought: what happened, where are we going?

ACKNOWLEDGEMENTS

The Publishers gratefully acknowledge Faber and Faber Ltd for permission to reprint the poem *Autumn Day, after Rilke* by Stephen Spender, from *Collected Poems 1928–1985*, and also Blackwell Publishers for permission to reprint the extracts on pages 162 and 163 from Ludwig Wittgenstein's *Philosophical Remarks* and *Philosophical Investigations*. Copyright Blackwell Publishers Limited.

Acknowledgements

[faded, largely illegible text]

Kate O'Riordan

Involved

'A striking debut by an original and strong writer.'

DERMOT BOLGER

When Kitty Fitzgerald falls for Danny O'Neill it seems nothing could spoil their perfect relationship. Not even their very different backgrounds. But the carefree Danny Kitty knows in Dublin is not the person she finds when they both travel North to meet his family.

The O'Neills – Ma, the formidable matriarch, her daughter Monica, and the disturbed and menacing eldest son Eamon – are bound by blood and history to a past they can never forget. As time goes on long-kept secrets rise to the surface and Kitty finds herself locked into a bitter struggle for the possession of Danny's soul. . .

A superb debut, *Involved* is an extraordinarily powerful novel about love and obsession, the intricate pull of family and blood, and the dangerous arrogance of those who seek to loosen the ties that bind.

'A truthfully imagined and gracefully tense first novel from a terrific storyteller.'

JOSEPH O'CONNOR

ISBN 0 00 654761 3

The North China Lover
Marguerite Duras

Acclaimed in France as 'an uncomparable pleasure', Marguerite Duras's new novel is a fascinating retelling of the dramatic experiences of her adolescence – as previously described in *The Lover* – that have shaped her life and work.

Far more daring and truthful than any book she has written before, *The North China Lover* emphasises the harsh realities of Duras's youth in Indochina and reveals much that her earlier works concealed. Gone are the romantic and nostalgic readings of the past. Here are the humiliations and passions of the poverty-ridden world in which Duras grew up; the intense sexuality of the young girls who were her friends and classmates, a group of adolescents impatient for the experiences of adult life, but still caught up in the passions of childhood.

Described by French critics as a return to 'the Duras of the great books and the great days', *The North China Lover* is an exciting and unexpected reading of the past life of one of Europe's greatest writers.

ISBN 0 00 654712 5

E. Annie Proulx

Postcards

'The richness of America is portrayed with memorable effect in this remarkable first novel – Faulkner springs to mind. *Postcards* is written from the heart and – for its raspy dialogue, laconic humour and beautiful description of the natural world – deserves to be widely read.'
Independent on Sunday

Postcards is the story of Loyal Blood, a man who spends a lifetime on the run from a crime so terrible that it renders him forever incapable of touching a woman. The odyssey begins on a freezing Vermont hillside in 1944 and propels Blood across the American West for forty years. Denied love and unable to settle, he lives a hundred different lives: mining gold, growing beans, hunting fossils, trapping, prospecting for uranium and ranching. His only contact with his past is through a series of postcards he sends home – not realising that in his absence disaster has befallen his family, and their deep-rooted connection with the land has been severed with devastating consequences . . .

'*Postcards* is a remarkable novel: poetic and yet driven by a strong narrative, tragic and yet scored with deep veins of humour. Loyal Blood is one of those rare, haunted characters who continue to live in the mind after you finish the book. *Postcards* is told in a fulsome and resonant prose that both soars and gets down in the dirt – a début which should be read by anyone who values fine, honest writing.'
Literary Review

flamingo

Dacia Maraini

The Silent Duchess

Winner of the bi-monthly *Independent* Foreign Fiction Award

'Set in eighteenth-century Italy the story of our heroine, Marianna, and of her family is a fascinating one which manages totally to overpower the reader with its narrative urgency. Maraini brilliantly conveys the mixture of luxury and squalor in which the Sicilian aristocracy lived, and with great skill, communicates every detail through the eyes and nostrils of her Silent Duchess.'

Francis King, *Evening Standard*

'Few other novelists have so forcefully expressed the sense that the age they describe is a shaping force in the conduct of their characters. *The Silent Duchess* has the richness of a saga, and Maraini weaves striking scenes into the narrative with an ease, both memorable and inevitable.' Joseph Farrell, *Independent*

'*The Silent Duchess* succeeds through its accretion of details. A vivid and hushed account, Maraini's portrayal of the Duchess Marianna's life is blanketed in a strange beauty, like the snow-muffled landscape of winter.' Nicci Gerrard, *Observer*

'Dacia Maraini is an artist of considerable power. *The Silent Duchess* is a novel that would have delighted Nabokov. It is brimming with detail, vividly presented in a style that is abrupt, spiky, and yet luxuriant. Every page presents one with the unexpected. It arouses intense feeling, it provokes thought.'

Allan Massie, *Scotsman*'

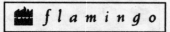

Carol Shields

Happenstance

'The biggest pleasure remains Shields' prose, at once dense and delicate. Her great strength is her ability to capture small moments and make them important . . . Shields displays in her careful delineation of her characters a tenderness for the ordinary which shines through the sheer cleverness of her work.' *Literary Review*

'A celebration of marriage as historical accident, *Happenstance* makes a delightful portrait of a partnership, full of quirky humour.' *The Times*

'The beautiful irony of *Happenstance* is that its novels are both bound together and held apart by the strength of the marriage they describe.' *Harpers & Queen*

'I highly recommend *Happenstance*. Both stories are funny – but compassionately so. Crucially, Carol Shields allows all the characters dignity. This is a tender, lovely book, about people who need each other. It is also superbly told.' *Marie Claire*

'With dazzling deftness Shields demonstrates the alienation innate in the most loving relationships . . . *Happenstance* is a remarkable, perceptive and painfully accurate work that yields more with each reading.' *Sunday Times*

flamingo

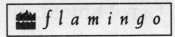
flamingo

Flamingo is a quality imprint publishing both fiction and non-fiction. Below are some recent titles.

Fiction

☐ No Other Life *Brian Moore* £5.99
☐ The Kitchen God's Wife *Amy Tan* £5.99
☐ A Thousand Acres *Jane Smiley* £5.99
☐ Dancing in Limbo *Edward Toman* £5.99
☐ Iced *Ray Shell* £5.99
☐ Split Skirt *Agnes Rossi* £5.99
☐ The Great Longing *Marcel Möring* £5.99
☐ Happenstance *Carol Shields* £5.99
☐ Miss Smilla's Feeling for Snow *Peter Høeg* £5.99
☐ Postcards *E. Annie Proulx* £5.99

Non-fiction

☐ Cyberia *Douglas Rushkoff* £6.99
☐ Sentimental Journeys *Joan Didion* £5.99
☐ Epstein *Stephen Gardiner* £8.99
☐ Love, Love and Love *Sandra Bernhard* £5.99
☐ City of Djinns *William Dalrymple* £5.99
☐ Dame Edna Everage *John Lahr* £5.99
☐ Tolstoy's Diaries *R. F. Christian* £7.99
☐ Wild Swans *Jung Chang* £7.99

You can buy Flamingo paperbacks at your local bookshop or newsagent. Or you can order them from HarperCollins Mail Order, Dept. 8, HarperCollins *Publishers*, Westerhill Road, Bishopbriggs, Glasgow G64 2QT. Please enclose a cheque or postal order, to the order of the cover price plus add £1.00 for the first and 25p for additional books ordered within the UK.

NAME (Block letters) _____

ADDRESS _____

_____